INVASION OF THE
Widows' Club

Dedication/Acknowledgment

I hope you enjoy reading this book as much as I enjoyed writing it. Each of these characters—Valentine, Reva, Sally and the others—have become so special to me; I feel like they're old friends. It makes no difference if a woman is young or old, has been married only a few short months or many years, widowhood is never easy. I have been a widow for over two years and I'm still hurting. Words can't express how much I miss my Don. But God has chosen to leave me behind. Why? Does this mean He has more books for me to write? Books to not only encourage and uplift those whose hearts who have been wounded, but to brighten their day? Books that will help be of help to those who struggle with the issues of life? To bring laughter, tears and joy, as well as many happy hours of entertainment, to those who read them? I hope so, because I truly believe my God-appointed ministry is to write books for Him.

As with every book I write, I dedicate this book to Don Livingston, my precious husband of many years, the hero of every story I have ever written or will ever write. I love you, Don. You may be gone, but our love will live forever.

I also want to dedicate *Invasion of the Widows' Club* to three of the lovely widows with whom I sit in Sunday school each Sunday. Their friendship and encouragement means more to me than they will ever know. So—Alberta Clark, Louise Stockhaus, and Judy Kasper—this book is for you.

And, dear reader, this blessing is for you: May you look to God as your Savior and walk with Him all of your days. May you turn to Him not only with the needs of life, but with a grateful heart. May God fill your life with joy and blessings untold, and may you worship Him in love and awe, for He is my Savior and I want Him to be your Savior, too.

CHAPTER 1

I giggled aloud as I beheld the flamboyantly attired woman reflected back at me in my front hall mirror. If anyone had told me a year ago that, by my own choice, I'd be going out in public in a red and purple pantsuit topped off with a red, wide-brimmed straw hat adorned with an oversized purple silk rose and accessorized with red chandelier earrings and a gaudy purple sequin-trimmed purse, I would have told them they were crazy. Not to mention the red-feathered boa draped around my neck. It wasn't because of the extravagant brightness of the colors that I wouldn't have dressed this way. I adored color! Especially anything in the pink, rose, red, and burgundy family. And I loved any shade of purple, from the palest of pale to the deep, deep purple I assumed kings wore in Bible times. But wear purple and red together? I'd only worn such a ridiculous outfit on one other occasion—the evening I attended my first Red Hat meeting with my friend—or should I say my high school nemesis?—Barbie Baxter.

With one final glance in the mirror, I grabbed up my purse,

the box I had prepared containing the decorations, and car keys and headed toward the restaurant Reva and Sally, my very best friends, and I had selected as the place for the first official meeting of the Widows' Club.

The manager greeted me at the door, all smiles. "You're early, but your tables are ready, Ms. Denay." He gestured for me to follow him to the area reserved for private parties, a lovely bright and cheery room done in white and green, featuring white lattice-work dividers woven with long strands of green ivy. I had dined in that restaurant a number of times but had never been in their private room. The pots of red geraniums wrapped in purple foil we had ordered as centerpieces sat invitingly on each table.

"You've added red and purple napkins!" I said with a burst of surprise, my palm flattening against my chest. "How nice! The ladies will love it."

He gave me a half bow. "We're pleased you selected The Southern Belle as the place to hold your first meeting. We've set the speaker's table for five and the round tables for twenty-seven, as you requested. Is there anything else I can do for you?"

I shook my head. "Looks like you have everything under control."

He backed toward the door. "I'll check back with you in a few minutes."

I opened the box I'd lugged in with me and set about taking care of last-minute details by placing the name cards Reva had made beside each plate and sprinkling some cute, sparkly red and purple confetti-type cutouts Sally had found at a stationery store around the base of the geranium pots. Then I added the crowning touch to each table—fat red and purple candles. Finally, I placed the little clear cellophane bags of the goodies that Reva, Sally, and I had assembled earlier, as favors beside each plate. I lit the candles, asked the manager to dim the lights to create a romantic ambience, then hid the box behind the piano and sat down at the speaker's table to await my guests. A feeling of satisfaction washed over me.

"You're already here!" I turned to see Sally coming through the door with Reva two steps behind. "Reva and I were going to help you add the things to the tables, but it looks as though we're too late." She quickly placed her purse on a chair, then did a graceful pirouette in front of me. "How do I look?"

Reva bustled past her before I could answer. "Weird! We both look weird. Like strawberry smoothies with a dab of pink-tinted whipped cream on top."

I grabbed onto Reva's arm. "You don't look weird—you look cute!"

She rolled her eyes. "Valentine, the word *cute* may fit Sally, but I am anything but cute! If my husband could see me now, he'd laugh his head off."

Sally snickered and gave Reva's arm a pinch. "I told her she could dye those white painter's pants of hers lavender and wear a pink T-shirt and ball cap instead of that fancy dress."

Reva sat down with a grunt. "Pink and lavender in any form, even painter's pants, are way too feminine for me. I don't see why I can't wear red, like Valentine. I don't like red, either, but even red would be more to my liking than pink."

"You're too young to wear red," Sally reminded her. "Until you and I reach fifty, if we want to be a part of this group, we're going to have to abide by the rules and wear lavender and pink."

Reva snorted. "Rules are made to be broken." Turning to me, she added, "I'll bet our Queen of Hearts could give me a special dispensation if she wanted to."

I gave my head a shake, then smiled at her. "Reva, don't even ask. Fortunately, there are very few rules in this official Red Hat Society with which we have chosen to identify. But there is a definite rule that says no one younger than fifty can wear the official red and purple, and we must abide by it. All ladies-in-waiting, those of you who have not reached that magical age, *have* to wear the pink and lavender. Is that so awful?"

Reva gave me one of her impish smiles. "So you're saying, as our queen, you won't give me a special dispensation?"

I nodded. "That's exactly what I'm saying. I couldn't if I wanted to. You'll be fifty in a couple of years; then you can wear red."

Reva repeated her impish grin. "So, only old ladies like you can wear red?"

I laughed aloud. Sometimes Reva could be such a tease. "Hey, girlfriend, from my vantage point, fifty-three is anything but old! Mind your tongue."

Sally glanced around the room. "Oh, Valentine, everything looks so pretty. The women are going to love it."

"I hope so. But I don't want anyone who plans a meeting in the future to think they have to do something frivolous and exotic like I plan to do next month. Since this is our organizational meeting, I thought it should be fairly simple." I couldn't hold back a broad smile as I thought about my plans for next month's meeting. Big plans. I wanted our first official Widows' Club outing to be extra special, an evening everyone would remember. I just hoped I had time to pull it off.

"So? Have you decided to tell us what you have planned for next month?"

I grinned at Sally. "Can't. I want it to be a surprise, even for you two. Let's just say—you wouldn't want to miss it." I gestured toward the speaker's table. "I want you two, Wendy, and Bitsy to sit up there with me."

It wasn't long before Wendy joined us, dressed in an old-fashioned, high-necked purple dress, the lovely cameo we knew had belonged to her mother at her neck, and a red pillbox-style hat perched jauntily upon her head. "You look adorable."

Her weathered hand fingered the brooch. "At eighty-one? Adorable?"

"Age is merely a state of mind," Sally reminded her.

"I felt like everyone in the restaurant was staring at me."

"They probably were," I told Wendy. "With that gorgeous smile of yours and your silver hair, you're beautiful."

"Hi, everyone!" We all grinned as Bitsy joined us. Though Bitsy was the youngest of our group, a mere twenty, soon to be twenty-one, and the mother of a newborn infant, she also was a widow, having lost her sweet husband, a member of our armed forces, to the war in Iraq. "Pink is definitely your color," I told her, meaning it. "You look lovely. I can't believe this is the last evening you'll be in town before you move away. I hate to see you leave, but I know you want to be closer to your in-laws."

"How's our precious baby Valentine?" Reva asked, the very question I, myself, was about to ask Bitsy since she had graciously named her precious baby girl, Valentine Denay Foster, in my honor. An honor I didn't deserve but wore proudly.

Bitsy beamed, as she did anytime anyone talked about her

baby. "She's amazing, Reva. My mom is keeping her tonight. She thought I needed a night out. But since I'm nursing my baby, I may skip out early. I hope no one minds. I don't want her to give my mother a hard time."

"You leave anytime you feel necessary," I told her. "Everyone will understand. We're just glad you're here."

Before we could ask any more questions, three other women from our church came into the room, followed by four more, each wearing a red hat and purple outfit. We'd barely had time to greet them before the room began to fill as the rest of those who had made reservations joined us, oohing and aahing over the way the room looked, admiring the perkiness of the red geraniums clothed in their purple foil, and exclaiming over the cute place cards they found on the tables.

I motioned toward Reva, Sally, Wendy, and Bitsy to join me at the head table, then moved to stand by my chair. "All right, ladies," I said, tapping my spoon against my water glass. "Take your seats. We have a lovely evening ahead of us. I know you want to visit, but there will be time for that later."

After everyone located her place card and was seated, I scanned the tables, taking in each happy, smiling face. Most of these women I had known for a number of years, though a few I knew only by name. Some were total strangers.

"Welcome, ladies. I can't tell you how happy I am you've chosen to join us this evening, the first official meeting of the Widows' Club." I gave them my best smile. "By the way, you all look beautiful in your official Red Hat colors. Most of you are aware of how this Red Hat chapter came into being. But for those of you who aren't, let me give you a brief history. As most of you know, our church,

Cooperville Community Church, recently held its first annual bazaar, which, I might add, was quite successful. Many of you had a large part in that success, but planning a bazaar takes a lot of work. I, along with my committee chairwomen, spent many weeks in the kitchen of my home, planning and implementing the ideas we had for our bazaar. Though we hadn't planned it that way, we soon realized many who worked on that committee were widows."

"Widows of all ages," Reva inserted, pointing toward Bitsy. "Some even with babies to raise."

I nodded. "Yes, unfortunately, that's true." I wanted to say more, but the timing didn't seem appropriate, so I continued on.

"Many of you know Barbie Baxter. She's been coming to our church lately and helped with hostessing at the bazaar. When she first moved to Nashville, she invited me to attend a Red Hat chapter meeting with her. I had an enjoyable time at that meeting and met a number of really nice ladies. I decided later that sometime in the future, I would like to start my own Red Hat chapter. I mentioned my desire to those of our bazaar committee members who were also widows, and they liked the idea. After we discussed it and made a list of how many widows there were in our church and how we as widows had our own set of needs and interests, it was decided we would limit our membership to widows only."

"So no one can belong and attend our meetings unless they are a widow, right, Valentine?" Karen Gamer, one of the newer members of our church, asked.

I gave my head a nod. "That's right. They can't hold membership in our group, but we decided they could come occasionally as guests."

"As the one who registered the group," Reva added, gesturing toward me, "Valentine is automatically our queen. We call her our Queen of Hearts."

Karen smiled. "Oh, I like that name."

"We even thought of calling ourselves the Merry Widows," Reva inserted. "But that sounded a bit cliché."

I quickly took hold of the discussion, afraid all this talk about what we *almost* named the group would spark a whole new list of ideas. "After much discussion, we decided the best name for our group would simply be the Widows' Club."

Helen Morgan stood to her feet. "I, for one, appreciate the fact that we are limiting membership to widows only. Unless you have personally been a widow yourself, you have no idea what happens and how you feel when you lose a spouse." Her hand rose to gesture about the room. "I am friends with many women, but I have a special kinship with the women in this room. We understand each other like no one else does. We—" She paused and dabbed her handkerchief to her eyes. "We need each other. Now, more than ever."

Phyllis Lytle, who was sitting next to her, rose and slipped an arm about her shoulders. "And we need some fun in our lives. Totally outrageous fun. I don't know about the rest of you, but the minute I slipped into this purple dress and cocked this red straw hat on my head, I felt like a new woman. I love wearing red and purple together. It makes me laugh. I haven't worn big earrings in years, but look at me." Her lips widened into a gigantic smile. "What do we care if people think we look eccentric? I say it's time we widows put aside the grief that has grasped us in its ugly, stifling clutches and start living again!" She grabbed hold of her water glass with her free hand, lifted it high into the air, and shouted. "Long live the Widows' Club!"

Thirty-two ladies, including those of us at the head table, lifted our glasses and joined in her salute, shouting in unison, "Long live the Widows' Club!"

The sea of purple and red before me was a remarkable sight, made even more beautiful with its touches of lavender and pink. A feeling of pride swelled within me. The Widows' Club was now officially a reality. Our chapter had taken on a life of its own. Something deep inside me made me know the Widows' Club was going to add much to my life and to the lives of my friends, and I was excited about it. Lifting my face heavenward, I breathed a thank-you to God for putting the idea into my head and for bringing it to fruition.

Our salute brought on a buzz of conversation and laughter as the women hugged each other and talked about our name. I hated to break things up—we were having so much fun—but we had to get on with our business. It took several loud taps on my water glass before the commotion finally began to quiet down.

"What about dues or membership fees?" someone asked, raising her voice so she could be heard over the few who had ignored the tinkling of my spoon and were still talking.

"We'll need to set some kind of membership fees, but since we each will be paying for our own meals, or whatever functions we attend each month, our costs should be minimal. I've already paid our registration fee."

Reva waved her hand. "You shouldn't have to pay for that, Valentine."

Sally nodded. "Why don't we pass the hat to cover the cost of our registration fee and to set up a miscellaneous fund that can cover things like postage?"

"I don't mind paying—"

Interrupting me by noisily jumping to her feet, nearly knocking over her chair, Phyllis pulled her hat from her head and ceremoniously passed it to the next person at her table. "It's only fair, Valentine. You must let us do our part. We're all in this together."

I honestly didn't mind paying the fee. It wasn't that much, but I agreed with what she was saying. We *were* in this together. I didn't want anyone to have the impression this was *my* chapter, just because I had come up with the idea and started the ball rolling.

Phyllis gave me a grin, then moved from table to table, holding out her hat as each woman pulled loose change and dollar bills from her purse and added her share.

"What about rules?" a woman I barely knew asked as the hat continued its journey about the room.

I couldn't contain a smile as I gazed at her. She was a tiny, small-boned woman, probably weighing not much over ninety pounds. Her oversized red hat was almost as big as she was and seemed to swallow her head. "At this time, other than our members being widows, we have only one other firm rule. Whatever we do, we must have fun! No one will be allowed to enter our meetings without a smile on her face."

"I like the sound of that," a rather large woman wearing a red cowboy hat with a purple leather hatband chimed in with enthusiasm. "What will we be doing at our monthly meetings? Just eating and visiting?"

"Yeah, and who will plan our meetings? Will we have committees?" another questioned.

"That's the beauty of this organization. No formal committees unless you want them, though we will have a few officers." I made a dramatic sweep of my hand, encompassing everyone in the room. "We'll all have a turn at planning our get-togethers and making the arrangements. I'm doing it next month, but I hope each of you will volunteer to take a turn." I nodded toward Reva. "I've asked Reva to start a clipboard around the room. On it, you will find a place to sign your name, address, and phone number, and be sure to add your e-mail address. Along the bottom of that sheet, I have listed the next twenty-four months and a place for you to sign if you would like to host one of our meetings. If you add your name, it will be up to you to find a place for us to have lunch or dinner, a program or an event for entertainment, and whatever else you think we widows would enjoy."

"Like what?" Belle Mitchell asked, looking perplexed.

"It could be a number of things," I explained, hoping I could make people realize that they didn't have to put a lot of money, time, and effort into the club unless they wanted to. "Our goal is to have fun and enjoy our friendship with one another." I laughed and fingered the brim of my hat. "You have to *want* to have fun to wear red hats and purple dresses or pantsuits and walk into places en masse, but let me give you some suggestions. Dinner theater is always fun. Or maybe a Christian concert. Or how about a movie, as long as it's funny and clean. The circus? A picnic in the park? Or maybe a barbeque in your backyard? The choices are endless. Even having it in your home and discussing a book you've read would be entertaining. It can be as simple or as complex as you want to make it. The variety will make our meetings interesting and keep people coming back. Please notice: A number of the things I've mentioned are free. As widows, quite a few of you are on a limited budget. Those who will be planning the meetings need to keep that in mind. In fact, several of you could work together to plan one of our meetings."

"Are we always going to meet on Thursday evenings?" Phyllis asked.

Reva snagged onto that question. "When I phoned each of you to invite you to this meeting, it seemed most people thought Thursday evening was a good time, or even Thursday afternoon, though some of you hold jobs or still have young children at home."

Phyllis shrugged, then sat back in her seat. "Thursday is good for me."

"Then it's settled," I said quickly, afraid opening the day of the week up for discussion could start a lengthy free-for-all that would probably lead nowhere.

"We'll need someone to call everyone with the details of each meeting." I scanned the group again, hoping someone dependable would volunteer.

Wendy lifted her hand. "I'm home all day; I'll do it."

I was glad she was the one who volunteered. You could depend on her to do what she said she would, plus her always-cheerful voice would put everyone in a good mood.

"Great!" I gave her a smile of appreciation. "Wendy will be our contact person. So when it's your month to plan activities, you will need to get your information to her at least a full week ahead of time so she can let people know what your plans are, the cost, and where to meet as well as the time. Okay?"

She nodded.

"Okay, Wendy is officially our E-mail-Female Damsel of Dialing. Now do we have a volunteer to be secretary?"

Sally giggled. "Give me a cute name like Wendy's and I'll take the job!"

I giggled back and pointed my finger at her. "You got it! How's this? I officially appoint you as our Royal Recorder!"

"Royal Recorder? I love it! Maybe I'll have one of those satin banners made to wear across my chest, like the beauty queens wear when they strut across the stage. Red satin with purple lettering, announcing to the world that I am officially the Royal Recorder."

We all loved Sally's sense of humor. Leave it to her to come up with an idea like that. Now, probably each woman would want her own job so she could have a banner. I wrinkled up my face. Not a bad idea! I hurriedly sent it to the back of my mind for future reference.

Dixie clapped her hands loudly. "This is so much fun! I'm glad I came."

"Dixie," I said, I myself caught up in the contagious enthusiasm permeating the room, "since you seem to be enjoying yourself, and I know you work in an accountant's office, how about a job for you? Would you like to be our money keeper?" I racked my brain for a title for her. "You could be. . .Duchess of Dollars!"

Her eyes sparkled. Dixie was one of those plain-Janes who often faded into the background, but she was one of the smartest women I knew. She literally glowed at my suggestion.

"I—I'd be honored. Are you sure you want me?"

Everyone nodded.

"Of course, we want you. You'd be perfect for the job."

Those around her began congratulating her.

I gave them all a coy smile. "Before we're through, each of you will have a royal name, so be thinking about it. If you have a special talent, like working with Web sites, doing art work, an interest in making sure we know whose birthday it is each month, you enjoy doing publicity, crafts, scrapbooking, anything that would be of value to our chapter, and you'd like to volunteer, we need you. If our Widows' Club is to be a success, we each need to take an active part."

I snapped my fingers. "I almost forgot to mention one of the most important jobs. We need someone to lead us in a short devotional thought or reading at the beginning of each meeting. You can do it yourself or ask others to do it, but we definitely want to include something inspirational each time."

Gloria Bright rose slowly. "That's one job I'd love to do. I've been going through some tough times lately, and my daily devotional readings are what have kept me going. If you allow me to do it, I promise I'll do the very best I can."

The commitment in her voice touched my heart, and I was sure the heart of every woman there. "I think I can speak for everyone when I say we'd be blessed to have you in that position."

As Sally and Reva began to applaud, all the others joined in.

"One more thing," I added quickly. "I want to remind everyone—it is mandatory that you wear the red and purple to all our get-togethers, or pink and lavender, depending on your age. Your attire doesn't always have to be dressy like it is tonight. Wear whatever is appropriate for the activity. Like red capris and a purple T-shirt to a picnic. Or simply jeans and a purple shirt and red ball cap. You could even tie a red bandanna—" I nodded toward Bitsy, Reva, and Sally. "Or a pink or lavender bandana—if you're lucky enough to be under fifty—but you must wear our colors. That's half the fun." Glad the business part of our evening was over and had gone so well, I gave everyone a smile. "We have a marvelous meal awaiting us. Let's all stand and hold hands as we ask the Lord to bless our food and fellowship."

After I prayed a simple prayer, I sat down, basking in the chattering roar that filled the room as we thirty-two women visited with one another. What a joyous sound. My heart reveled in it. This was exactly what we widows needed—a place to share our hearts, our joys, our up times, and our down times with those who understood.

"Serve the head table first," I heard a familiar voice say with authority. "And be quick about it. We're already running behind. Their preliminaries took far too long."

No! It can't be!

I turned quickly and stared into a very familiar face.

"Barbie Baxter? What are *you* doing here?"

$\mathscr{C}$HAPTER 2

Barbie gave me a coquettish grin. "Didn't expect to see me here, did you?"

I drew in a deep, calming breath. Surely she didn't come to crash the party after I'd explained to her that we were a widows-only group. But then I took a look at what she was wearing. Her outfit was not the traditional purple and red the rest of us were wearing. Her dress was almost sky blue, a lightweight chiffon cut on the bias, and it clung to her magnificent figure like water seeking its level.

"Pierre, the owner of this magnificent restaurant, is an old friend of mine. I'd heard you ladies were having your meeting here tonight and mentioned it to Pierre when I was having lunch here the other day. He thought it would be nice to have someone act as your hostess to make sure everything went smoothly for your dinner. So, here I am!"

I stared at her in amazement. "We really don't need a hostess—"

"I'm not exactly a *hostess*. I'm doing this on behalf of the restaurant. Pierre wanted me to make you feel welcome and ensure you get good service." She turned to one of the waiters, snapped her fingers, and called out with the aplomb of a drill sergeant, "The ladies at this table need their water glasses filled."

I glanced at our glasses. None of them were less than half full. "He needn't do that now," I told her, sending a placating smile to the waiter. "We have plenty of water."

She gave her slim shoulders a slight shrug, then moved quickly to stand by another waiter as he reached to place a basket of rolls on one of the tables. "Are those rolls hot?"

He gave her a blank stare. "I don't know."

She took one of the rolls from the basket, then frowned up at him. "Take them back to the kitchen. They're cold."

I placed my napkin on the table and, trying to be inconspicuous, walked over to her. "It's okay. They're probably cold because our meeting ran longer than expected. I don't think any of our ladies mind cold rolls."

She spun around and glared at me, her hands anchoring on her hips. "It's not okay, Valentine. Barbie's Babes," which happened to be the name of her Red Hat chapter, "meet here once or twice a year, and we get excellent food *and* service, and our rolls are always hot. As tonight's representative for The Southern Belle, it is my duty and responsibility to see that your group gets the same excellent food and service."

The owner sidled up beside us. I hadn't even noticed he'd come into the room. "Is there a problem?"

I started to say, "No, everything is fine," but Barbie butted in ahead of me.

"The rolls are cold," she blurted out, as if it were a national disaster. "I told the waiter to take them back to the kitchen."

The man bowed low toward me. "I'm so sorry, Ms. Denay. I'll see to the problem immediately."

"But—"

"I was sure you wouldn't want your patrons served cold rolls," Barbie told him, her tone changing from demanding to sticky sweet as she smiled up at him. "Aren't you glad I'm here to hostess this group for you? Otherwise, you may not have known those rolls were cold."

Poor man. I felt sorry for him.

He glanced at me.

I shrugged.

He glanced at Reva and Sally.

They shrugged.

Cupping his hands together, he turned back to Barbie. "I'll personally go to the kitchen and make sure only hot rolls are being served."

She gave him a flirtatious smile. "Thank you, Pierre. You're such a nice man."

As soon as he disappeared through a doorway and I'd returned to my chair, Barbie sent those of us at the head table a victorious grin. "See how much better the service is when I'm in charge? If you don't watch these people, they'll walk all over you."

I bit my tongue. After many inward struggles with myself and my attitude, and much prayer to God, I'd finally come to think of Barbie as a friend. I was truly concerned about her and her relationship with God—or maybe I should have said *lack* of a relationship with Him. I know He placed her in my life for a purpose, but sometimes I wanted to strangle her. She was the most self-centered woman I had ever met. To her, her needs and wants superseded any needs others may have. There were moments in my life when I wished I'd never met Barbie Baxter. I couldn't count the times she had embarrassed me by her words and actions. I should have realized she'd figure out an excuse to wheedle her way into our meeting.

"Did you hear me, Valentine?"

I bobbed my head. "Yes, I heard you."

She moved to stand directly in front of me. "So you ladies are still determined to keep your group limited to widows? I heard you discussing it earlier."

My mouth gaped. "You heard us?"

"Of course."

I felt my feathers ruffle. "You were here? In the room? I didn't see you."

"Not exactly *in* the room." She nodded toward the ivy-covered latticework. "I was behind the lattice partition. Is it my fault your voices carry? By the way, you really should appoint all your officers tonight and not put it off. That way they can assume their responsibilities right away."

I glared at her. She was queen of her own Red Hat chapter and could run it any way she chose, but I was the queen of this chapter. "Oh, you think so, huh?" I shuddered as I heard that sentence come out of my mouth. It was as though we were back in high school again.

"Yes. And everyone needs to pay dues," she said curtly, as if she were the absolute authority on the subject. "An organization, even a small one like yours, can't function without a treasury. There are always unplanned expenses that need to be taken care of."

"I'll keep that in mind," I said as nicely as I could through gritted teeth, though I had thought of a few other words I would like to have added.

"You could learn a lot from me, Valentine," she rambled on, apparently still not realizing she was treading on my territory. "My chapter is one of the best-run chapters in the country, a real model for the other queens."

"Like I said, I'll keep your suggestions in mind."

Outwardly, I was smiling. Inwardly, I was seething. The audacity of that woman to listen in on our business meeting and then tell us how to run things. If I hadn't been a Christian and concerned about being a testimony to Barbie, I might have said something I'd later regret. But, thankfully, I didn't. I learned a long time ago, words spoken in haste could come back to haunt me, and I sure didn't want that to happen. Barbie and I had already had our run-ins, and I didn't want another one. No matter how they turned out, I always felt I came out the loser and was ashamed because I hadn't responded in a Christlike way.

It was then that I realized the room was as silent as a broken phone connection. All conversation among the women at the tables had ceased, and everyone was staring at us. I felt about six inches tall.

Lifting my shoulders, I stood and smiled at the lovely women seated in front of me. "Thanks to Barbie, our water glasses are being filled, we'll soon be served hot rolls, and our salads look delicious. Let's enjoy our meal."

As I sat back down and lifted my salad fork, I gazed fondly at the vast array of friendly faces engulfed in the sea of purple and red, and I knew, even with Barbie's unexpected presence and the tenseness it had caused, we were truly blessed. How could I have let such a little thing upset me so? Even though I was Valentine Denay, Queen of Hearts, it was God who was in control of the Widows' Club. Not me. It was up to Him to fight my battles. Hadn't I started the Widows' Club as a ministry to Him?

I sucked up my pride, smiled at Barbie, and gestured toward a nearby chair. "Maybe you can have dessert with us later," I told her, trying to sound gracious.

The surprised look she gave me was priceless. "Thank you. I–I'd love to."

With Barbie acting as overseer, the entrée reached each person without a hitch, though it was obvious the waiters weren't too happy having her bark out orders and look over their shoulders. As soon as each woman had finished her main course and had received the luscious-looking cherry pie à la mode, Barbie pulled a chair up beside the speaker's table and sat down, setting her pie in front of her. "So," she asked, twisting in her chair toward me, "what are you going to do at your next meeting?"

I responded with a slight frown. I wasn't sure it would be wise to tell her, especially since I hadn't told the others. Besides, I didn't want to announce that it was going to be a backyard Tuscany-themed party until I was absolutely sure my new landscape job could be completed in time. "It's still in the planning stage."

"The Red Parrott is an excellent restaurant, and they cater to Red Hat groups. They have amazing facilities. My group, Barbie's Babes, love to go there."

I picked up the purple pencil and pad I'd placed beside my plate earlier and wrote the name on the scratch pad. "Thanks for the suggestion. I'll keep it in mind."

Barbie's expression brightened. "If you decide to go to The Red Parrott, I'm sure I can talk the manager into letting me hostess like I'm doing tonight. That way you'll be assured great service."

Sally flashed me a questioning glance.

"It may be several months before we go to another restaurant," I said quickly, hoping she would let the subject drop. "But thank you for the suggestion. I'll be sure to pass it on."

"And there's another great restaurant we use quite often. It's a little pricey but has great ambience. It's. . .ah. . .ah." She gave her hand a flip. "I can't think of the name right now, but it'll come to me later. I have so many important things on my mind these days, I have a tendency to forget the mundane. I'll call you." Barbie speared a single cherry then, smiling at me, twirled her fork in the air. "I'm really glad you and I have become friends, Valentine. We have so much in common."

I nearly sputtered ice cream down the front of my dress at that remark. *So much in common?* In most ways, we are as opposite as a piece of cherry pie and a dish of spinach!

She turned her attention toward the others at the table. "Isn't it amazing that Valentine and I decorated our homes in the same color and the same style? What a coincidence!"

This time I *did* sputter pie onto my dress. Our homes were similar because Barbie had copied nearly everything I had already done to my house when she redecorated hers! Mine had been that way for a full year, long before she even moved into the neighborhood.

I was convinced that when she told a lie she thought it somehow magically turned into the truth just because she voiced it.

Giving me one of her plastic smiles, she pointed a perfectly manicured fingernail in my direction. "Oh, by the way, Valentine, I had lunch with Robert today."

She had lunch with Robert? My Robert?

Barbie fanned her hand through the air. "Now don't get all hot and bothered. Everything was perfectly innocent. As usual, he conducted himself like a gentleman."

I couldn't stand it. I had to know more about this innocent lunch. "He'd told me he was going to stop by McDonald's for a quick bite to eat. Is that where you saw him?" I tried to make it sound like a casual question, but I wasn't sure I succeeded. Barbie had done everything she could to get Robert to pay attention to her. As beautiful as she was, I was amazed her flirting schemes hadn't worked. Or had they? He hadn't mentioned Barbie was the one he'd be meeting when he'd phoned that morning. Was he trying to keep it a secret from me?

"Like I said, I didn't just *see* him, we had lunch together. I just love that man. He certainly knows how to treat women."

Grrr! The old jealousy we'd felt toward each other during our high school days, the jealousy I thought I'd squashed and put aside, grabbed hold of me and wouldn't turn loose. I decided rather than ask her about it, which was exactly what I knew she wanted me to do, I'd wait until I talked to Robert and let him tell me. Surely, since he and I were nearly engaged, he would mention it to me.

"Robert is definitely one of a kind," Sally said, giving me the eye. "I'm so glad he and Valentine—"

I narrowed my eyes in a way I knew Sally would interpret as *Keep your mouth shut!* Thankfully, she got the message.

I took Barbie's revelation about Robert as a cue to begin our program. Rising, I tapped my water glass again. "Ladies! Ladies! May I have your attention?"

I tapped it a second time, then waited for everyone to quiet down. "I know this meeting was to be our organizational meeting, but I thought it would be nice if we also had a short program. I've asked Debra Stone to share her magnificent talent with us and give us a mini-concert on the piano. We hear her at church quite often, but I understand that in addition to worship music, she also has a passion for the romantic songs of the fifties." I gave Debra a wide sweep of my hand. "Debra, it's all yours."

As Debra moved to the piano, Barbie leaned toward me and whispered, "I think I'll be going. I'm expecting a gentleman to stop by for a nightcap." She grinned that mischievous grin of hers. "I wouldn't want to miss him."

I wish I could say I was surprised by the way she conspicuously sashayed her way through the tables, pausing at each one to whisper a good night and blow everyone kisses, but I wasn't. That girl loved attention.

Debra's concert was even better than I had expected. When she played her final number, she invited us to sing along, a song we all loved—"Let Me Call You Sweetheart." I glanced at each face as we sang, and I could tell, for many of them, that song had a special meaning in their life. Mine, too. Carter had sung it to me many times during our years together, and I'm sure many of the other widows' husbands had sung it to them, as well. At the conclusion, I thanked everyone for coming, reminded them to take the favors we'd packaged for them, and said good night. Though everyone else left, Sally and Reva stayed behind.

Sally grabbed onto my arm, her big, innocent eyes gazing into mine. "I'm sorry, Valentine, I never meant to mention you and Robert, but I get so frazzled when Barbie is around. It's like she baits me to say something I'll regret."

Sally was notorious for speaking before thinking. "Don't worry about it, sweetie. No harm done."

"I feel like a dork around her. She's so beautiful. And look at me. My hair is a mousy brown. I'm short." She gestured toward her ample hips. "And no matter what I do, I can't seem to get rid of the extra ten pounds I've carried since my last baby was born. I hate being fat."

"You're not fat. You're. . .curvy. . .and beautiful. And you have one of the prettiest smiles I have ever seen." Naive as they come but loyal to the core, our sweet, innocent Sally always seemed to need the approval of her friends.

Reva sized her up. "You look okay to me, but if you're concerned, you should join the Y. I've heard they have some great exercise classes. Maybe that would help you."

I cringed. Leave it to Reva not to leave well enough alone. Unlike Sally, Reva, in her customary attire of blue jeans and chambray shirt, her light brown hair cut into a mannish style, and her speak-your-piece kind of attitude, at five feet eight inches could stand nose to nose with Barbie and put her in her place if she had a mind to. But, as brusque and outspoken as Reva was, she was as gentle as an autumn breeze to those of us who loved her. The kind of friend you always knew you could count on to stand by you. Through thick and thin, she was with you. Not only was she loyal, but she was amazing with tools, a real Ms. Fix-it. As chairman of the booth committee for our church bazaar last year, she and a handful of other women had built all the booths by themselves and had done a masterful job. Everyone was impressed with their skills.

When Sally didn't respond to her comment with more than a downward turn of the corners of her mouth, Reva stood and pushed her chair up against the table. Then, after picking up one of the pots of geraniums I'd told my friends to take, gave her head a shake. "Why in the world would Barbie make that statement about decorating her house? Everyone knows she copied you."

Relieved the conversation had shifted away from Sally's hips, I shrugged. "Why does Barbie do anything she does?"

Sally picked up her pot, then chimed in. "I feel sorry for her."

Reva did a double take. "Why?"

"She works so hard at trying to get folks to like her then she does things that make you want to hate her."

"Sally!"

"Well, she does, Valentine. Look at the shameful way she's always throwing herself at Robert. Everyone knows he's in love with you."

Then why did he have lunch with her today?

"He *is* in love with you, Valentine," Reva said, putting in her two cents' worth. "And everyone knows you're in love with him."

I felt as if my face had turned as red as the pot of geraniums Reva held in her hand. I hated it that I blushed so easily. Were my feelings for Robert that obvious? "Okay, I admit I have feelings for him, and we've even discussed how nice it would be to get married and spend the rest of our lives together, but even though Carter is gone, I can't help it, I still feel married. I've told Robert we're going to have to wait. I'm just not ready to commit myself to him yet."

"He's a real catch, Val. Everyone at church thinks you two belong together." A scowl worked its way across her face. "Are you sure waiting is wise? Knowing Barbie like you do?"

"Yeah, he might get tired of waiting for you if you put him off too long," Sally reminded me. "He's a man. Most men want to remarry after they've lost a spouse. I wouldn't let Barbie get too close to him if I were you."

"I hear what you're saying, and it does concern me that Barbie is so determined in her desire to win Robert for herself—" I lowered my eyes and fingered the wedding ring I still wore on my left hand. "But I can't even bring myself to take off my ring, let alone remarry." I didn't want to mention the fact that, at times, his patience with me did seem to be wearing thin. I hoped it was only my imagination.

Reva pulled her keys from her purse and stood staring at me. "I feel that way, too. My ring is a part of me. Like the one tie I have left to Manny."

Both Reva and I gasped as Sally thrust out her hand, revealing her ringless finger. "It was hard, but at my kids' request, I finally took mine off yesterday. They think I should start dating again."

"You're quite a bit younger than me," I reminded Sally. "I'm kind of surprised your children want you to start dating. Especially Jessica. I'd think most sixteen-year-olds would hate the idea of having another man come into their home." I slung my purse strap over my shoulder, picked up my box, and the three of us headed for the door.

"I was surprised, too, but I guess one of her friends has a new stepdad who is going out of his way to impress his new stepdaughter. He goes to all her games and has even bought her a car. I tried to tell Jessica not every stepdad is like that or can afford to be."

"But your kids are right, Sally." Reva said, looking back over her shoulder. "It is time for you to start dating. You have young children to raise, and you're going to need help. Besides, you were never meant to be alone."

Sally squiggled up her face. "But I could never marry, or even date, a man who didn't share my faith. A good man like that is hard to find."

I nodded. "Yeah, I know what you mean. That's one of the things that drew me to Robert." I mentally ran through the list of single men in our church. Although there were a number of nice ones, I couldn't visualize Sally with any of them. They just weren't her type.

Reva muffled a giggle. "Maybe you could try a dating service, Sal. I've heard there are some Christian ones out there."

"Jessica mentioned that very thing."

Reva did a half turn. "I was only kidding, Sal. You aren't going to do it, are you?"

"Of course not! I'm still pretty uncomfortable with the idea of dating at all, so I can't imagine dating a stranger."

The three of us moved out into the main section of the restaurant, which was now empty except for two couples lingering over coffee at a corner table.

The owner hurried toward us. "Was everything satisfactory?"

I nodded. "Yes, thank you, everything was quite nice. We had a lovely evening. I'm sure our group will want to come back to The Southern Belle again sometime in the future."

"I was slightly taken aback when Ms. Baxter showed up tonight, since she wasn't on the guest list you'd given me. But when she told me you'd requested that she act as hostess for your group, I figured it would be okay."

Reva, Sally, and I sent glances to one another.

I couldn't resist. "She told me she had lunch here a few days ago. I'm surprised she didn't mention it to you then."

He gave me a mystified look. "Lunch here a few days ago? I don't recall seeing her since her Red Hat group was here several months ago. She's not the kind of woman you'd easily forget."

That's for sure.

"I'm sorry the rolls weren't as warm as they should have been," he went on. "If your group comes back again, I'll add dessert to your menu at no additional cost to make up for it. I want my customers to be happy."

"Don't worry about it." I managed a smile, though inside I was thinking about the lie Barbie had told us about seeing the man at lunch. "The rolls were delicious."

"And you were satisfied with your entrée ?"

"Absolutely."

"I'm confused. *You* requested Barbie as hostess for our dinner?" Sally asked when we three reached the parking lot.

"Of course not, Sally! She lied when she told him that. I would never ask Barbie to come and hostess after we'd decided this was to be a widows-only group. She invited herself! She probably thought we'd never find out the truth."

"I thought the two of you had made peace."

"Reva," I said, well remembering that day, only a week before, when I'd gone to Barbie to apologize for my short patience with her and the way I'd been treating her, "I thought we *had*, too, especially since I apologized. I'd even admitted I was jealous of her, not only because of her vow to *get* Robert for herself, but also because of her beauty, her gorgeous, voluminous head of blond hair, her incredible smile, her willowy figure, her winsome personality, and a lot of other things she has going for her."

"And she accepted your apology?"

"Yes. She even went so far as to compliment me back and tell me how grateful she was for the way I'd stepped in and taken care of her when she was sick."

"Barbie actually said that?"

"Though they were a long time coming, those were her very words." I opened my car door, took the box from Reva's hands, and placed it on the seat. "I know this is going to surprise you, but I told her I thought it was time the two of us became friends—real friends—and I said I was glad she had moved in next door to me."

Sally's jaw dropped. "How could you say such a thing? She's caused you nothing but trouble. I thought you hated it that she'd moved in next door."

I considered my words carefully. "I did hate it, up until I came to the realization that God had put her there so I could be a witness to her and lead her to Him. I'm afraid that before Barbie and I had that talk, I'd been a willing stumbling block instead of the loving stepping-stone God had called me to be. What she saw in me—my actions, my words—was anything but a true reflection of my Lord."

Reva placed a loving hand on my shoulder. "You weren't that bad."

"I was, Reva. You know I was. I've been terrible. Though I

didn't deserve her forgiveness, I thought sure, after Barbie and I had apologized to each other, we could be friends—" I smiled first at Reva, then at Sally. "Though she could never be as close a friend as you two are." I shrugged. "But when she pulls something like she did tonight, showing up uninvited and then lying about it?" I tossed my purse onto the car seat, then lifted my hands in discouragement. "I just don't know. You should be able to trust a friend, yet I wonder if I'll ever be able to trust Barbie."

"Then there's the matter of Robert."

Reva was right. There *was* the matter of Robert. Robert's and my relationship had started out on a casual basis when I had been asked to be the chairperson of our church's first annual bazaar and the church board had appointed Robert as the bazaar liaison. But without either of us expecting it, our relationship soon developed into something much more.

"I don't think you should put his offer of marriage off too long," Reva said.

Sally huffed. "It's obvious Robert loves you. But he's a man, Valentine. Granted, a godly man, but look how many men have been led astray by beautiful women. Not only David, Solomon, and other men in the Bible, but pastors in our own city. Men who should be grounded enough in God's Word to resist that kind of temptation."

"Sally's right, Val. Not that I think Robert is weak enough to succumb to her charms, especially since she doesn't share his faith like you do, but—" She clamped her lips and gazed into my eyes. I could see kindness there.

I knew what she was about to say—it could happen—even with as fine a man as Robert. But as afraid as I was that there was even the slightest possibility of that happening, I still wasn't ready to commit my life to another man, not even him. I'd finally admitted to myself that I loved Robert, but even though Carter had died, I still loved him, too. I couldn't help myself.

I dragged my weary self into the driver's seat, then looked up at my friends. "Look, you two wonderful, caring women, the best friends a gal could ever have, I appreciate your concern, and I know you're right, but I can't jump into something I'm not ready for because I'm afraid of what Barbie might do. I pray about Robert's and my relationship all the time. If God wants the two of us together, He'll work it out. I'm not saying that will keep Barbie from doing her best to take him away from me. It probably won't. But if Robert should happen to succumb to her charms and decide she was the one for him instead of me—which, knowing him, I'm sure he wouldn't do unless she became a true, born-again Christian—then, even though it would hurt me terribly, I would have to accept the fact that those two belonged together. Does that make sense?"

Reva nodded. "I guess so."

"But, Valentine—" Sally protested.

I lifted my hand to halt her words. "No more, Sally, please." After making sure they were out of the way, I closed my door and rolled down my window. "I'm beat, and I'll bet you two are, too. Let's call it a night." I inserted the key in the ignition, then gave it a twist. "Thanks to you and all your help, I think our first meeting was a success. Wanna come by in the morning for coffee?"

Reva grinned, then slipped an arm around Sally. "You bet. We'll both be there, and I'll bring some of those poppy seed muffins you girls like so well."

We'd launched the Widows' Club.

It was now a reality.

I could hardly wait for the next meeting.

But as I pulled into my driveway, my heart sank.

$\mathscr{C}$HAPTER 3

Robert's truck was sitting in Barbie's driveway!

Robert? He was the man she'd expected to stop by for a nightcap?

Maybe I didn't know him as well as I thought.

Rather than park in my garage, which was my usual mode of operation, I parked in my driveway and stared out my windshield. I couldn't help wondering what was going on in that house as all sorts of scenarios ran through my mind. I grabbed up my purse, then slammed my door, half hoping they'd hear it and come out to see what all the noise was about. . .but no one appeared in her doorway. I craned my neck, hoping to catch a glimpse of them through the big plate-glass windows in Barbie's living room, but the windows were dark. She'd either closed the drapery or hadn't turned on the lights. No wonder she didn't mention who she was expecting. She hadn't wanted *me* to know who it was! And Robert certainly hadn't mentioned planning on going to her house when he'd phoned me that morning. Of course he hadn't mentioned having lunch with her, either. Sometimes he seemed so secretive. I suddenly realized I knew very little about Robert. Other than the two years he'd lived in Nashville and attended my church, I knew practically nothing of his past, other than the fact his deceased wife's name was Lydia and he'd lost his son in the war in Iraq.

Feeling angry and betrayed by both Barbie *and* Robert, I grabbed the box from my backseat and pranced toward my front door with plans to slip into my nightgown, go to bed, and pull the covers over my head.

I discovered later that pulling the covers over my head didn't block out the vision that kept nagging at me, of Robert and Barbie together in that house alone at that late hour. I felt a slight sense of relief when I heard his Avalanche start up and pull out of the driveway, but I still had to wonder why he was there and whether his visit was his idea or Barbie's.

"Hey, girlfriend, why the long face?"

I rallied a smile for Reva as we gathered around my kitchen table the next morning, surprised I'd been so transparent. "Nothing. Didn't sleep well, that's all. Too big a night last night, I guess. But we did have fun, didn't we?" When I felt soft fur press against my leg, I bent and patted Sprinkles, the stray cat that had wandered into my yard several months before. I'd done everything I could to find the owner, but when no one would claim him, I'd allowed him to stay, even though I wasn't a cat person. He'd won his way into my heart, and I couldn't imagine life without him. "Out with you, you spoiled thing," I told him as I opened the storm door. "And don't bother the birds."

Reva watched, then shook her finger at me. "I can't believe how you spoil that cat."

I huffed. "I can't believe it either."

Sally filled three cups from my coffeepot, then set them down before us in the center of my bright yellow and white daisy-trimmed place mats. "We did have fun, didn't we? I think the Widows' Club is exactly what we've all needed." She gestured toward my back door. "By the way, Barbie waved at me when I got here. She said she'd be over in a few minutes."

I grimaced. Oh, terrific! Just what I needed to start my day!

Reva lifted her cup and peered over the top at me. "Even knowing how brazen she can be, I'm still surprised she showed up like that last night."

Sally nodded in agreement. "Nothing that woman does surprises me."

"I feel that way, too." *Seeing Robert's car in her driveway had been an even worse surprise.* "I guess we should be complimented that she wants to be a part of us," I said, trying to sound nice while keeping my true feelings to myself.

"Like the way she throws herself at Robert?"

I rubbed at my forehead, then let out a sigh. "Yeah, like that." I almost mentioned his truck being in her driveway, but I didn't. Sharing my anger and frustration with them would serve no purpose but to cause more trouble.

Our three heads turned as my back door opened. It was her, in all her glory. Flowing white caftan, huge gold hoop earrings, a heavy gold chain about her neck, stiletto sandals, and that voluminous, gorgeous, bleached-blond head of hair that always reminded me of a gypsy. As was typical, even this early in the morning, her makeup had been meticulously applied. Despite being fifty-three, she always looked like an ad out of a leading fashion magazine, and today was no exception. I hurriedly tucked my shirttail into my jeans while wishing I'd at least applied a dab of lipstick before my friends had arrived.

As if she were on stage in a play, Barbie waved toward the sun streaming in through my kitchen window. "Isn't this the most magnificent day you have ever seen? The sun is shining, the birds are singing, the flowers are blooming. What a wonderful day to be alive."

That's easy for you to say. You spent the evening with Robert!

Reva selected a poppy seed muffin from the plate I'd set on the table and began to peel off the pleated paper. "You're cheerful this morning."

Barbie twirled around, her long caftan billowing out about her slim legs, then seated herself with the grand move of a princess. "Why shouldn't I be? Everything is going so well in my life."

What you mean is—you somehow conned Robert to coming over to your house last night.

Reva pushed the plate of muffins toward Barbie.

The twig of a woman turned away from it as if it contained rotten apples. "Too sugary for me! I have to watch my figure, or no one else will!"

Why did that statement bring up visions of Robert? What was it Reva had said? *"Robert loves you. But he's a man. Look how many men have been led astray by beautiful women."* Her words haunted me like a bad omen.

For a moment, no one spoke. Finally, Sally, bless her heart, took the plunge. "Did the man you were expecting stop by for that nightcap last night?"

"Of course he did, Sally. I can't remember a time when a man stood me up."

Reva leaned toward her conspiratorially. "Was it someone we know?"

"Maybe Jake Gorman?" Sally inserted. "He was the foreman on your landscaping job, wasn't he? He'd certainly be a nice catch."

Barbie nodded. "Oh, yes. That Jake is one handsome man. I could go for him in a big way." Then, with a smile I perceived as a smirk, she added, "If I didn't already have someone else in mind."

"So it wasn't Jake?"

Barbie feigned shyness, which must have been difficult for her. "A girl never kisses and tells. You should know that, Reva."

Kisses and tells? No, Robert wouldn't kiss her. Not yet anyway. Or would he? She is an attractive woman. Get that notion out of your mind, Valentine. You know him better than that. She's simply playing it coy. I wish she would go after Jake. Maybe if she did, she would leave Robert alone.

Sally leaned forward in her chair. "Was it your Realtor friend?"

Barbie gave a twirl of her long, manicured-in-red fingers. "Like I said, a girl never kisses and tells."

But you'd love to, right?

"By the way, Barbie, when is your next Red Hat Barbie's Babes meeting?"

I was glad for a change in the subject before I said something I might later regret. I just hoped my face didn't betray my true feelings. "Next week, but I have no idea what we are going to do. The woman who is planning it is keeping it a secret."

Sally proudly pointed her finger at me. "We're calling our queen the Queen of Hearts. Don't you just love that name?"

The smile on Barbie's face quickly morphed into a narrow line. "I know. I overheard it at the restaurant last night." She twisted in her seat to face me. "Being the queen is a huge responsibility, Valentine. People expect you to be perfect. Are you sure you're up to it?"

Me? Up to it? I'd taken on far more responsibility than leader of a Red Hat group when I'd organized the church bazaar. "I'm sure I won't be perfect, but I'll do my best," I said evenly, hoping the rest of her time with us wouldn't be spent giving me more advice.

Barbie leaned forward, her elbows resting on the table, her face serious. "You'd never guess who I heard from. Can you believe it? My last ex's sister. He's on oxygen full-time now. The doctor says he may not last a year."

Sally's eyes widened. "That's awful. Are you going to go see him?"

Barbie huffed. "No, although she said he'd asked about me. But why would I want to go see him? He left me for that brazen hussy, and his sister said they're still together. If I never see that man again, it'll be too soon."

"Maybe he asked her to call you. A lot of people want to try to right the wrongs they've done when they face death."

Glaring at Sally, she huffed again. "Not that man. He's too self-centered. He'd never admit to doing anything wrong, even on his deathbed. I'm sure he's convinced everyone our divorce was my fault, when the truth is, I was the innocent party. I was the perfect wife to all three of my husbands. They were the ones with the problems."

I nearly spewed my coffee on that one. Sally, Reva, and I exchanged glances.

"If he dies," she went on, blissfully oblivious to our response to her statement, "I'll be a widow. Then I can join the Widows' Club, so the news of his bad health wasn't all bad."

Our jaws dropped. How could she speak so cavalierly about someone's death? Even an ex-husband whom she hated?

"Of course," she continued, "knowing him, he'll probably live to a ripe old age. As they say, only the good die young."

What could we say to a statement like that?

Reva rose, then picked up her and Sally's cups and placed them in my dishwasher. "Hate to rush off, but Sal and I need to go. I promised my mother-in-law I'd take her to Wal-Mart, and even with me pushing her in the wheelchair, that's still a two-hour process."

Sally scooped the muffin crumbs from the table into her cupped hand, then stood and dropped them in the wastebasket I kept by the fridge. "And I've got laundry to do." She bent and kissed my cheek. "See you in the morning, Queen Valentine."

Barbie rose, too, her hands moving to finger her hair. "And I have to get to the beauty shop."

Everyone was deserting me. I walked them to the door, then watched as Sally and Reva crawled into Sally's car and Barbie walked across the lawn to her house.

Barbie hadn't even mentioned Robert's late-night visit. Surely she knew I'd seen his truck. Curiosity was killing me. What, if anything, was going on between those two?

I went about my tasks, cleaning the kitchen, sweeping the patio, picking the faded petals from the petunia baskets that hung on my porch, but all the time my mind was on Robert. I seemed to be thinking less about Carter and more about him these days. Surely that was a good sign. Could it be that I was finally putting aside the guilt feelings for my deceased husband?

It was a beautiful morning, the kind that makes you certain God is in control. Unable to resist its lure, I pulled off my work gloves, seated myself on the porch swing, and began to swing. There was something about swinging in my porch swing that was soothing, almost cathartic. As I had done so many times in the past, I swiveled around and swung my legs onto the seat, then leaned back and rested my head against the pillow I kept there, and closed my eyes. I loved hearing the sound of the birds in the trees. I wondered if they could actually communicate or if they ever had disagreements like we mortals do.

I yawned, then stretched my arms one way and then the other before wrapping them over my chest, crossing my legs at the ankles, and snuggling down into the comfort of the pillow. This was the laziest day I'd had in months, and despite my concern about Robert and Barbie being together the night before, I was enjoying every minute of simply relaxing.

I must have drifted off, because the next thing I knew, someone kissed me on the cheek. Startled, I lifted my head and stared into eyes so blue they could have competed with the clear blue waters of the Caribbean and won hands down. "Robert! How long have you been here?"

He snickered. "Long enough to watch you drool."

I let out a gasp as my hand went to my chin. "I drooled?"

He threw back his head with a boisterous laugh, then grabbed hold of my wrist. "I'm only kidding, Valentine. You weren't drooling.

Beautiful, put-together women like you don't drool." He slipped his finger beneath my chin and lifted my face to his. "Did anyone ever tell you how cute you are when you're asleep?"

I hurriedly swung my feet to the ground and raised myself to a sitting position. "Why are you here?"

His brows raised as he sat down on the swing beside me. "Aren't I welcome?"

"Of course you are. I was just surprised, that's all."

"I was going to call you this morning to see how the Widows' Club meeting went, but I decided to stop by instead, since I was coming this way to check on a landscaping job. I would have stopped when I left Barbie's last night, but your house was dark. You must have already gone to bed."

Feigning innocence, I gazed up at him. "You were at Barbie's last night?"

"You didn't see my truck when you got home?"

"I had my hands full and was anxious to get into the house. I—I guess I never noticed." Why didn't I tell him the truth? What difference did it make if I saw him there? I had no say in what he did.

"She phoned me when she got back from your meeting. The water in the toilet in her upstairs bathroom wouldn't shut off, and it was too late to call a plumber."

That's why he was at her house? "Why didn't she let it go until morning?" I asked, as if I didn't know the answer. "She has four bathrooms in that house."

He shrugged. "It was the bathroom off her bedroom. I guess the noise bothered her."

"So? Were you able to fix it?"

He huffed. "Yeah, it wasn't that big a deal."

His shy grin made me think there was more to the story. "Oh?"

"She sure didn't look like she was expecting the plumber when I showed up at her door. Valentine, she had the lights turned low, music playing on the CD player, and she was dressed in some skimpy, feathery thing. I was embarrassed to even look in her direction."

"But she wasn't expecting the plumber. She was expecting *you*," I reminded him, pleased to learn he hadn't gone to Barbie's for that nightcap. "That makes a big difference."

"Well, let me tell you, once I got that thing fixed, I got out of there as fast as I could. So fast, I left my favorite pliers in her bathroom. I bought a new pair this morning. She can keep that pair, though I doubt she'd know how to use them." He slipped his arm around my shoulders and pulled me close as he set the swing to rocking with his foot. "So, how did the meeting go?"

I told him about the restaurant, the decorated tables, the decisions we'd made.

"Barbie told me the manager had asked her to be your hostess for the evening."

"He didn't ask her, Robert. That was a lie. She told him *I'd* asked her."

"I suspected as much. Did she behave herself?"

"Except for barking out orders to the restaurant staff, she was the perfect hostess. I'm sure all our ladies, except those of us who really know her, were impressed with her efficiency."

"Did she tell you I saw her at lunch yesterday?"

"Yes, she said the two of you had lunch together." I tried to sound casual, like it really didn't matter.

49

A slight frown creased his suntanned brow. "If you call sharing a table for fifteen minutes in McDonald's having lunch together, then, yes, I guess we did."

My jaw dropped. "*She* had lunch at McDonald's?"

He nodded. "Yeah, she likes their salads and their low-fat dressing. I was surprised to see her there."

She probably happened to see you drive in and followed you. I wanted to slap myself for that thought. Why did I always suspect the worst where Barbie was concerned?

Maybe because you're jealous of her and her beauty, a voice said from somewhere deep inside me.

"So when is your next meeting?"

"Four weeks from today. It's going to be at my house. I want to make it a really festive occasion." Putting all thoughts of Barbie aside, I turned and gave him a coquettish grin. "But I'm going to need your help."

A tingle went clear to my toes when he pulled me even closer.

"For you, Valentine, I'd do anything."

My smile widened. "Even turn my backyard into an Italian villa?"

"It could be a challenge, but it sounds like fun. Grapevines, arbors, and fountains are my specialty. Besides, it'd give me an excuse to spend more time with you."

He wasn't kidding about the specialty part. As the owner of Chase's Landscape and Garden business, Robert certainly had the know-how, as well as access to anything and everything necessary to make over my backyard into the masterpiece I had in mind.

"I don't want the Tuscany look to be a temporary thing. I want it to be permanent and beautiful, with what you said—grapevines,

arbors, and a fountain," I explained. "I've wanted to redo my backyard ever since you remodeled and landscaped Barbie's yard."

"I've got some great magazines and catalogs. I'll bring them
over so you can take a look at them. The Tuscany look is one of
my favorite themes." His cheek touched mine as he whispered, "If
you'd marry me, we could go to Italy for our honeymoon and take
an even better look at the Tuscany décor."

If I loved this man like I thought I did, why did the image of
my deceased husband's face always come to haunt me whenever
Robert brought up the subject of marriage? According to God's
Word, as a widow, I was free to marry again, but that terrible
feeling of guilt always plagued me for even thinking about having
a relationship with someone else.

Robert gave me a slight squeeze. "Valentine? Did you hear me?"

I closed my eyes, trying to blot out Carter's image. "Yes, I
heard you."

"I didn't mean for my words to upset you, sweetheart." I felt
the tip of his finger slide gently beneath my chin. "They were
wishful thinking on my part. I can hardly wait to see your sweet
face smiling at me over the breakfast table every morning."

I opened my eyes, then pressed my forehead lightly against
his. "I wish I *was* ready to marry you, but—"

"But you're not. The memory of Carter is still standing between us."

"Yes."

He kissed my cheek with a kiss so sweet and gentle it touched
the innermost recesses of my heart.

I lifted misty eyes to his. "I'm trying to—"

He put a finger to my lips. "I know you are, and I love you for it. There's nothing I want more than to make you my bride."

I had to ask. I had to know. I didn't want to lose him. "Are you sure? You could have your pick of women. Beautiful, godly women who wouldn't hesitate one minute to accept your proposal and do all they could to make you happy."

"I don't want any of those women, dearest. I'm in love with you."

I wanted to hold on to those words forever, to etch them upon my heart, especially since I felt unworthy of this good man. That he would be willing to wait was truly amazing. I knew several women who had married within three months of their husbands' deaths. Why hadn't I reacted that way? But in my heart, I knew the answer. Those women hadn't been married to my Carter. Even without the children we had both longed for, Carter's and my marriage had been more than I ever could have hoped for.

"I could never be Carter, and I may not have his wonderful attributes, but I love you, Valentine, and I love our Lord. I promise you, sweetheart, I will strive with every ounce of strength God gives me and with everything in my being to be the husband you deserve. I would never try to replace Carter, my love. I want you to continue to cherish the years you had with him, even as I cherish the years I spent with Lydia. You shared the biggest part of your life with that man. I'm not asking you to forget the past. I'm asking you to share the future with me."

For a brief moment, the image of Carter that separated me from Robert seemed to fade into the distance. "I do love you, Robert." I'd no more than said those words when the image reappeared, strong as ever. "But—but I need more time."

He released a deep sigh, then, pulling his arm from about me, he rose and tugged me up beside him. "I know, and I am trying to be patient. It's just that I want to whisk you off to some exotic place as my bride. Some place where we can be alone. Without anyone or anything making demands on our lives. To me, that would be as close to heaven as I could get here on earth. I think the Tuscany valley would be the perfect place for our honeymoon, but I'd be willing and happy to go wherever you choose." His lips lightly grazed mine, then turning aside, he nodded toward my backyard. "This landscaping job of yours could be a lot of work and expensive. Are you sure you want to go to all that trouble? Your house should sell quickly the way it is."

I gasped. "My house sell?"

He shrugged. "I figured, when we married, we'd both sell our houses and get a home of our own."

"I could never leave this house and all the memories it holds. It's a part of me!"

A deep frown creased his brow. "Surely you don't expect me to move in here."

"I—I don't know what I thought."

"I'd never be comfortable living in this house, and I wouldn't think you'd want me living here, either." He gestured toward the kitchen door. "Face it, Valentine. It'd be like *three* people living here. You, me, and Carter."

"But. . .how could I ever leave it?"

"Maybe you should have thought of that before you led me to believe we could have a life together. I'm a patient man, but only if I'm convinced what I am waiting on is actually going to happen. The fact that you can't bring yourself to accept my marriage proposal, and the fact that you refuse to leave this house and I can't live here in Carter's shadow makes our situation seem impossible. Maybe it's time we reevaluated our relationship. I know I promised I'd wait as long as it takes, but I can't wait forever, especially if it seems nothing is going to happen."

His sigh and the sober expression on his face said it all.

We had a problem, a major problem.

And I, for one, had no solution.

For a moment, we simply stared at one another.

Then slowly, without a kiss good-bye or even a backward glance, he turned and hurried toward his truck, leaving me standing alone on the porch with an aching heart. I watched until the Avalanche disappeared, hoping, wishing he'd come back. But even if he had, what difference would it have made? I couldn't give up my home, and he couldn't live here.

Though it was a beautiful day and there was plenty of gardening I needed to do, I couldn't. My heart wasn't in it. All I could think about as I aimlessly wandered inside, feeling sorry for myself and taking on mundane tasks to keep my hands busy, was that I may have lost Robert. Not because of Barbie and anything she'd done, but because of me.

Three times over the next hour I dialed Robert's cell phone, and three times I hung up before he answered. I half hoped he'd see my number on the missed-call list and phone me, but what would I say if he did call? Nothing had changed since he'd left me. My nerves were a basket case of jangles.

About four I fixed myself a low-cal, low-fat frozen dinner, which I ate in front of the TV while I watched some program on the affect of stress on your health. Talk about perfect timing. I felt totally stressed out. Eventually, after I cranked open a window to enjoy the light breeze that had gently begun flicking at the leaves on the trees, I picked up the new novel I'd been wanting to read, hoping it would make me forget my woes, and pushed back in the recliner. I'd gotten no farther than the first paragraph on the first page when I heard a vehicle of some kind pull into Barbie's driveway.

I cringed.

Surely not her toilet again!

CHAPTER 4

After hurriedly folding down the corner of the page in my book, I lowered the footrest and rushed to the window, relieved to see an unfamiliar car parked in Barbie's driveway instead of the Avalanche. Curiosity getting the better of me, I lingered long enough to see if I could recognize Barbie's late afternoon caller.

I watched as the willowy figure of a woman, whose beauty nearly equaled that of Barbie's, climbed gracefully out of her silver Mercedes convertible, walked up onto Barbie's porch, and pressed the doorbell. When no one answered, she pressed it a second time. Finally, Barbie appeared in the doorway. I couldn't hear what they were saying, eavesdropper that I had become, but from the blank expression on my neighbor's face, I got the impression she didn't know the woman. After exchanging a few more words, Barbie pushed open the storm door and motioned her in. From the looks of her expensive car and her couture garments, I doubted she was the Avon lady. Since it wasn't any of my business anyway,

I went back to my book.

I'd barely settled in the chair again when the phone rang. It was Sally.

"Valentine, I feel really stupid," she began without taking time to even say hello. "Something has happened, and I'm not sure how to handle it. I need your advice."

Knowing the trouble Sally's teenage daughter, Jessica, had caused her in the past, I feared the worst. "I'm not one to be giving you advice on child rearing. Maybe you should talk to—"

"This isn't on child rearing. It's about me."

I could tell from the tone of her voice that whatever was troubling her was serious. "Okay," I said, momentarily putting my own troubles aside, "tell me about it. Maybe the two of us can put our heads together and work something out."

"I feel sorta silly for even mentioning it."

"You know you can tell me anything."

"I should have told you about it this morning."

"Quit procrastinating. Out with it, Sal. What's troubling you?"

"I got a phone call last night."

"So? Who was it from?"

"Remember that new George guy who has been coming to our Motivators class on Sunday mornings?"

Though she couldn't see me, I nodded. "Yeah, what about him?"

"He—ah—he asked me for a date! For next Thursday night."

I sucked in a quick breath. "He did? A real date?"

"Yep, a real date. I've already told Reva about it. He's such a nice man, and he loves the Lord. That's really important to me."

It took me a few seconds to digest what she'd said. "Are you going?"

"That's why I called you. Reva made fun of me at first, but then she said she thought I should go. What do you think? Should I?"

"Sally, you're in your midforties. You don't need my permission. Do you want to?"

"Kinda, but I'm not really sure."

I dog-eared my page again, then closed my book and set it on the table next to my chair. That was serious stuff we were talking about and demanded my full attention. "I—I didn't realize you were ready to date again."

"I'm not sure I am, especially after seeing all the turmoil you're going through with Robert." She paused. "But, Valentine, even though I live in a house with three noisy kids, I'm lonely. A night out, being treated like a real woman and not just my kids' mom, sounds really appealing at this point in my life. I need something new."

Dear me. Who was I to be giving advice on the subject of dating? Especially now.

"He's talking about dinner at a nice place and a movie afterward."

"It sounds to me like you've already decided."

Another pause. "At first I refused, but after we'd had a chance to talk and he explained how lonely he's been since his wife left him and remarried, I sorta reconsidered. I told him to let me think about it and call me this afternoon."

"I don't really know him that well, but he seems nice."

"Does that mean you think I should accept his invitation?"

I tightened my grip on the phone. "What was your children's reaction, or haven't you told them yet?"

"Actually, all three of them were in the room when he called.

They heard my side of the conversation, every word. Amazingly, they didn't seem the least bit upset and even encouraged me to go. I thought sure Jessica would throw a fit that a man would even call me, but she didn't."

I lifted my shoulders in a shrug. "Well, if *you* want to go and your children want you to go, then maybe you should. One date doesn't commit you to anything."

"I hate to turn him down. He may never ask me again."

"Then don't turn him down. Go, Sally. A night out on the town with a male companion might be just what you need. You have seemed a bit down lately. Have you prayed about going?"

She responded with a giggle. "Not yet. I wanted to call you first."

"God is a much better adviser than I could ever think of being, Sally. You'd better ask His advice."

"Everyone keeps reminding me God's Word says I'm free to date again."

"That's the way I understand it." How many times had I tried to convince myself of that very thing?

"Thank you, Valentine. I knew you'd know what to do. I'm going to tell him yes."

I could hear the excitement in her voice. Then a click sounded and our conversation was over. Sally was going on a date! I guessed I shouldn't have been so surprised. She had a lot going for her. She was quite a bit younger than me, was pretty, and had a great personality and a smile that would wilt any man's heart. Granted, she was a wee bit insecure, and sometimes airheaded and naive, but she was a jewel. Any man would have been fortunate to have her in his life. But somehow I couldn't picture her with anyone else but Eric. Those two had been a wonderfully matched couple.

As my gaze fell upon the framed photograph of Carter and me that I kept on the mantel, I tried to imagine Robert's face in that picture, in Carter's place. A shudder coursed through my body, and I turned away, unable to bear the guilt I felt from Carter's image. I had always supposed he would want me to marry again and be happy, but we never really talked about it. Maybe he wouldn't feel that way. Then I tried to imagine what it would be like for Carter if he were the one who had lived and *I* had died. If he were sitting in my place, staring at that same photograph and trying to imagine another woman in my place, how would he have reacted? If only we *had* talked about those things. Maybe, if we had, I wouldn't have felt so guilty about marrying Robert. Sometimes life was the pits.

Reva rolled her eyes. "So you're gonna do it? You're really gonna go on a date?"

A slight blush appeared on Sally's cheeks as we sat in my kitchen the next morning. "I told him yes. Do you think I'm doing the right thing?"

Reva, wearing her customary solid-color chambray shirt and blue jeans, leaned back in her chair, frowned, and crossed her arms, her lower lip rolling down. "You girls make me feel like an old maid. You with your George and Valentine with her Robert."

Sally grinned. "You want us to find a man for you?"

Reva rolled her eyes again, then turned her head away. "I have enough troubles with my crotchety mother-in-law living with me.

Can you imagine what she'd do if some man showed up at my door? She never thought I was worthy of Manny, but she sure wouldn't want any other man to have me."

Sally leaned forward and placed her hand on Reva's shoulder. "But wouldn't it be nice to have someone pay attention to you, tell you how special you are, take you to nice places?"

Reva huffed. "Sal! You haven't even been on that date yet and you're already talking like—"

"Like a woman who is tired of carrying the ball by herself, tired of trying to do the repairs around the house when I have no idea what I'm doing? I'm ready for someone to take me out to dinner, tell me I look nice, talk to me like I'm an adult, and treat me with the respect I rarely get from my kids." Sally let out a long, slow sigh. "I went from my father's house to becoming a wife, then a mother, and now a widow. I was there when my parents needed me, when my husband needed me, and when my kids needed me. I've spent all my time and energy since Eric died keeping our home together and trying to sell our business. It may sound selfish, but when is it going to be time for just me? I never thought I'd even consider dating again, but I'm excited about my date with George. If you think that makes me a bad person, then so be it. You're entitled to your opinion. But, as for me? I plan to have the time of my life. I'm going to have my hair and nails done and buy a new dress. I may even purchase a pair of fashionable shoes. This may be the only date I'll ever have, but I plan to make the most of it!"

I couldn't help myself—despite the sorrow tugging at my own heart, I stood and applauded. "Bravo, Sally. I'm proud of you. I didn't know you had it in you."

Reva gave her a half salute with her coffee cup. "Wow, Sal.

What are you on? I've never heard you talk like that."

Sally grinned. "I don't know what's gotten into me, but I felt like a schoolgirl when I got out of bed this morning. It was like the sun shone more brightly, the sky was bluer. Like there was a rainbow, which there couldn't have been, because it hadn't rained. I haven't felt like that in years." Her grin broadened. "And you know what? I like the feeling. I wish it would last forever."

She stopped long enough to let out a giggle. "I didn't even holler at my kids when they nearly missed the school bus. That was a first. Normally, when something like that happened, I'd go into a tirade. Today, I just smiled. If they missed the bus, so what? No big deal. I'd just drive them to school."

Reva gave her head a shake. "Wow, Sal, if one simple date makes you feel like that, maybe I should consider putting myself on the market again."

Glad for friends who could make me laugh in spite of my problems and the fact I hadn't heard a word from Robert since he'd walked out on me, I gave Reva a playful nudge. "On the market?"

"You know what I mean, Valentine." She raised a brow. "I've gotten a few overtures from men."

Both Sally and I gasped. Our plain, more-interested-in-new-tools-than-a-new-dress Reva was getting overtures from a man? Unthinkable! "Who?"

She treated us to a mischievous smile. "A lady never kisses and tells."

Sally grabbed onto her arm. "You kissed someone?"

"Sal—it's a figure of speech, not a statement of a truth. I didn't say I'd kissed anyone, but—"

Her big eyes rounded, Sally leaned closer. "But what?"

"But a few men *have* asked me to sit with them in church."

Now I leaned closer. "Are you serious? I've never seen you sit with a man in church. You and Sally usually sit together."

Reva huffed. "You girls don't listen. I didn't say I'd *sat* with them. I said they'd *asked* me to sit with them."

"What men?" It was obvious Sally's interest had been piqued. Mine had been, too. "Name them."

Reva crossed her arms. "I'd prefer not to say."

"You should have sat with them, Reva," I told her. "Sitting with a man would do no harm."

"I still feel married."

Boy, did those words hit home.

"Manny's not coming back, Reva. You have to face that fact."

"It's not that Manny wouldn't want me to date, and even marry again, because he always told me that if anything ever happened to him he'd want me to go on with my life."

"Then why not date one of them?" Sally asked. "If that's what Manny wanted you to do?"

"He never liked any of those guys. He always called them Sunday-morning Christians. You know. People who make it to church on Sundays but have no real spiritual depth in their lives. If I ever get involved with a man, it will be with someone who loves the Lord. Someone I'm sure Manny would approve of. But don't hold your breath until that happens. Most of the good ones are already taken."

"Manny would only be picky because he would want the very best for you."

Reva smiled, then became somber. "All three of us were fortunate to have had men who loved us like our husbands did.

Every woman should be so blessed. Eric, Manny, and Carter are not easily replaced. They were each one of a kind."

Sally, too, became somber. "I thought Eric and I would be together forever. I really miss him."

Reva leaned back in her chair and stared off into space. "I hate the idea of growing old alone."

"I think everyone feels that way. I know I do. We all need someone."

She turned her attention toward me. "That's why you shouldn't keep Robert waiting. He wants to marry you, Val."

"I know, and I'm grateful.." I filled everyone's cup, then sat back down and slowly began buttering my muffin. "But I wish life wasn't so complicated. One day, I think I'm ready to move forward with my relationship with Robert. The next day, I'm back to my old guilt feelings for even considering it."

Sally patted my hand. "You're a lovely woman. Carter wouldn't want you to waste your years mourning for him."

"She's right, Valentine. I've been thinking a lot lately about my own situation. I know it would freak Mother Billingham out if I even talked about dating, but—" She paused long enough to take a sip of coffee before going on. "But my resolve is beginning to weaken. Maybe it's time I should consider it. I want to keep my options open. You know, maybe be ready to say yes if someone just happens to ask me out. David will be in college soon, and the way my mother-in-law's health is deteriorating, she may end up in a nursing home within weeks. Do I really want to rattle around in that house by myself?"

I sighed. "Let me tell you, it's no fun living alone. I can't believe your son is getting so grown-up."

"He's given me a few gray hairs these past two years, but he's finally beginning to be the boy I wanted him to be. Not perfect, mind you, but better."

Sally rolled her eyes. "Tell me about it. Now if that daughter of mine would just straighten up. One day Jessica is obedient and loving. The next day she's stubborn and moody. Living with her is an ongoing adventure. I just hope my younger kids don't follow in her footsteps."

"Even with the grief they give you, you and Reva are lucky to have your children with you. I don't know what I'd do if you two and our other friends stopped coming by for coffee. Some days this big house seems like a mausoleum."

"It won't feel that way after you and Robert are married. Coming here is the highlight of my day, too," Reva went on to confess. "I leave your house every morning feeling refreshed and like I can face the day."

Sally added, "Me, too, Reva. I'm glad the three of us live on this cul-de-sac."

My mind overflowing with thoughts of my own situation, I took a slow sip of coffee. "Agreeing to marry Robert would be the beginning of even more problems."

My friends' brows rose. "What do you mean—more problems?" Sally asked.

I gestured around the room. "Even though this house sometimes seems like a mausoleum, I can't give it up. Carter built it for me. Everything in here is exactly as I'd wanted it. I could never live here with Robert. I'm afraid he'd always seem like an intruder. It would be as though Carter was watching our every move, listening to our every conversation. Plus, I'd be comparing him to Carter or

65

begrudging him for trying to take Carter's place."

"You and Robert could always buy or build another house."

"Reva, even if I could bring myself to give up this home that means so much to me, that's not the only problem. Every piece of furniture, every lamp, every picture on the wall, and nearly every knickknack Carter and I selected together or he gave me as a gift. I couldn't bear to give them up, not a single piece. But even moving to another house, taking it all with me and living with it, wouldn't be fair to Robert. Can you imagine how uncomfortable it would be for him? Being surrounded by all of those remembrances? I'm sure one or two of Carter's pictures around the house would be acceptable, but all of this?" I gave my head a shake. "No. It would be a constant reminder of the life I had with another man. It would be a constant contention between us. I know how I'd feel if he regarded everything around us as a memorial to Lydia."

Without commenting, both my friends just sat and stared at me. I knew why. It was an impossible situation. "The first time Robert came to my home," I continued with the emotional lump rising in my throat, "he sat down in Carter's recliner and lifted the footrest. Just seeing him there nearly killed me. I can't tell you the emotions that surged through me. *That* chair had always been reserved for Carter. No one else ever sat in it. It was like Robert was invading my privacy, taking something meant only for my husband. Of course, Robert didn't know it had been my husband's favorite chair. He'd never been in our house when Carter was alive."

"Did you mention the chair to him?"

"No, he would have felt awful if he'd known. I almost said something before he sat down, but I didn't. I'd had no idea how much his sitting there would affect me."

Reva asked. "Have you two ever discussed where you will live?"

A lump rose in my throat, making it difficult to answer without crying. "Not until yesterday."

Sally leaned toward me, her face filled with concern. "What did he say?"

"That he could never live here."

Get-to-the-point Reva gave my shoulder a shake. "Then move. What's more important to you? A wonderful life with Robert, the man you love? Or this house?"

Her question brought forth a burst of emotions I'd been holding back since Robert and I had discussed the situation and he'd walked out. I began to cry. "That's the problem, Reva. I don't know!"

Reva grabbed onto my hand and squeezed it tight. "Girlfriend, you have got to snap out of this funk of yours. You'd better get your act together and decide before you blow the whole thing."

I blotted the tears away with my sleeve. "I know you're right, and I'm trying, but—"

Sally tugged at Reva's arm. "You're being too hard on her. This is a beautiful home filled with happy memories. Walking away from it, even for a wonderful man like Robert, isn't going to be easy."

"*If* I can bring myself to walk away. And we haven't even discussed my furniture and all the memorabilia I'd want to take with me."

Reva gave her head a shake. "All I can say is you'd better weigh the consequences then make up your mind once and for all. I'm just glad I'm not faced with your decision."

Sally nodded in agreement. "She's right, Valentine. You know where Robert stands. The next step is up to you. I love this house and the way you've fixed it up, but I'm not sure I'd want to live here the rest of my life if it meant living alone."

Long after my friends had placed their plates and coffee cups in my dishwasher and had gone back to their own lives, their words kept ringing in my ears. I didn't want to lose Robert, but try as I may, I just wasn't ready yet to say yes, knowing it would mean leaving this place.

Though I still had no solution, I had to see Robert. I couldn't let this silence between us continue. Since he had been taking me out to dinner most of the evenings we were together, I decided it was time to cook another meal for him. I hoped he would accept my invitation. I dialed his cell phone number and waited.

"Hi, gorgeous. I always love it when I see your name on caller ID."

Not that I thought I was gorgeous, because I didn't, but I loved it when he called me that and his other pet names for me, and I was so relieved he sounded glad to hear from me. "Hi, Robert."

"What's up?"

"I was hoping you'd come over tonight for dinner. About six? That way we can talk about that Tuscany theme I mentioned to you and. . .ah, other things."

"Sounds good, but make it six thirty and I'll have time for a shower. Remember, I play in the dirt all day. I can assure you, you wouldn't want me to come as is."

I loved his sense of humor, especially considering the abrupt way we parted. The man was almost always upbeat and ready for anything. I just hoped I could be the same way by the time he arrived.

"Six thirty it is."

As was his style, Robert arrived a few minutes ahead of the appointed time. Neither of us mentioned our earlier conversation. After a leisurely dinner, which had included all his favorites, we carried our second cup of coffee out onto my patio. He placed his on the picnic table, then stood staring out into my yard. "What exactly did you have in mind for this Tuscany look of yours?"

I placed my cup alongside his and sidled up to him. "Well, over there"—I pointed toward the back wall—"I thought a grape arbor would be nice. Since the vines will need time to grow, I thought this year, for the party, I could embellish it with fake vines and plastic grapes to add a little ambience."

Robert tilted his head and narrowed his eyes, as if in thought. "What would you say to two arbors?"

"Two? Are you serious?" Did his interest in going ahead with my landscaping mean he'd changed his mind and might consent to live in this house?

"One in each corner of the two far corners of your yard. Then, in the center, I could build a large rectangular pergola-type structure with natural stone columns on all four corners to hold up the roof. Only instead of open beams, I'd like to use terra-cotta–looking tiles so it would block out the sun and be useful even when it's raining. I've done some research since you first mentioned this project, and I've located some fiberglass tiles that look like the clay ones they use in Italy but don't have the extra weight."

My enthusiasm grew with each new idea he mentioned. "And a statue? Every picture I've ever seen of the Tuscany area had statues."

He nodded. "Oh yes, definitely a statue, and several concrete pedestal planters filled with flowers and trailing vines. I also envision a three-tiered fountain at this end of the pool."

I gazed at the faded blue vinyl cover blanketing my swimming pool. I hadn't opened the pool since Carter died. He'd been the swimmer in the family. I just puttered in the water or paddled around on my floating lounge chair. Without him to share the pool with me, it had seemed nothing more than a gigantic eyesore.

Robert must have read my mind, because he smiled at me and gave me a gentle nudge. "It's a beautiful pool, sweetheart. Don't you think it's about time you took the cover off and enjoyed it? We could make it the focal point of your yard."

Of course it was time. How long was I going to go on like this—as if time stood still? Like the world should stop because I'd suffered a loss. I was in a rut of my own making, and I was the only one who could get me out. Smiling back, I leaned into him. "Absolutely. I'll call the pool maintenance company first thing in the morning."

He bent and kissed my cheek. "Good. I was hoping you'd say that."

"Be patient with me, Robert. I'm trying, honest I am."

He kissed my other cheek. "I'm sorry I behaved like a spoiled child last night, walking out on you like I did."

Suddenly, I felt all warm and cozy. Comfortable. That's the way I always felt when Robert was around, and I liked the feeling.

"But my apology doesn't mean I've changed my mind. I'd be willing to live most anywhere, but I cannot live in this house as your husband. You and I have too much going for us to throw it all away because we can't agree on where to live. We need time to consider our options. I propose we continue to spend time together but give ourselves a couple of weeks to think things over and try to come up with a solution."

"And if we can't?"

He shrugged. "Then, as bad as I hate to admit it, perhaps the best thing we can do for one another is to move on."

His words shocked me. "You'd actually break up with me?"

The long pause before he responded gave me his answer before he even voiced it.

"If we can't agree on where to live, what other choice would we have?"

I found myself speechless. I'd never considered that we might break up over something like this. The thought hit me that I was asking way too much of him to even consider that he would be comfortable living in this house, yet how could I ever leave it?

Taking on the sideways grin that always made me smile, he reached for my hand. "But like I said, let's give ourselves time to think this over and come up with a solution. It might not be a bad idea for us to take a look at the homes for sale in this area just to see what is available. Who knows? We might fall in love with one of them and our problem would be solved."

"But—"

Using his free hand, he put a finger to my lips. "Please, Valentine. Let's forget about it for now and concentrate on your yard. Now that I know you like my ideas, I'll get that sketch worked up and we can get started. Four weeks isn't a lot of time, but we'll get her done in time for your party."

"Are you sure you want to do that much? We could limit it to an arbor, a statue, and a small fountain."

He pulled me into his arms and nuzzled his chin in my hair. I was glad I hadn't sprayed on extra hairspray like I usually did.

"Valentine," he said in that soft, husky tone he sometimes used when speaking to me, "I want to do this up right. It will be my pleasure to landscape your yard for you. Fortunately, my best crew is finishing one of our bigger jobs tomorrow. Most of the workmen can start work here on the retaining wall and the concrete work the next day. I'll order all the supplies, and within four weeks you'll have your Tuscany backyard, which will be lighted for nighttime use, of course."

"Oh, Robert, it sounds amazing. I can hardly wait to see it. Carter—" I almost wished I hadn't said Carter's name, but it was too late. I'd already blurted it out. "Carter had set aside the money to redo the landscaping, but we never got around to deciding on how we wanted it. I still have it, so don't worry about the expense."

"We'll worry about that later. You'll be getting a big discount. Right now, let's concentrate on what kind of fountain you'd like." He gave me a shy grin. "I was hoping that perhaps by transforming your yard, we might be married here before moving into a place of our own. It'd be a beautiful place for our wedding. It's definitely something we should consider. Of course, if we can't work out our living situation, there will be no wedding."

I let out a gasp. "No wedding? Surely you don't really mean that."

Lowering his arms and taking a step back from me, he gazed off into the distance and seemed to be searching his heart before answering. Finally, he answered in a firm whisper, "Yes, I do."

"I wondered where you were when you didn't answer your doorbell."

We'd both been so caught up in conversation we hadn't noticed Barbie coming through my gate. Why did that woman always show up at the most inopportune times? After Robert's last comment about calling off our wedding, I wanted to kick, scream, cry—anything but visit with Barbie. Then I noticed there was someone with her, which made the situation even more difficult. A strikingly beautiful woman donned in a tightly fitted white sheath that barely came down to her deeply tanned knees. A wide black-and-white belt cinched in her tiny waist. On her feet were black stilettos that had to be either Manolo Blahniks or Christian Diors. Her thick blond hair was swooped back into an elegantly swirled French twist that emphasized her long, slender neck and flawless complexion. As I gazed at her slim figure, I couldn't help but wonder if, like Barbie, she took diet pills to keep down her weight. When she looked directly at me, I immediately remembered who she was. The woman who had been driving the silver convertible!

Wearing a big smile, Barbie grabbed hold of her hand and tugged her toward us. "I want you to meet my new friend, Diamond Jenson." She gestured toward me. "Diamond, this is Valentine, my neighbor."

Next, without giving either her new friend or me time to respond, she turned her attention toward Robert. "And this is Robert, the sweet, handsome man I told you about."

Robert and I, in almost unison, said, "Hello, nice to meet you," then he shook her hand.

Diamond Jenson kept hold of Robert's hand and smiled at him in the same overly exuberant way Barbie did each time she was near him, which made me wonder what she had told her about him. I watched in amazement, infuriated as the woman began to fawn all over him, batting her eyelashes like some teenager.

"Diamond," I said, hoping my mention of her name would draw her attention away from him. "What a lovely name."

Without so much as a glance my way, she answered. "I never liked my birth name, so when I was in junior high and my family moved, I changed it to Diamond. And I've been known as Diamond ever since. Besides, my birthstone is the diamond, so it was quite appropriate."

"Well, it's a truly lovely name."

Trailing a finger down Robert's arm, she smiled up at him with gleaming white teeth. "I'm totally impressed by the marvelous landscaping job you did on Barbie's yard."

"Thank you. It did come out well."

"And you were so nice to care for Barbie when she was sick. I'll just bet you were better for her than her medicine."

"I—I didn't do that much." He sent me a look of embarrassment. If I hadn't been so miffed by the attention she was paying him, I might have been amused.

"Not that much?" she fairly cooed. "I'd say you were her knight in shining armor."

He responded with a simple, "She's giving me credit I don't deserve."

"Of course you deserve it. You even rushed to her aid late at night to fix her toilet! I just wish I had a knight in shining armor who would come to rescue me when I get in trouble."

Who was this woman?

Was I imagining things, or was she making a play for Robert, too? Or was it simply my jealousy because of her beauty, her youth, and her sparkling personality? It was hard to tell her age. I guessed her to be in her late twenties, maybe even her early thirties. Nothing about her had gone south. She had the dewy radiant skin and perfect figure that often come with youth. Had she really been fawning over him? Or was it only my overactive imagination where Robert was concerned? Especially now, since things between the two of us were so strained.

"Please. I really didn't do that much," he told her, nodding his head toward me. "Valentine did far more than I."

Though I hadn't added anything to their conversation, I had hoped Barbie would come back with a word of praise for all the time and effort *I* had expended when she'd been ill, but she didn't. Not that I wanted or expected praise. I'd done it on behalf of the Lord, but it was nice to know you had been appreciated. I helped people out quite often when they had a need, and I enjoyed doing it.

Diamond slipped her hand into the crook of his arm, leaned into him, and gave him a smile that would have sent most men into orbit. "You sweet man. You're being entirely too modest."

Barbie, as if upset by being left out of things, moved closer to the pair. "Diamond and I are having the best time together. We are so much alike. We like the same foods and the same movies. Even our tastes in fashion are the same. We're like sisters." From the way she reached out and grabbed Diamond's free hand, I wasn't sure if she merely wanted Diamond's attention or if she, too, was jealous of the way the woman clung to Robert.

My mind still on Robert's and my situation, I responded with a simple obligatory, "That's nice."

"We met in a most unusual way," Barbie went on. "When an old friend of mine from Atlanta, whom I haven't seen in years, heard that Diamond was moving to Nashville, she told her to look me up immediately—even before she checked into a hotel and started house hunting—so I could tell her where the best areas were. Poor Diamond knew almost nothing about our beautiful city. And, of course, she needed to know the best restaurants and places to shop. Wasn't that just the kindest thing our mutual friend did? Sending her to me?"

Finally, Diamond released Robert's hand—not that I was watching.

"I so appreciated our friend's recommendation," Diamond said, "though I did think it rude to expect a total stranger to drop whatever they were doing to help me make the right decision about where I should live. But my new friend Barbie welcomed me with open arms. She invited me into her home and—"

"And we've been together nearly every minute since!" Barbie said proudly, patting Diamond's shoulder. "I've never met another woman with whom I could relate like Diamond." She let out a girlish giggle. "We even finish each other's sentences!"

Diamond beamed. "It's like our minds are geared to think alike. And I love Barbie's home. She did an outstanding job decorating it."

Did she tell you her home decor is an exact copy of mine?

Barbie gave her a demure smile. "Diamond is so complimentary about everything. My house. My clothes. Even my makeup. She's just the most darling person I've ever met."

"Have you found a house yet?" I asked. For some reason I felt compelled to put a stop to the mutual-admiration-society thing they had going on between them before it got any more out of hand.

Diamond shrugged her slim shoulders. "No, not yet. In fact,

Barbie and I have been so busy getting acquainted, eating in Nashville's finest restaurants, and—"

"And shopping!" Barbie inserted, pointing her finger into the air. "She loves to shop as much as I do."

Now it was Diamond's turn for a girlish giggle. "Yes—and shopping. We two do that so well! We've been so busy doing things together I haven't had time to look for a house."

"So are you staying at a hotel?" Robert asked.

"No. Barbie has been kind enough to open up her home to this wandering traveler. I'm staying with her!"

CHAPTER 5

"You're *staying* at her house?" I'm sure my eyes bugged out at her comment. Barbie took in a complete stranger? Although Diamond seemed nice enough and they were so much alike, I couldn't help but wonder how much Barbie knew about this woman. Not many people would invite someone they'd never met to stay in their home, merely because someone they hadn't seen in years suggested they contact that person. I hoped she hadn't made a wrong decision. She'd already told me how hurt she'd been when her trust had been betrayed by one of her ex-husbands. I'd think she'd be more careful than to take in a stranger. Even a pretty one.

Barbie gave me a frown. "Of course she's staying with me. Why shouldn't she? I have plenty of room, and she *is* the friend of a friend of mine. A hotel is fine for a few days, but it gets old very quickly. Besides, I like her company. Every night is going to be just like a pajama party. I don't know when I laughed as much as I have since she's been here. Diamond is like the sister I never had and always wanted. She's even allergic to strawberries like I am. She's going with me to my next Red Hat meeting. Isn't that amazing? I know all of Barbie's Red Hat Babes will love her as much as I do."

For the first time, Diamond's attention focused totally on me. "Barbie mentioned you've started a Red Hat chapter. I'd like to join."

"Oh," I said, raising my hands in front of me, "I'm sorry. Maybe Barbie forgot to tell you, but my group voted to keep our membership limited to widows."

"But I *am* a widow."

"She lost her husband six months ago." Barbie's face saddened. "That's why she's moving to Nashville."

Diamond became a widow only six months ago? The poor thing. I felt an instant kinship. "Then you'll have to come to our next meeting. It's going to be at my house."

"I'll come, too!" Barbie inserted quickly. "As a guest, of course."

Diamond gave me a smile. She'd smiled at me before, but this one seemed genuine and not as plastic. "I'd love to attend your meeting, Valentine. Thank you for inviting me. It'll be nice to be around other widows. I don't think anyone who isn't a widow can truly understand our plight."

I suddenly found my opinion of this new woman changing. Maybe I had judged her too quickly. "Where were my manners? Can I get you ladies some coffee?"

Barbie gave her head a vigorous shake. "I don't drink coffee anymore. Diamond is into health foods. She's convinced me it's not good for me."

"Then perhaps some iced tea?"

"No, we're going to hit some of Nashville's late-night music spots. Diamond loves country western. We'll get something to drink there."

Diamond raised her brow and gave Robert a playful, which could have been interpreted as *flirty*, smile. "Why don't you come with us, Robert?" She bobbed her head toward me. "You *and* Valentine." I couldn't help but note her amazing head of hair. Though it wasn't as flighty as Barbie's, it was blond, quite thick, and feathered around her face like a gold-gilded frame. There was no doubt about it, Diamond was an extremely attractive woman.

Robert answered for both of us. "Thanks for the invitation, but I still have paperwork to do yet tonight."

Barbie puckered up her face. "You're always busy. You need to take some time off to just have fun."

"My work *is* my fun. I enjoy what I do."

Then, like a small child curtsying at the conclusion of her recital, Barbie took hold of her skirt with both hands, twirled around, and slightly dipped one knee. "You're usually so observant, Robert, yet you haven't said a word about my new dress. Diamond picked it out. She said it brings out the blue in my eyes and does wonders for my figure. Do you like it?"

He let out a nervous laugh. I was sure he was as upset with them interrupting our intense conversation as I was. "It's pretty, Barbie, but I'm afraid I'm not up on the latest fashions."

After nearly ignoring my presence, Barbie swirled toward me. "That reminds me, Valentine. Did I leave my turquoise sweater at your house?"

"I haven't seen it."

A slight frown wedged itself between her rounded eyes. "I wonder where I left it."

Diamond did an exaggerated glance at the delicate gem-encrusted watch on her wrist, then grabbed onto Barbie's hand. "We'd better be going." She turned to me. "It's been nice to meet you, Valentine. I hope we'll become good friends."

To Robert she said, "And it's very nice to meet you, too, Robert. Barbie speaks of you so often I feel like I already know you. I do hope you'll stop by the house. I'd like to hear more about the plants and trees you used in Barbie's yard and how you came up with its spectacular layout. Maybe you could come and have lunch with the two of us soon."

"Thank you for the invitation, but I'm afraid my every moment is going to be taken up for the next four weeks with a special project I'm working on."

Diamond and Barbie exchanged disappointed glances.

"Maybe once that's over I'll have time to stop by," he added. "I would like to see how all the trees and plants are doing."

Barbie's eyes lit up. "You really must come and see them. Even if you don't have time for lunch, you know you can stop by anytime. You're always welcome."

After Barbie said her customary, "Toodles," and Diamond a traditional "Good-bye," the two of them made their way across the yard and disappeared through the gate.

Robert gave his head a slight shake. "That woman never ceases to amaze me."

"Barbie has done some strange things since moving in next door, but inviting a woman she doesn't know to stay in her home has to be one of the strangest. Diamond seemed nice enough, and I'm probably worrying needlessly, but I hope Barbie's blind generosity doesn't come back to haunt her."

"I'd better go, too. I haven't even opened this week's mail." Robert pulled me into his arms and held me close. "I'm sorry for being so abrupt earlier. I never meant my words to hurt you, but I'm serious about both of us giving our situation more thought. Because—if these things aren't resolved—"

Fighting back tears, I lifted my face and gazed into his blue, blue eyes. "Do you have to go now? We've so much to talk about. I hate for you to leave like this."

"When you let me hold you like this, I'm tempted to forget about the unopened mail and the bills that need paying, and stay, but at this point, I think we've both said all we can say, unless you have an idea we haven't discussed."

"No, I don't," I admitted.

"Then I'd better go. I'm the boss, and if I don't get my paperwork done, my bills paid, and my orders in, my crews won't be able to work. Besides, I want to get that sketch drawn for you so I can get the supplies ordered for your job."

He lessened his hold on me, but I grabbed onto his arm and leaned into him. "What if I won't let you go?"

The expression in his eyes as his arms tightened around me gave me goose bumps. "My greatest desire is that we can somehow work things out and I can make you my wife."

I thought I would die as his lips sought mine and he kissed me. I couldn't imagine life without him. I locked my hands behind his head and rested my forehead against his. "I want that, too, dearest. More than you know. You're everything I could ever hope for. I praise God daily for bringing you into my life. I do want to marry you."

"But we have a lot to figure out before that dream can come true." He kissed me again, deeply, passionately. "We belong together, you and I. There's an old song that says something about love being sweeter the second time around. I don't know if that's true, but considering the wonderful first marriages we both had, I'd say that if we can work past our barriers and our love is only half as sweet as the first time, we'll be mighty blessed."

What a precious thing to say, and how true. His lips sought mine in a good-night kiss that set my heart a skittering.

I walked him to the door and watched until I could no longer see his truck, then moved back inside before jolting myself out of those happy thoughts as my mind returned to the one thing so important it could sink our ship of love.

Where would we live?

I'd half expected Barbie to show up at church and bring her new friend with her the next morning, but she didn't. Maybe they'd been out house hunting.

"She actually invited a stranger to stay with her?" Reva asked, pouring herself a cup of coffee when she and Sally dropped by later that afternoon to pick up a book on the life of Esther I'd promised to loan Sally. "Isn't that like sending *trouble* an invitation?"

Sally reached her empty cup toward Reva. "Doesn't she realize how dangerous it is to do something stupid like that? She should watch Lifetime TV."

"You know Barbie. She's famous for doing impetuous things." I leaned forward in my chair. "I wasn't sure I was going to like Diamond at first, but she's really nice. She's going to join our Red Hat chapter."

Sally gave me a blank stare. "I thought we were limiting our membership to widows."

"She *is* a widow. She lost her husband six months ago."

Reva flinched. "Ow-wee. Six months ago? Poor thing. She must be miserable. How's she coping?"

I lifted my shoulders in a shrug. "I wasn't around her very long, but I'm sure she's like the rest of us. Smiley, smiley when around people, but sad and blue when she's alone."

"We've got to help her."

"That's exactly the way I feel, Sally, though I'm not sure how Barbie would like it. She is so enamored with Diamond it's ridiculous. She's even given up coffee because of her. She's like a kid, and Diamond is her new toy."

"What's this Diamond person look like?"

I grinned. "She's gorgeous. Even prettier than Barbie. She has what looks to be natural blond hair, kinda full and flighty like Barbie's, but much more under control. Slender. An amazing complexion. Long, beautiful nails, but they may be fake. And eyes so pale blue they remind you of the soft, innocent blue of a newborn's baby blanket. I tell you, this gal is a real looker."

"But is she nice?"

"Reva, I was only with her a few minutes, but I liked her. She seems a bit on the airheaded side like Barbie, but even though she's got to be at least twenty years younger, she seemed more mature, even more considerate than her." I rolled my eyes. "Even if she did make a play for Robert."

Both Sally and Reva gasped, then said in unison, "She didn't!"

"Well, not exactly a play, but you could tell she was a bit too interested in him. That, or I perceived it that way. Maybe it was just my jealousy kicking up." I wanted so much to tell my friends of the ultimatum Robert had give me, but I couldn't bring myself to do it.

Reva clasped my wrist. "He loves you, honey. It's written all over his face every time you're together. I wish I—"

Sally and I both looked at her when she paused.

"You wish what?" For some reason I had the notion something was going on in Reva's life that she wasn't telling us.

"Nothing. Forget it."

Sally huffed. "Forget it? You've got to be kidding. What is it you're not telling us?"

Reva avoided our gaze and twiddled with her fingernails. "How do you two always know when something is happening in my life?"

Sally crooked her neck and looked up into Reva's eyes. "Because we're your friends. Friends know those things."

"Out with it, Reva," I told her, as concerned as Sally. "We've always bared our innermost feelings to you. Now it's your turn."

"I haven't been completely honest with you two."

What? What did she say? I couldn't imagine Reva having a secret of any kind. She was about as transparent as the glass in my patio door; a true what-you-see-is-what-you-get kind of person. We three had always confided in each other about everything.

"What do you mean—'haven't been completely honest'?"

CHAPTER 6

"Remember when I told you several men had asked me to sit with them in church?"

Again Sally and I nodded.

"They really did ask me. I wasn't kidding about that part." Without lifting her eyes, Reva took in a deep breath. "I didn't sit with either of them. I turned them both down, explaining I always sat with Sally."

Sally lifted her hands in the air. "That's it? Your big revelation? You've already told us that much."

Reva paused, as if deciding whether she should continue her story or just drop it there. "Not quite. One of them, a man who helped us rebuild the kitchen after the church fire, caught me in the foyer later that morning and asked me to have coffee with him."

Sally's big eyes rounded in question. "And you didn't tell us?"

"I was afraid you'd laugh at me for even considering it. I told him yes."

I gaped at her. "You're really going to do it?"

"No. Not do it." She lifted her face and gave us a timid smile. "I already did. Twice."

Sally's jaw dropped. "Twice, and you never told us?"

"See, you are making fun of me, just like I thought you would."

I grabbed onto her other arm. "Oh, Reva honey, we might have teased you, but we'd never make fun of you."

Sally gave her head a shake. "I still can't believe you did it without telling us."

I smiled at her, with hopes of setting her at ease. I truly was happy for her, but I wanted to know all the details. "You are going to tell us who he is, aren't you?"

"Chuck Clemson," she said with a nervous grin. "He's really nice. He's going to show me his tools sometime."

Sally and I flashed a grin at each other. No wonder Reva and Chuck got along so well. Tools were one of her main interests. The woman had her own workbench and a much better collection of tools than most men, from a cordless drill to the most expensive laser-equipped miter saw. I knew because she'd proudly dragged me to her house so she could show them to me the day she'd purchased them and set them up. I had oohed and aahed over those funny-looking things, even though I had no idea what they were for or how to use them. The woman was a master at anything that drilled, sanded, or sawed. "How did your son react to you having a date?"

Reva pursed her lips. "David doesn't know yet."

Sally gasped. "Oh, Reva, you are going to tell him, aren't you?"

"Yeah, I'm planning to tonight. I think now that he's worked on Robert's crew and has been around him so much, he's missed having a father even more. Robert has been a great influence on him. I'm not the most feminine female in the world, but I'm still a female. I know that as a teenager, David finds it hard to talk to me about some of the things he'd prefer to talk about to a man."

I smiled at my friend. "I'm really excited that David seems to be straightening up. You deserve some happiness in your life."

"I'm not overly concerned about how David will respond when I tell him. It's Mother Billingham I'm worried about. She's crankier than ever. Which reminds me, I'd better not forget to pick up her cigarettes, or she'll go into one of her rages. I hate going into a store to buy those things, but since she can't get around on her own, I'm elected. David's too young to buy them for her, and I wouldn't want him doing it anyway."

Sally gave Reva a wistful look. "I know she's Manny's mother, and you are doing your best to provide a home for her now that her health has failed, but, sweetie, you can't live your life just for her. Especially since she doesn't seem to appreciate it."

"She's right, Reva," I tacked on. "It's obvious Manny's mother belongs in a nursing home. I know you hate to put her there, but she's beginning to need more care than you can give her. Her health has been on a downhill slide since long before the day she came to live with you, despite the excellent care you've given her."

Reva sighed. "The doctor has warned her dozens of times she absolutely has to give up smoking, but she won't listen. He's already told her she's soon going to be on oxygen and will have to carry around one of those portable tanks. She hacks and coughs all the time, then blames it on me, saying the dust in my house is causing it because I'm a bad housekeeper."

Sally frowned. "That's mean! You're a wonderful housekeeper and a fabulous cook."

INVASION OF THE *Widows' Club*

"She doesn't think so. That woman literally lives on ice cream and soft drinks, snack cakes, potato chips—anything sweet—and refuses to eat the nutritious meals I prepare, saying I'm a bad cook. I've tried refusing to buy those things, but she has a so-called friend who shops for her when I won't or when her supply runs low. Even though she's fairly small boned, she's gained more than thirty pounds since she's been with me. And she gets light-headed so easily. I'm afraid she'll lose her balance and fall and break a hip. But what can I do?" She lifted her arms in despair. "She won't even talk about going to a nursing home, despite her own doctor telling her that's where she needs to be."

"I think the three of us should move your mother-in-law to the top-priority section of our prayer list. Only God can touch that woman's heart and make her appreciate you." I gave Reva a hug. "I'm glad you decided to go out with Chuck. Are you going to see him again?"

Reva rubbed at her eyes, then let a small smile tilt at her lips. "Yes, tonight. We're going to the Big Dipper for banana splits. Fortunately, every time I leave the house in the evening, she assumes I'm going to some activity at the church, though I'd never even suggest such a thing. She's always complaining I spend too much time there as it is. I refuse to lie to her. I don't know what I'd do if my sweet next-door neighbor hadn't offered to sit with her anytime I need some time to myself. She does fairly well in the daytime, since most of her attention is focused on her soap operas, but not after the sun goes down. That's when she gets depressed and does her worst complaining. Even though there is a phone right beside her bed and she wears one of those call button things around her neck, I always make it a point never to leave unless someone is with her."

Sally let out a chuckle. "Look at us. Aren't we some trio? Three lonely widows who said they'd never marry again, yet we each have a man on the string."

Reva's expression turned sober. "I don't exactly have Chuck on a string. We've only spent a few hours together."

Sally gave Reva's arm a playful pinch. "Reva, don't be offended. That was only a figure of speech, like 'kiss and tell.' I merely meant that we each have finally, despite our resolve, allowed a man into our lives. That's all."

I gazed at those two, so opposite in personalities and appearance, who had come to mean so much to me. We three had shared countless experiences together, held one another up when others failed us. We'd each felt the same pangs of guilt as we thought about the possibility of allowing another man to take our beloved husband's place. And we were each lonely, even lonelier than we cared to admit to one another. And because of that loneliness, we were each slowly opening our lives and our hearts to someone else, someone with whom we might share our remaining years now that our husbands were gone.

I was happy for Reva, glad she'd accepted Chuck's offer.

I was happy for Sally and her upcoming date with George.

And Robert and I were struggling to find a way to salvage our relationship.

Maybe, just maybe, we three widows were beginning to move on with our lives.

CHAPTER 7

When I caught sight of someone crossing my yard the next morning, I assumed it was Barbie coming to tell me all about her night out on the town with Diamond.

But I was wrong.

When I realized it was Diamond, I pushed open the storm door and greeted her.

"Good morning, Valentine. I hope you don't mind me coming over uninvited. I left Barbie at the beauty shop having her eyebrows and legs waxed, so I thought it would be a good time for the two of us to get acquainted."

She moved on inside without even asking if I was busy, which surprised me, especially since we'd met only briefly the day before. However, I put on a gracious smile. "No, I don't mind. Usually my friends are here for coffee about this time, but one of them has a special evening planned, so she's having her hair and nails done. Another is taking her mother-in-law to the doctor. And Wendy, a third regular, is out of town for a week." I motioned toward the table where we usually gathered. "So, it's just me. Would you like a cup of coffee?" I suddenly remembered what Barbie had said about Diamond talking her into quitting coffee for her health's sake. "Or juice? I have either cranberry or orange."

"Cranberry would be nice, unless it's the kind laden with sugar; then I'd prefer orange juice." She glanced around my kitchen. "Nice. I like the yellow, green, and white daisy dishes." After moving to my range, she picked up the spoon rest. "You even have a spoon rest to match? How adorable."

"I bought them when I was on a bus tour to St. Louis."

"When I find a house here in Nashville, I'm going to turn it into a real home—" She paused and did a complete three-sixty. "Like you have here. I love this kitchen. If the rest of your house is anything like it, I'm sure it's lovely."

I pulled the orange juice container from the fridge, filled two glasses, and placed them on the table. "Would you like to see the rest of my house? I could give you a quick tour."

"You wouldn't mind? I'd love to see it."

"It'd be my pleasure." I gestured toward our glasses. "It won't take long. We can drink these when we get back."

She crossed my kitchen and hurried to my side. "Where shall we start?"

First, I took her into my dining room. "When Carter was alive, we entertained guests in this room nearly every week. Now it just sits here, but I love it. This room holds many precious memories."

Diamond trailed her fingers over the table's shiny surface. "Oh, Valentine, this room is so special. I love the carved legs on the table and chairs, the tapestry fabric on the seats, the drapery, the Aubusson area rug—all of it." She moved to my china cabinet, smiled, then opened the door and carefully took out a cup and saucer. "What an amazing pattern. It's Royal Stafford's Celebrity pattern, isn't it? I love the gilt edge and the way the white rose and other flowers are hand painted into the cup."

"Wow, you do know your china. I'm impressed." That pattern dated back to the mid-nineteenth century. It had taken me years to accumulate the minimal four place settings I had been able to find.

"I love old china. Collecting old china teacups and saucers is one of my vices. But, unlike you, my collection of the Celebrity pattern is only one teacup and one saucer."

I had to admit, the woman had excellent taste. From there, I led her into the living room I also rarely used now. As with most of my home, I'd decorated it in a near-Victorian theme. Burgundy walls, gilded candleholders and wall sconces, an oversized beige sofa topped with an array of beige and burgundy pillows, glass-topped iron tables garnished with huge bouquets of burgundy, pink, and rose-colored silk flowers and plants. Lots and lots of green plants.

She stopped in the doorway and steepled her hands. "Oh, Valentine, what a magnificent room! Now I understand what Barbie meant when she told me you both loved the same colors and had decorated your living rooms nearly alike. I love this room. It's exquisite."

"I'm glad you like it."

Though I didn't take her into all the bedrooms, I did take her to the one Carter and I had shared and to the family room before going back to my kitchen.

"Your home is gorgeous, Valentine. I know you have to be

lonely living here in this big house by yourself, but I can't imagine you ever leaving it. It's a gracious reflection of you." Her face took on an expression of sadness. "My husband was in the import-export business. It took him to places all over the world, and I had the good fortune of being able to go with him. We lived short terms in Japan, Germany, Italy, France, Canada, Hawaii, and even South Africa, but we never had a home we could really call our own. At least not until we purchased the house in Atlanta. It had everything we'd ever hoped for and then some. Since my husband had planned to be there for at least a year—" She dipped her head as her voice trailed off.

I wanted to say something, she looked so sad, but I wasn't exactly sure what to say. Instead, I pulled out the fresh tissue I'd placed in my pocket earlier and handed it to her. She gave me a grateful smile, then dabbed at her eyes.

"A drunk hit his car the day after we moved in. Needless to say, that home lost its meaning to me after that. No special memories, nothing. We'd hadn't even been there long enough to unpack our suitcases."

Though I didn't know her well, I slipped my arm about her shoulders. "I'm so sorry, Diamond," I said, keeping my voice to a whisper. "How awful that must have been for you."

She blinked hard. "It was, Valentine. As a widow yourself, I'm sure you can understand the heartache and turmoil his death caused. Though I wasn't sure I could ever face life without him, fortunately for me, in addition to his successful business, he had stocks and bonds and a number of other investments, so he left me quite well off. I stayed in Atlanta long enough to sell the house and his business, wind up his affairs, and spend some time grieving. If I hadn't been a Christian and hadn't had the support of my church friends, I don't know what I would have done. God and His strength was all that kept me going."

"You're a Christian?" I was so happy I nearly shouted the question.

"Oh, yes, since I was a child. Barbie tells me you are, too. I just wish Barbie knew Him like we do."

Suddenly, I felt an even closer kinship with this woman who had so quickly come into our lives. "I've tried to be a witness to her, but she just doesn't get it. She's been attending my church, even helped with our church bazaar, but she has never been able to accept the fact that, like the rest of us, she is a sinner. I keep praying for her but—"

She took a few sips of her juice. "I know. I try to talk to her about it, too, but she gets upset and we end up in a heated discussion. I've concluded the best thing I can do is try to live a Christian life in front of her. And pray, of course."

Her words gave me great hope for Barbie. Perhaps Diamond could reach her in a way I hadn't been able to.

"I'm planning on going to your church with her Sunday, so I guess I'll see you there." She placed her glass on the table, crossed my kitchen, and headed for the door. "I'd better scoot. I don't want to keep her waiting. I can't tell you how nice it is to have met you, Valentine. You and I have so much in common. I'm hoping this is the beginning of a long and beautiful friendship."

Donning a sincere smile, I nodded. "Me, too."

I watched as she crossed my lawn then exited through the gate. Praise the Lord. Amazing! Barbie's new friend was a Christian. I could hardly wait to tell Reva and Sally.

Other than an occasional phone call or a break to drink a glass of iced tea, I saw very little of Robert for the next four days. In some ways it seemed as though he was avoiding me. I hoped that wasn't true. And though I never had a chance to visit with Diamond again, I did catch sight of her occasionally, buzzing out of Barbie's driveway in either Barbie's or her convertible with the top down, probably off on some shopping trip to Dillard's or Nordstrom's or one of the fancy boutiques for which Nashville had become famous. Though some of the appeal of shopping for the latest fashions had gone out of my life with Carter gone, I found myself disappointed they hadn't invited me to go along. But I had plenty to do with the planning of my yard. Already, the men who were to lay up the retaining wall were at work. I couldn't believe they had been able to begin the work so quickly.

When my two best friends appeared at my back door on Friday morning, Sally's face literally glowed. "From that smile, I'd say you and George must have hit it off pretty well last night," I told her as the three of us sat down around my table. "I want to hear all about it."

Sally let out a high-pitched giggle. "I was so nervous about the whole thing I almost canceled at the last minute, but I'm glad I didn't. I had a great time. George is so funny. He kept me laughing all evening."

I shoved a pack of sugar substitute toward her. "I like seeing that smile on your face. No feelings of regret or pangs of guilt?"

Her smile subsided. "At first, but I had been psyching myself up all day by convincing my concerned side that what I was doing was okay. Okay with the Lord, and, I hope, okay with Eric. So—I put those anxious feelings aside and concentrated on having a wonderful evening."

"You going to date him again?"

Sally nodded toward Reva. "Yes, Saturday night. This time we're taking my children with us. Even Jessica agreed to go when I told her we would be having dinner at the Macaroni Grill. She loves what they call their Penne from Heaven. After that Jessica is going to a movie with her friends, but the rest of us are going to the Ryman Auditorium to see Garth Brooks. Doesn't that sound terrific?"

"It sounds more than terrific." I cupped her hand in mine and gave it an affectionate squeeze. "It's nice your evening went well." I have to admit I had a few reservations. I sure didn't want Sally rushing into something simply because she was lonely. Granted, George was a nice man who loved the Lord, but even that didn't ensure happiness. But I wasn't about to burst her bubble now that she'd finally ventured out on the dating scene, and I kept my concern to myself. Instead, I vowed I would pray for her that whatever she did would be right in God's eyes.

When Sunday morning rolled around, I almost wished I'd called Diamond and invited her to attend my Sunday school class with me. But she was Barbie's houseguest. Not mine. Barbie only attended the morning worship service when she came to church, so I decided it was probably best that I hadn't. I'd learned from experience that

Barbie was excessively possessive about her friends, and I certainly didn't want to upset her. But I did decide if the opportunity arose I would casually invite both her and Barbie to go with me the following Sunday.

As soon as my class ended, I scurried out into the foyer, just in time to see the two walk in through the double doors. I smiled a welcome and gave Diamond's hand a warm shake. I was ready to shake Barbie's, too, when she suddenly grabbed onto Diamond's hand and yanked her past me.

I turned quickly to see what had attracted her.

I should have known.

When would I learn?

It was Robert.

In true Barbie fashion, she slipped her hand into the crook of his arm and smiled up at him, batting those long, sooty lashes. He shot me a quick glance over his shoulder, then, in his gentlemanly way, politely greeted both Barbie and Diamond. I hated to barge in by joining them and almost didn't, but since Robert and I always sat together in church, it seemed the right thing to do. I couldn't just stand there awkwardly twiddling my thumbs as if I were invisible.

"You must sit with us," Barbie told him, still holding onto his arm as I sauntered up beside them. "I want Diamond to feel at home."

For the first time, I gave the twosome a closer look. As expected, Barbie was dressed to the hilt, clad in a gorgeous, tight, sheath dress in the palest of green, with a delicate matching chiffon scarf draped around her slender neck, its long tails dangling gracefully down her back to below the dress's hemline, which fell just above her knees. And, as always, her purse and shoes matched perfectly. She looked lovely, but it was Diamond's outfit that really caught my eye. Adorned in all pristine white, right down to the white jewelry on her wrist, about her neck, and dangling from her ears, she looked amazing. I'd never realized how striking all white could be.

"Wouldn't we, Valentine?"

I quickly lifted my eyes to Robert. I'd been so caught up in my silly evaluation of their appearance, I'd missed his question. "Wouldn't we—what?" I asked, afraid I was blushing with embarrassment.

"I just told these ladies we'd be honored if they'd sit with us in church."

"Ah, sure. I mean—that'd be nice." Duh! I should have been listening; then I wouldn't be bungling my words.

We made our way up the center aisle to the fourth-row seats Robert and I had begun to claim as ours. Though Robert motioned Barbie in first, she told him she and Diamond would prefer to sit in the aisle seats. He nodded, then gestured toward me. I scooted in, then Robert. Diamond started in next, but Barbie grabbed onto her arm, wedged herself in front of her, and seated herself next to Robert like some teenage girl staking out her claim, leaving Diamond to occupy the aisle seat. It reminded me of the musical chairs game I'd played as a kid.

My dander rose. I had hoped, now that Robert and I had become so close, that Barbie had given up on him and was concentrating on one of her other suitors, but apparently I was wrong. I was confident that if she knew the two of us were having trouble, she'd make an all-out, no-holds-barred rush to get him away from me. When I glanced at Sally and Reva, who were sitting two rows ahead of us, they each gave me a mischievous smile that let me know they had witnessed the seating fiasco.

Despite all that, I soon fell into a worshipful mood. I loved everything about the worship service at Cooperville Community Church. The orchestra, the choir, the worship team, the special music, and most of all, I loved our pastor. It always amazed me the way he could take even the smallest portion of God's Word and deliver a message that could touch hearts with such depth. I was pleased to see how attentive Diamond was as she seemed to hang on to every word the pastor said.

"I really enjoyed the service, and the people were so friendly," Diamond told us as we all walked into the foyer at the close of the service. "Your church reminds me of the church I attended in Atlanta."

"I hope you'll come back again," I told her, meaning it. "You'd make a wonderful addition to our congregation."

"Oh, I'll be back. You can count on it."

"I consider Cooperville Community *my* church, too," Barbie inserted, smiling proudly. "I even helped Valentine with the bazaar. She said I made a wonderful hostess."

I smiled back. "You did make a wonderful hostess. Everyone said so."

We chatted a few more minutes, then said our good-byes and went our separate ways, since Barbie and Diamond had plans to visit a number of open houses that afternoon.

"Diamond seems nice," Robert told me as he opened the car door for me. "She could be a good influence on Barbie."

"That, or a threat to her."

He frowned. "A threat? What do you mean?"

"Face it, Robert. Diamond is not only beautiful, she's years younger than Barbie and could be real competition for her. I'm sure you weren't aware of it, but Barbie was giving Diamond the eye when you were introducing her to Jake Gorman." I gave him a flirty smile. "I think, since she was afraid she couldn't woo you away from me, she may have had designs on that man ever since he worked as foreman on her landscaping job. You know, like a backup in case plans to snag you didn't work out."

"Rough-and-tumble Jake? You really think so?"

I shrugged. "Who can anticipate what Barbie does or feels? But it sure looked that way to me. Those two got along really well when he worked on her yard. She was always taking cold drinks out to him when he was working, carrying on long conversations with him, and of course she was always dressed in one of her cute little outfits and wearing her best smile. What man could resist that?"

He appeared thoughtful. "Jake's a good man, and you're right—they did spend a lot of time together."

"She needs someone like him in her life instead of the party boys she seems to attract. Someone stable who she can depend on."

"Jake might be interested in her, too, but I doubt he'd consider *dating* a woman on more than a friendly basis if she wasn't a true Christian. I hate to say it, but I get the impression Barbie's only playing church."

I sighed. "I'm afraid I have to agree."

Robert and I had lunch together, and then he took me home. I was hoping we could spend the rest of the day together, but he left me at the door, so I was surprised when he phoned an hour later.

"Guess who I got a call from?" he asked as soon as I'd said hello.

"I don't know. Who?"

"Barbie, and she had the strangest request. You were right

about her being attracted to Jake Gorman. She wants me to set up a date for her with Jake and—"

My jaw dropped. "She actually asked you to set up a date for her? The audacity of that woman!"

"Yes, but that's only half of it. She also wants me to set up a blind date for Diamond with Ward Davis so they can double date to some dinner theater thing she wants to attend."

"Oh, Robert, that really puts you on the spot. You're not going to do it, are you?"

He huffed. "I already have. I'd no sooner hung up the phone from talking to her when Jake called me. So, thinking he'd be flattered and then refuse, I told him about her request, and he said he'd give her a call."

"What about Ward Davis and Diamond?"

"Jake said *if* he decided to do it, he'd give Ward a call. Guess we'll have to wait and see what happens."

Concerned about Jake, I stared at the phone after the connection severed. It wasn't as if I should warn him about her. He'd spent weeks working as foreman on her landscaping job, hearing her endless chatter, and listening to her excessive demands when she changed her mind about something. I shrugged. I had no business interfering in anyone's life. My time would be best spent taking care of my own. If Jake should happen to say yes, he'd certainly know what he was getting himself into.

Considering the conversation I'd had with Robert about Jake and Ward, I shouldn't have been surprised when Barbie came fluttering into my house a few minutes before ten the next morning without even knocking. "Valentine," she said, drawing out my name, "you'll never guess what happened. That gorgeous hunk of a man Jake Gorman has asked me for a date!"

Surely this woman wasn't so naive as to think Robert hadn't told me about her call.

"He's taking me to The Best of Country Music Dinner Theatre. Doesn't that sound like fun?" She clutched her hands to her chest. "And guess what else. Ward Davis has asked to take Diamond. We're double-dating. Isn't that just the nicest thing?"

Suck it up, girl. What does it hurt if she stretches the truth a little? A little? A lot would be more like it. Let her have her fun. "Yes, it does sound like fun. I'm sure you'll have a great time."

"I knew you'd be happy for me." She nodded toward the door. "I need to get back. I left Diamond scanning the morning newspaper. She's having a terrible time finding the right house."

"None of the open houses you visited Sunday looked promising?"

She lifted her shoulders in a shrug. "I thought two of them would be perfect for her, but she didn't like either one."

"Sometimes the right house isn't easy to find. She may be with you for a long time, longer than you anticipated when you invited her to stay with you."

"It isn't that I mind her staying with me. We have a great time together. But I have to admit, it is a bit stressful having someone live with you twenty-four hours a day when you're used to living alone. More stressful than I ever imagined it would be." She gave her hand a flip. "Like, some mornings when I'd like to sleep in, I feel like I have to get up because Diamond is already up. And I normally eat when the mood strikes me. Now I feel obligated to try to plan for at least two meals a day, which means, since neither of us is too handy in the kitchen, we have to get dressed up and go out most of the time, when I'd much prefer to relax and eat an apple. That sort of thing. Plus, I like to stay up late and watch TV in bed. She doesn't. She'd rather sit up and talk or listen to music on the CD player. That woman is a bundle of energy. She wears me out just trying to keep up with her. This whole thing of having a houseguest isn't nearly as easy as I'd thought it would be."

She latched onto my arm. "Please don't say anything about this to Diamond. I value her as a friend."

I promised I wouldn't, then watched as she tiptoed across the lawn, which was still damp from the sprinklers, and disappeared through the doorway of her home. Could the *sparkle* possibly be wearing thin on their newfound friendship?

I saw very little of Reva or Sally that week. With Wendy back but feeling a bit under the weather and Bitsy gone now that she had moved out of town, Reva having extra things to do for her mother-in-law, Sally spending time with the lawyer who was helping to finalize the sale of her and Eric's business, and me in my backyard every moment of the day watching its transformation, we put a temporary hiatus on our morning coffee times. Though I missed those morning chats with my friends, I was glad to be able to spend the time with Robert as he personally supervised and worked on my job.

When he showed up Friday morning, he was all smiles. "Did Barbie tell you about their double date?"

I shook my head as I picked up Sprinkles and cradled him in my arms. "No, it's been several days since I've seen either her or Diamond."

"It happened last night. Jake told me."

"Oh? How'd it go? Did he say?"

"He said they had a great time, and that Diamond and Ward really hit it off. The four of them have made plans to sit together in church Sunday morning."

I gaped at him. "Really? That's great."

"I'm not so sure Barbie is the right woman for Jake, and I think he's only dating her to help her better understand God's Word, but he sure seemed impressed with her. He said she was a totally different woman on their date than she had been when he was working on her landscape." He snickered. "On her best behavior, I bet."

"I'd like to see Barbie find a really nice man," I said. "From what she says, all three of her husbands were louses."

He tapped my chin playfully. "That's her version. You haven't heard their side of the story."

"True," I said, remembering how badly one of her ex-husbands had treated her when she'd gone to Florida to visit him and return a ring at his request. I'd seen the bruises on her face, neck, and arms for which he'd been responsible. The poor woman could barely get around when I picked her up at the airport. "I know she stretches the truth, but I believed her about the way her husbands treated her."

"Well, she'd never have to worry about Jake harming her. That man wouldn't lift a finger to anyone." Robert took hold of my hand and led me through the house and out into my backyard. "You have to see the pergola, or should I say 'gazebo'? It's almost finished."

I couldn't believe how beautiful the pergola had become. With the addition of its red-tiled roof and rough-hewn posts, it was a more perfect addition than I'd dared hoped for. I could almost see myself relaxing in a comfortable lawn chair reading a book, sipping iced tea, and watching it rain. "I love it."

Robert pointed toward the planters he'd placed near each outer post. "By this time next year, these will be covered with vines."

His words brought me back to reality. Next year? Where would I be at this time next year? Living alone in this house because he and I couldn't agree on where we would live? Or would I relent and sell my house and be living in the new house he had promised to build for me. Life was full of uncertainties, and this was surely one of them. He must have sensed my discomfort at his words, for he slipped his arm around my waist and pulled me close. "Vines do fine, sometimes even better when they're dug up and moved to a new place."

No explanation necessary. His message came through loud and clear.

Several hours later when I was on my knees planting some of the flowers Robert had brought, Barbie pushed open my gate and hurried toward me, all gussied-up in a pale pink top and capri set and pink sandals, a tall glass of what looked to be lemonade in her hand. The woman was actually radiant.

"Where is Jake? I've brought him something cold to drink."

I lifted my glove-clad hand and gestured toward the fountain they had just delivered. "Over there." I couldn't resist. "How'd the double date go?"

She grinned at me. "It was stupendous. I've always liked Jake, but I had no idea he was such a great conversationalist. The four of us are going to church together this Sunday."

I gave her a genuine smile. It was good to see her happy. "I'm glad it worked out well for you. There aren't many men as kind and considerate as Jake."

"I've never met a man like him, Valentine. He's so—so sweet. I'm so glad he asked me out."

I gazed at her and let out a slow breath. *Oh, Barbie, why do you always find it necessary to lie?*

"I'd better get this drink to Jake before the ice melts."

I really was glad Barbie and Jake had gotten together, but I couldn't help wondering how he felt about dating someone who had failed at three marriages. Did any man want to be someone's fourth? But I had to admit, when Jake turned around and spotted Barbie coming toward him in that pink outfit, with that tall glass of cold lemonade, his face lit up. I wasn't sure if it was her or the lemonade that caused such a pleasant reaction, but he seemed very glad to see her. I wanted to gawk, but knowing how rude it would be, I turned my head away and went back to my planting.

"See what I mean?" Robert gestured in Jake's direction, then knelt down beside me and placed a new flat of flowers beside the one I'd nearly finished planting. "I told you they have a thing for each other."

"You don't think the three ex-husbands concern him?"

He shrugged. "The way I read the scriptures, the woman's not free to marry. But I think we're getting way ahead of ourselves here. They've only had one date. Jake is a smart man. He may enjoy her company, but I doubt he'll let their relationship get to the serious state."

"I don't want to see him get hurt, and I don't want Barbie hurt, either."

"Neither do I." He motioned toward Barbie's house. "It's different with Diamond and Ward. They've both lost their spouses and they're both believers. A permanent relationship between those two would be more than proper."

"You really think they'll continue to date?"

He pursed his lips as his brows rose. "Guess we'll have to wait and see."

As soon as my Sunday school class ended, I hurried to the sanctuary to see if the double-daters had arrived. Sure enough, directly across from the pew from where Robert and I had staked our claim sat Jake, then Barbie, Diamond, and Ward.

"From the way you're all smiling, I guess you had a great time together last night," I told the foursome before taking my seat.

Still wearing his smile, Jake nodded toward Barbie. "Sure did. I had no idea this little gal and me had so much in common. She's as crazy about football as I am."

I raised a brow. "Oh? I didn't know that." Not one time had Barbie ever mentioned being a sports fan.

Giving Jake one of her most alluring smiles, she nodded. "I love football. There's nothing so exciting as sitting in the stadium along with all those other fans and rooting for your favorite team. Jake's promised to take me to a game. Isn't he just the most considerate thing?"

Grinning a toothy grin, Jake sat up straight and squared his shoulders. "See why we get along so well? She loves football and she's great for a guy's ego."

Robert, who had been filling in for the high school class teacher, came hurrying down the aisle and reached out to shake hands with Jake and Ward, then nodded a hello to Diamond and Barbie. "Good morning, folks." Then as the beginning anthem sounded, he added, "Looks like church is starting. We'd better get into our seats."

Once we were seated I cupped my hand and whispered in his ear, "That's some foursome. Maybe now that Barbie has Jake to sit with, she'll be more regular in her attendance." I realized my comment had been snippier than I had intended when I was instantly hit with a sharp pang of guilt.

"If she's going to have anything to do with Jake, she'll be in church," he whispered back. "He constantly warns the people in his singles' class about missionary dating. I doubt he'd want to get tangled up in something like that himself."

I took a final glance at Barbie, then Diamond, then settled myself down and dedicated my full attention to the worship team who were already leading the first praise song of the service. I loved praising the Lord through music, especially when the words came directly from scripture. I smiled up at Robert when he took my hand and enfolded it in his. His rich baritone voice never ceased to amaze me. He sang each word as if it came from the very depths of his heart, much like my Carter had done when he was alive and we'd sat side by side in church holding hands.

I swallowed hard at the lump rising in my throat. I had to stop comparing those two. Though there were many similarities between them, they were two very different people.

My glance went again to Barbie and Diamond. Although, at times, Diamond seemed almost as flighty as Barbie and as caught up in the fashion scene as she was, it was good that God had brought her into Barbie's life. I had to admit I loved dressing in the latest fashions, so long as they were modest, but my apparel and my appearance weren't the uppermost things on my mind. Well, not as much as they used to be. As I watched Diamond singing, my heart rejoiced that she was a Christian and that Barbie looked to her with such admiration.

My next glance went to Jake. I liked Jake. He was a fine man, a real spiritual leader among the singles in our church. If anyone could be a witness to Barbie and win her to our Lord, it would be him. With all the men who had taken advantage of her and treated her with disrespect, Jake must seem like a saint to her. No wonder she found men like Jake and Robert so appealing.

My gaze roved to Ward as he stood by Diamond. They made a marvelous-looking couple. Tall, strong, soft-spoken Ward—what a treasure he was. Many of our congregation's women had tried to win him, but he'd grieved long and hard after he'd lost his wife. He had only recently begun to date again.

Pastor Wyman's message was from Proverbs about how charm was deceptive and beauty fleeting, but a woman who feared the Lord was to be praised. I wasn't sure how much charm I had, but I knew, even though I'd used expensive moisturizers and the finest of cosmetics on my skin and had shielded my face from the sun, whatever beauty I may have was quickly fading. Tiny crow's feet had begun to form at the corners of my eyes; laugh lines had permanently etched themselves on my face; my hair was rapidly losing its youthful luster; and I didn't like to think about the body parts that had already moved south. But I did fear the Lord. I was in awe of His power and His majesty.

With a look of concern, Barbie hurried over to me at the close of the service. "Was I wearing a brooch when I hosted your meeting at that restaurant?"

I gave her a blank stare. "A brooch? I don't remember for sure, but it seems like you had one pinned to your shoulder. A bird or butterfly maybe? Why?"

She sighed. "I was sure I wore it, but I can't find it anywhere. It was one of my favorites, not to mention expensive."

"Did you call the restaurant?"

"Yes, no one turned it in."

"And you've searched your jewelry cabinet?"

"Three times. I even crawled around on my bedroom floor and shone a flashlight under the bed."

"What about your car?"

"Checked that thoroughly, too."

I placed a consoling hand on her arm. "Don't fret too much about it. It'll turn up. Things like that usually do."

She shrugged. "You're probably right. Diamond seems to think I took it off and laid it down somewhere. It does seem like I've been a bit forgetful lately."

We joined the others who were wrapped up in conversation, laughing over a comment the pastor had made in his sermon. Barbie gave me a smile, then pulled her arm away and moved to stand by Jake.

Diamond turned to me and asked in a near whisper, "Did she ask you about her brooch?"

I nodded.

A slight frown creased her brow. "That's the third thing she's misplaced this week. I found the other two exactly where she kept them after she said she'd looked there. I'm getting worried about her. It's like her memory is failing her."

"Maybe some of the medication or the diet pills she's been taking are causing it. Some drugs do strange things to a person.

"Maybe."

Although the others invited us to have lunch with them, Robert and I opted for a quick meal of leftovers at my house so we could spend the afternoon going over the last-minute changes in my Tuscany renovation. By five o'clock he was gone and I was alone. For some reason, I couldn't get Barbie off my mind. I'd been concerned for some time about those pills she'd been taking to keep weight off. Maybe they were the culprit causing her memory lapses. I made up my mind that if and when the right time appeared, I would talk to her about it.

The next morning, when I saw her heading toward her mailbox with letters in her hand, I called out to her. After she'd placed them in the box, she hurried across the yard toward me. "I am so frazzled." She pushed a lock of hair from her forehead, then stared at me with those big blue eyes of hers. "I don't know what's gotten into me. I thought sure I'd mailed those checks last week, but they turned up on my kitchen counter this morning. Now I'll probably have to pay late fees."

I chose my words carefully. "I've read that some medications can make a person forgetful."

She lifted her shoulders in a slow shrug, as if giving my comment some thought. "I've read that, too. Do you think my diet pills could be causing it? I've been taking them for a long time, but they've never caused a problem before."

"Maybe. You might ask your doctor."

"Did Diamond say anything to you about my memory lapses?"

I couldn't lie, but I didn't want to cause any problems between the two of them. "We all forget things," I said, trying to avoid directly answering her question.

She glanced back at her house, then leaned toward me. "I really wish she could find a house. I like Diamond, and we get along like sisters. I never thought I'd feel this way, but I really don't like having someone living with me."

Oh, oh. I was afraid of that. "Does she have any interesting prospects? I've seen FOR SALE signs in front of some really nice homes over in that new development."

"We've looked at those. I think they'd be perfect for her, but she doesn't like any of them. She wants one on Morning Glory Circle."

I felt my eyes widen. "The only house that has been for sale around here was the one Sally bought over a year ago. I haven't heard of anyone who is even thinking of selling. It could be years before another one goes on the market."

"I know."

"Surely Diamond doesn't expect to live with you until one of those opens up."

She lifted her hands, palms toward me. "Who knows?"

I wanted to remind her that I'd advised her against letting a stranger stay in her home when Diamond showed up at her door, but I didn't. "Maybe she'll find something she'll like even better than Morning Glory Circle."

Barbie rolled her eyes. "Not unless she looks for it."

"She's not house hunting at all?"

"Not really. She spends her mornings on my treadmill while

watching TV, or playing tennis with some guy she met at the health club. The rest of the time she expects me to go to the country club with her since she doesn't have a membership, to the beauty shop, shopping, or sunning in my backyard."

"Can't you tell her you have plans of your own?"

"I've tried, but she grabs my hand and tells me how much fun she has with me, and I end up doing what *she* wants."

I smiled inwardly. That was exactly what had happened to me when Barbie moved in next door and I had tried to befriend her. "Maybe you should just put your foot down and tell her it's time for her to find her own place."

She paused, then glanced back toward her house before answering, "I sorta did that. She all but refused to leave."

My jaw dropped. "You told her and she refused to leave? You could have her evicted."

"Evicted? I could never do that. She's my friend! Besides, she didn't exactly refuse to leave. She said she'd prefer to stay until she can find a house. I had to agree. It would be foolish for her to put all the personal items and the mountain of clothing she brought with her to my house into the place where she has her furniture stored, temporarily move into a hotel, and then have to move everything all over again."

I lifted my hands in surrender. I had no other solution to offer. "Well, all I can say is, come over and visit me whenever you want. You're always welcome." *Even if you do drive me crazy sometimes!*

To my surprise, she threw her arms about my neck and gave me a hug. "Thanks, Valentine. I know I can always count on you. You're a true friend."

My guilt over the way I'd treated her hit me like a Mack truck.

"I—I know we've had our differences, but I do think of us as friends." Despite my guilt, I managed a smile. "Hang in there. Things are bound to get better. Surely Diamond will get tired of not having her own place and start looking for a house again."

"I hope so. Thanks for listening. I'd better get back."

She had no more than crossed her lawn when Diamond came flying out of the house. "I wondered where you were!" She waited until Barbie stepped onto the porch, then reached out and grabbed hold of her arm. "Why didn't you tell me you were going outside?"

When Barbie glanced back over her shoulder, Diamond looked in my direction, smiled, and gave me a wave. Apparently she hadn't realized I was there, within shouting distance. I waved back, then went into my house. I'd barely pushed the START button on the washing machine when I heard a tap on my back door. Thinking perhaps it was Reva or Sally, I called out, "It's open!"

"Valentine?" a voice responded. "It's me, Diamond. Where are you?"

I tapped the button on the dryer, then hurried into the kitchen. "Hi, Diamond."

"Have you got a minute? I need to talk to you."

I pointed to a chair, then sat down at the table. I would have poured her a cup of coffee, but I knew she wouldn't drink it. "What's up?"

She scooted into the chair next to me. "I know Barbie came over to see you this morning, and I wanted to set a few things straight."

I frowned. "Like what?"

"I'm sure she told you I refused to move out, which is the truth, but I doubt she told you why."

I smoothed out the place mat in front of me. "She mentioned you hadn't bought a house because you'd prefer to find one on Morning Glory Circle."

"That part is true. I would prefer to find a house here, but that's only part of it." She leaned toward me, her eyes narrowed. "I'm afraid to leave her alone. She's been doing some strange things."

"What kind of strange things?"

$\mathcal{C}$HAPTER 8

I mentioned the problem of the brooch to you the other day, but that's only one thing. For nearly a week now, the envelopes containing the checks Barbie had made out for her bills have been on the kitchen counter in plain sight, right where she'd put them. Yet she came bursting into my room early this morning, claiming she was sure she'd mailed them last Tuesday and couldn't imagine how they'd gotten back onto the counter."

I shrugged. "Maybe she was so used to seeing them there, she'd overlooked them."

"Maybe, but there's more. When her MasterCard statement came in this morning's mail, she screamed out like a mad woman, claiming she hadn't charged most of the dozens of items that were listed there."

"Maybe they'd billed her by mistake or someone had used her numbers."

Diamond scrunched up her face. "Valentine. Get real. I think the woman is losing it. I'm worried about her."

I was worried about her, especially since I'd personally witnessed several of her forgetful times in the past few weeks. "Did she phone the credit card company?"

"Yes, and they told her every charge had borne her signature. Not only that, the charges were all from her favorite stores, the purchases all in her size and by her favorite designers. Isn't it slightly unreasonable to believe a thief would wear her size and have the exact same tastes in clothing?"

"I suppose it could happen," I said slowly, not wanting to believe Barbie might have a serious problem.

"Not likely."

The two of us sat silently for a time, then Diamond spoke. "I've thought of moving into an apartment until I can find the right house, but"—she tightly closed her eyelids—"I'm afraid for her. I think leaving Barbie alone in that house might be a big mistake. I'd never forgive myself if something happened to her."

"You think it's that serious?"

She shrugged. "I honestly don't know, but I'm afraid to take a chance. I think she needs someone staying with her, to keep an eye on her. I'm trying to monitor those diet pills of hers to make sure she doesn't overdose on them, but I have no idea what other pills she may have in the house. She puts on a happy smile when she's around people, but at home she's terribly moody and wants to sleep all day. That has to be a sign of deep depression. I make up all sorts of excuses to get her out of the house, but if she had her way, she'd stay in her room all day with the draperies closed and the lights out."

I didn't like the sound of that one bit. "Maybe she needs to have a checkup by a different doctor. Have some tests run to see what's causing her depression."

"See a different doctor? I think that may be part of her problem. She's seen too many doctors. I'm sure she has dozens of prescriptions hidden in her bedroom. Some of them may not be compatible with the others." She lowered her gaze and fiddled with the salt and pepper shakers on the table. "I'm afraid she'll take a handful of those things and it will be all over for her before anyone can get to her."

I trembled at her words. I knew Barbie was eccentric and had an obsession about keeping her weight down—but trying to end it all? Would she consider doing something so foolish?

Diamond lifted her face and stared directly into my eyes. "You do think I should stay with her, don't you, Valentine?"

At that point, I didn't know what I thought.

"I need to get on with my life," she continued, not waiting for my answer. "But Barbie has been so good to me, I feel obligated to stay as long as she needs me."

Under the circumstances, it did seem best for someone to keep a constant vigil on her. "You will keep me posted, won't you?" I said. "And call me whenever she needs help of any kind, day or night. It makes no difference."

Diamond nodded. "I'd better get back before she misses me. Thanks, Valentine, for letting me unburden on you. It's wonderful to have a Christian friend like you."

"I'll be praying for her. For both of you."

"Thanks, I knew you would." She hurried out my door, closing it behind her, leaving me in a state of shock.

"Did you believe her?" Robert asked an hour later when he took a break to drink the glass of iced tea I'd carried out to him. I'd told him about the conversations I'd had with both Diamond and Barbie.

"Why would Diamond lie? What could she gain by it?"

"Maybe she's having financial problems and can't really afford to buy a house."

I sighed. "No, I doubt that's true. Both she and Barbie said her deceased husband was an extremely wealthy man, plus she was the sole beneficiary to his million-dollar life insurance policy. Though she'd sold the home they'd lived in, she still owns a beachfront house in Florida she's trying to sell. I think she said they owned a large group of rental houses, too."

"That rules out the money problem."

"If Diamond is on the up and up, and I have no reason to doubt she isn't, what other reason would there be for her wanting to live in Barbie's house, other than to help her and keep watch over her?"

"Got me." He took a long, slow sip of tea. "I know Jake's original intent was to simply share his faith with Barbie, but I think he's falling for her. They spent a lot of time together when he was working on her yard."

"She seems really interested in him, too, which I find pretty amazing. Every man she's ever talked about being drawn to, including her three ex-husbands, has been domineering, flamboyant, a playboy-type risk taker"—I nudged his side with my elbow—"except you and Jake, of course. None of those terms apply to either of you."

Robert screwed up his face. "Are you saying Jake and I are wimps, plain, too staid in our actions, dull?"

I sidled up close to him and smiled up into his face. "I'm saying you're handsome, steadfast, dependable, strong—"

He rolled his eyes. "Somehow, those terms sound almost boring. Maybe I should buy me a motorcycle and hang gold chains around my neck. Make myself more attractive to women."

With a giggle, I cupped his cheeks between my hands. "Don't you even consider doing such a thing, Robert Chase! There are too many women after you already. Barbie may have eyes for Jake, but she'd be falling at your feet in a heartbeat if she thought she had a chance with you."

He huffed. "You flatter me too much." Then, smiling, he added, "But keep it up. I like it."

I became serious again. "I know she wants Diamond to leave, but do you really think Barbie is in danger?"

After handing me his empty glass, Robert pulled his work gloves from his pocket and tugged them on. "I have no idea."

I sucked in a deep breath and expelled it slowly, not sure if I should voice the idea that popped into my head. "I—I guess I could invite Diamond to stay with me. That way she'd be close enough to check on Barbie, but Barbie could have some space and privacy."

"And *we'd* have no privacy." Robert gave his head a shake. "Not only that, but you'd be stressed out all the time. No way. Forget it. Besides, you know Barbie would never hear of it. She's the one who invited a stranger into her home, not you. She may want her space, but it's obvious she considers Diamond a friend. Suggesting Diamond stay with you would be like putting her new friend out, and Barbie would never do that. Mainly because it would be like admitting she'd made a mistake, and we both know admitting to anything is not her style."

I nodded. "I guess you're right."

"We just have to keep praying for her. God can touch, bend, and break even the strongest of wills." After wiping the sweat from his brow with his sleeve, he grabbed the spade from where he'd leaned it against the new retaining wall, then bent and gave my cheek a sweaty kiss. "Love you, babe. Thanks for the tea."

"Love you, too."

He grinned that silly grin, the one that always gave me goose bumps. "You mean it?"

I grinned back. "I mean it."

"Then why don't you marry me—now?"

"I will—in time."

He gestured to the cell phone holster on his belt. "I have the preacher's number on speed dial. Say the word, and I'll call him and have him mark a day on his calendar."

"You make it sound mighty tempting."

"I want you to be tempted."

"If only saying yes would end all of our problems. But we both know that isn't the only thing keeping us apart."

He was right. Setting a wedding date would only compound those problems.

He started to say something else but stopped, frowning, like there was something I should know but he didn't want to tell me. I hated it when he did that. It always made me wonder if perhaps he wasn't as perfect as we all thought.

Taking on a smile that almost seemed forced, he backed away and gave me a salute with his free hand. "Like I said, lovely lady, thanks for the tea."

I watched as he moved back out to join his crew, leaving me with an empty glass, questions on my mind, and an ache in my heart.

I almost wanted to shout for joy when Sally came bustling into my kitchen right after lunch. Though I was busy every minute of the day preparing for my upcoming Red Hat meeting and serving as the sidewalk superintendent of my landscape project, I missed her and Reva terribly. They'd been my rocks during so many hard times, as well as fellow gigglers when things were going well.

I grabbed the pitcher from the fridge and poured each of us a glass of iced tea before settling down at the table beside her. "What's with you today? You're literally beaming."

"Oh, Valentine, so much is happening. I had to come over and tell you about it."

I took a pink package of sweetener from the container and shoved it toward her. "Like what?"

"Jessica, for one. Remember when Reva's son stole those things from that discount house and I thought Jessica had been involved?"

I nodded. How well I remembered. If Robert hadn't stepped in and spoken with the judge, promising to sponsor David and hire him for one of his crews, that young man would have spent time in a detention center.

"I'm not saying Jessica has all of a sudden turned perfect, because she hasn't, but, Valentine, she's quit smudging those awful rings of black makeup around her eyes, and she's wearing colors other than black. She looks almost normal now, and the best part is that the two of us are talking again."

"What? How did that happen? You'd done everything, short of locking her in her room, to get her to quit wearing that stuff."

Sally giggled. "David did it."

I frowned. "David? What did he have to do with it?"

"Actually, I guess I should have said Robert did it."

I gave my head a shake. "Now I'm really confused. Robert got Jessica to quit wearing that makeup? I didn't even know he'd talked to her."

"He didn't, but it was his influence on David that caused the difference. From what Jessica said, I guess David told her she looked like a clown with all that stuff on. If I'd said that to her, she would have exploded and put on even more, but praise the Lord, she listened to David and didn't even get mad." Her eyes sparkling with joy, she grabbed hold of my wrist. "The change in that boy has been nothing short of a miracle. He's working here at your house every day. Haven't you noticed it?"

I shrugged. "Robert has kept his crew so busy I rarely see David. I'm surprised Reva hasn't mentioned it. I know that son of hers has been a constant worry to her. But then, I haven't talked to her for several days, either. I intended to call her, but—"

Sally gave a snort. "She's so tied up trying to keep her mother-in-law happy she barely has time for anything else in her life. I've never seen such a cranky woman. She's on a constant tirade. Reva keeps tactfully suggesting it may be time for her to go into a nursing home, but each time she mentions it, her mother-in-law starts screaming and swearing at her, saying now that Manny is gone, Reva is trying to get rid of her. And, you know Reva.

Though that woman's words hurt her and break her heart, she hangs in there and continues to smile. I don't know how she takes it. It's to the point she can't even leave the house without her mother-in-law going into a tizzy. In addition to all of that, now that the woman is beginning to have memory lapses and wanders out into the yard, Reva has to watch her every second. She's almost afraid to leave home, even with her neighbor there, which is really sad now that Chuck has shown an interest in her."

"I should have called her. I've been so busy with my own life and my yard remodeling project, I'm afraid I haven't been as concerned as I should be about the difficulties she's going through." I determined to phone her as soon as Sally left.

Sally swallowed down her last gulp of tea, then rose and dumped the ice in the sink before placing her glass in the dishwasher. "Gotta go. I told the kids I'd be right back."

I followed her to the door. "If Reva can't make it over here, maybe you and I should show up at her door tomorrow morning with coffee and rolls from Starbucks."

She stopped in her tracks and stared at me. "You wanna risk being screamed at by Mrs. Billingham? Surely you haven't forgotten the tongue-lashing that woman gave us a few months ago when we went with Reva to tell her about David's arrest."

I well remembered that incident. When I'd opened my mouth to defend Reva's mothering skills, her mother-in-law had reminded me, and not very nicely, that since I had never been a mother I had no idea what I was talking about, I had best keep my opinions to myself. Then she'd gone on to attack Sally for the way she had raised Jessica. I sighed. "I'd hate to be screamed at again, but I think Reva needs us, Sal."

"I'm game if you are. I'll meet you here about nine thirty, and we'll walk over together. That work for you?"

I nodded. "Nine thirty is perfect. Maybe we should take coffee and a roll for Mrs. Billingham, too."

"Good idea. See you in the morning."

Since I had already planted all the flowers Robert had brought, I decided to take a nice leisurely bath, then stretch out on the bed and watch *Oprah*. I'd barely settled into the tub when I heard my doorbell. Deciding whoever it was would probably be gone by the time I dried off and slipped into my robe, I sat and listened as it rang over and over and over. "Okay!" I shouted, knowing whoever it was couldn't hear me. "I'm coming!"

I grabbed the bath towel from the stool where I had laid it, dried off, then pulled on my robe, tying it as I headed down the stairs. Whatever it was that kept some person incessantly ringing my doorbell had better be good.

Curious and slightly irritated, I flung open the door.

CHAPTER 9

"Mrs. Denay?"

Surprised by his presence, I glanced at the officer standing on my porch, then pulled my robe more tightly around me. "Yes, I'm Mrs. Denay. Is there something wrong?"

"It seems your neighbor, a Ms. Baxter, has reported a missing sapphire necklace. She thinks it, along with several other items missing from her house, may have been stolen. Since you live next door, I was wondering if you'd seen anything or anyone suspicious in the neighborhood. Maybe a car cruising the area or people who are unfamiliar walking the street."

His words frightened me. "No, not that I can think of. Since we live on a cul-de-sac, there really isn't any traffic, except for those of us who live here, and our friends. She told me about her missing diamond brooch, but I figured it had been misplaced. I hadn't realized other items were missing, too."

He glanced toward the two trucks in my driveway. "Looks like you're having some landscaping done. What about the workmen?"

"I doubt it would be any of them. They're busy from the moment they arrive until it's time for them to leave." Though I knew several of the men who were toiling in my backyard, I had to admit I'd never met the others.

He pulled a card from his pocket and handed it to me. "If you think of something, give me a call. Even the tiniest bit of information could be important."

I assured him I would, then shut the door. When the diamond brooch was missing, I'd assumed, as Diamond had said, Barbie had misplaced it, but the sapphire necklace? Surely she wouldn't misplace two such precious pieces of jewelry. And he'd said there were other things. What was going on? Could someone actually be getting into her house and stealing those things? As long as I'd been living on Morning Glory Circle, we'd never had a theft or break-in of any kind. Just the thought of it happening here in our comfortable neighborhood made my blood run cold.

I hurried upstairs to finish my bath, slipped into a clean pair of jeans and a T-shirt, then headed next door.

"I'm so sorry to hear about Barbie's missing jewelry," I told Diamond when she opened the front door. "Surely someone didn't take it."

Diamond huffed. "*Missing* jewelry? Maybe. But the way she's been putting things away and then forgetting where she put them, I wouldn't be surprised if they were still in the house."

I stared at her. "You really think her forgetfulness is getting that bad?"

"Valentine, if I didn't know better, I'd think her mind was slipping. Just this morning she raved that her favorite coral silk shirt was missing. Later I went up to her room and found it hanging in her closet. Yesterday it was her purse with all her credit cards, checkbook, and cash in it. It turned up later under the foot of her bed. The other day, it was that gold compact one of her husbands had given her. I found that in the top drawer in her bathroom. I'll bet if we'd go up to her room right now, we'd find her sapphire necklace."

"Is that you, Valentine?"

I glanced up the stairway and found Barbie leaning over the railing, staring at me with eyes that seemed almost glazed over. "Yes, I wanted to make sure you were all right. I know how upset you must be about your missing jewelry."

She waved her hand at me. "Come on up. I need to lie down. I'm feeling a bit weak."

I ascended the stairs, then took her arm and assisted her into her room. "I hate to ask again, but are you still taking those diet pills?"

She grabbed onto her bed's footboard, then lowered herself slowly onto the mattress. "I was afraid they might be what was causing me to be weak, so I've cut down on them, but they've never bothered me before."

I circled my fingers around her wrist. "Do you realize how thin you've become?"

She gave me a feeble smile. "Don't they say you can never be too rich or too thin?"

I rolled my eyes. "Whoever made that silly statement didn't have good health in mind. I'm worried about you. Are you eating anything?"

"I eat. Occasionally."

I sat down beside her and slid my arm about her shoulders.

"When was the last time you've had a full meal? Meat, potatoes, a salad, a buttered roll?"

She shuddered. "Those things are fattening."

"Those things are what your body needs. You can't go on like this. You have to eat. Let me fix you something. What sounds good?"

"I couldn't keep it down."

"What? Why not?"

"That's one of the reasons I'm not eating. Everything I eat comes right back up."

"Have you told your doctor about this?"

"I—I was afraid he'd tell me I'd have to have surgery."

"Surgery? For what?"

"Stomach cancer. Remove my gallbladder. Maybe even a hysterectomy. I don't know. I just know I feel lousy most of the time."

I grabbed hold of her frail shoulders and spun her around to face me. "Barbie! You have to get some help. You can't go on like this. If you don't call your doctor, I'm going to call him for you."

Her face filled with terror. "No, please don't. I don't want you to. I'll be fine. I'm feeling better already."

That was a lie! Anyone could see the woman was sick.

"I've told her she needs to eat." I turned at Diamond's voice. "I fixed her a baked potato for lunch, but she didn't touch it."

Barbie rose slowly. "I need to go to the bathroom."

I reached out my hand. "You want me to help you?"

"No, I can make it on my own."

I watched her trudge slowly across the room, then after she had reached the bathroom and shut the door, I turned to Diamond.

"When did all this start? She seemed fine Sunday."

"She's not quite as bad as she's leading you to believe. She doesn't eat much, but she did eat half a grapefruit for breakfast and a small dish of oatmeal. Yesterday she consumed a half can of chicken noodle soup and five or six crackers, not to mention several low-fat, low-calorie ice cream bars."

"Still, that's not a lot of food. She's nothing but skin and bones," I countered.

"That's the work of those diet pills." Diamond gestured toward Barbie's jewelry cabinet. "I hate to say it, but I think this whole story about her missing jewelry is nothing more than a ploy to get attention. I'll bet she has those pieces stashed away somewhere so they can't be found."

I gave my head a vigorous shake. "No, I can't believe that. I know Barbie loves attention, but she'd never resort to something like faking a jewelry theft."

"Then explain the charges on her credit card. How can a woman charge as many clothing purchases as she has and claim she didn't, when they're hanging in her closet?"

I had no answer, but I still found it hard to believe even Barbie would do such a thing, unless—I tried to block out the thought, but it surfaced anyway—unless she had a mental problem.

Barbie looked more like herself when she returned from the bathroom. Though she was still pale, she'd run a comb through her hair and applied a fresh coat of lipstick. I assisted her back to her bed, then sat down beside her and stroked her hand. "An officer came to my door this morning," I said. "He said your sapphire necklace is missing."

She gave me a look of irritation. "Not missing. Stolen."

131

"And you still haven't found your diamond brooch?"

She shook her head. "No, and I doubt I ever will."

"Don't say that."

She looked sad, almost beaten down. Forlorn. Dejected. Not at all like the vivacious woman who had moved into that house only months earlier.

She shrugged. "Why not? It's the truth. Why won't anyone believe me? Diamond thinks I've misplaced them. Though that officer didn't say it, I'm sure he thought I had, too. Now you."

I gave her hand a consoling pat. "I didn't say I thought you'd misplaced them, Barbie."

"But that's what you think, isn't it?"

I didn't want to lie, but I didn't want to upset her, either.

"Well, isn't it?"

"We all misplace things," I began, "but—"

"Go ahead, Valentine. Join the crowd. Accuse me of lying. I'm used to my friends turning their backs on me."

Now I felt awful. I couldn't think of one reason—except for the one Diamond had given, about her doing it for attention—that would cause Barbie to lie about her missing jewelry. Even though I knew from experience how she loved to be the center of things, I honestly couldn't believe she would go so far as to report a fake theft to the police. "I'm not accusing you, Barbie. If you say that jewelry has been stolen, that's good enough for me."

Her eyes misted up as her expression transformed from one of anger to one that reminded me of an innocent child. "You believe me?"

I nodded. Though I wasn't 100 percent convinced she was telling the truth, I was 99 percent sure, and that was enough for me to say, "Yes, I believe you."

As weak as she was, with tears flowing freely, she threw her arms around me and buried her face in my neck, sobbing like a baby. "I can't tell you how much it means to me that you believe me, Valentine. You're the only one!"

"I'm sure others believe you, too." I glanced up at Diamond and found her scowling. When she realized I was looking at her, she rolled her eyes, then turned and left the room. Even though Barbie had hoped Diamond would be gone by then, I was glad she was still there. Barbie needed someone with her, and Diamond was willing to do whatever was necessary to help her. I just wished she would be more considerate and understanding toward Barbie at times. But, if I were living with Barbie twenty-four hours a day, I doubt I'd have nearly as much patience as Diamond. Barbie, with her egotistical, whimsical ways, could wear out anyone's patience. I gave her a hug, then pulled her arms from about my neck. "Why don't you take a nap? You've had an eventful morning. The rest would be good for you."

She gave me a slight nod. "I am tired."

I pulled back the comforter and sheet, plumped up her pillow, then helped her climb beneath the covers. Once she had settled, I tucked the comforter beneath her chin much like I would have done for the child I'd always wanted. She looked so frail and helpless lying in that king-sized bed. My heart went out to her. She had so much and yet so little.

"Would you read to me, Valentine? It might help me go to sleep."

I glanced around but didn't see a sign of a book. "What would you like me to read?"

"I think that Bible you gave me is in the top drawer of my nightstand."

I pulled open the drawer, expecting to see the bright red leather cover of the Bible I had bought for her.

But that wasn't what I found.

CHAPTER 10

I gasped when I saw it. It was a book on witchcraft! Though I hated to even handle it, I grabbed it from the drawer and, trembling, held it up for her to see. "Barbie, what are you doing with this? Are you into witchcraft?"

She gave me a blank stare. "Witchcraft? No. Why would you even ask me that?"

"You had this book in your drawer, that's why."

She lifted her head from the pillow and stared at me. "I don't have my contacts in. What book is it?"

Concerned by her blatant denial, I held the book even closer. "It's a book on witchcraft. I can't believe you'd bring something like this into your home."

She blinked hard, as if trying to focus. "I didn't. I have no idea where it came from. You have to believe me, Valentine."

"Believe you? The book was right here in your nightstand."

More tears began to flow as she wearily laid her head back onto her pillow. "I don't know what's happening to me. I've been charging

135

things on my credit card without remembering I'd purchased them, my jewelry is missing and everyone thinks I've misplaced it, and now you're telling me I have a book on witchcraft. Am I going crazy?"

My heart pounding, I stared at her. Though, like everyone else, I'd heard about witchcraft, even read articles about it and how rampant it was in certain parts of our country, I'd never actually met anyone who was involved in it. Could witchcraft be the reason for all the unexplained things going on in her life? Was her brain so addled from her exposure to it that it had begun to affect her in ways we mortals couldn't understand? I prayed that wasn't so.

"Well, am I?"

"I—I don't know," I finally managed to stammer. "But if you aren't the one who placed this book in your drawer, then you won't mind if I take it and burn it, right?"

She nodded. "Take it. Burn it. I have no interest in keeping it around."

"Good. You'll never see it again." I tucked the book under my arm. "I doubt you're going crazy, Barbie, but it is obvious you're having health problems. Don't you think it's time you went to a good doctor for a checkup? One who doesn't dole out diet pills so freely? I know you hate it when I say it, but I'm concerned about what they might be doing to your body."

"I'll go when I get to feeling better."

"Feeling better? That's ridiculous," I nearly shouted at her. "You should be going now."

She shifted her body away from me and onto her side. "I'm sleepy. I'll think about it after I take a nap."

I lifted my hands in frustration. "I'm going home. I'll read to you later. Have Diamond call if you need me, okay?"

When she didn't answer, I wondered if she'd been so exhausted she'd already drifted off, so rather than take a chance on waking her, I tiptoed toward the door.

"Thanks, Valentine," she said in an almost whisper. "You're a good friend. I knew if anyone would believe me, it would be you."

"I *am* your friend, Barbie," I whispered back. "I love you, and God loves you. Never forget it." Then I moved out into the hall, closing her bedroom door behind me.

"Sorry to have deserted you in there," Diamond said, surprising me. I hadn't noticed her standing in the hall. "I want to believe her, I really do, but she lies so much, I can never tell the truth from something she's fabricated."

I sighed. "I know." I took the book from under my arm and held it up so she could see the title. "Ever seen this before?"

Her eyes widened. "A book on witchcraft? No! Where did you get it?"

"It was in her room."

She took the book and leafed through its pages. "Barbie had it? I didn't know she was into witchcraft. She never said anything about it."

"She said she wasn't, but it was in her nightstand."

Diamond's free hand flew to cover her mouth. "Oh, my! Fooling around with that stuff could be dangerous. Do you think that's what has been causing some of her problems? She seems to have a great deal of trouble facing reality."

"I hope not, but who knows?"

She handed the book back to me. "What are you going to do with it?"

"Burn it. She said I could."

"I hope she doesn't go out and buy another one."

"When and if she feels like going out again, you might keep an eye on any purchases she makes. None of us has any right to tell her what she can and cannot do, but as her friends, we want what's best for her. Witchcraft is the last thing she needs."

"I try to witness to her, Valentine. I so want her to become a dedicated Christian like you and me, but she's so stubborn. She looks at going to church as entertainment instead of a chance to worship God, grow in the Word, and fellowship with other believers. Getting Barbie to admit she's a sinner like the rest of us and in need of forgiveness is an uphill battle."

"We just have to keep praying for her. We may not be able to reach her, but God can."

Her eyes narrowing, she tilted her head thoughtfully. "Did she tell you about the other things that have been missing? Beside the jewelry?"

I frowned. "No. What other things?"

"Her journal. Her silver hairbrush. Her favorite nightgown. Items like that. Usually they turn up in a day or two, but the way she raves about them when she can't find them, you'd think gremlins were coming in through the windows and purposely hiding them from her."

"Now you really have me worried." I headed down the stairs. "I hate to leave you with her, but I've got to get back home and burn this thing, and Robert is waiting for me to make some decisions on the shrubs he's planting. Call me if she needs me."

"I will."

I'd barely reached my yard when Robert came around the corner of my house. Just the sight of him calmed my frazzled nerves.

"Whatcha got there?"

I held the book toward him.

"Witchcraft? Where'd you get that?"

"It was in Barbie's nightstand."

His face troubled, he took it from my hand and thumbed through its pages, stopping at one place long enough to look at the table of contents. "She actually reads this stuff?"

I gave my shoulders a slight lift. "She says she never saw it before and had no idea where it came from, but it was right there beside her bed. I want to believe her but—"

"But she hasn't exactly proven worthy of belief, right?"

"Yeah, sad to say. Besides that, she's missing another piece of jewelry. The expensive sapphire necklace one of her ex-husbands bought her. She even reported it to the police. An officer came to my door asking if I'd seen anything going on in the neighborhood that might help them find whoever took it. He even asked about your work crew."

"That's not surprising, but I'm sure it's part of his job. She never found that diamond brooch?"

"Nope. Still missing."

He handed the book back to me. "What are you going to do with that?"

"Burn it in my fireplace as quick as I can set a match to it."

"Good idea. Do you want me burn it for you?"

"Would you?"

He took my hand and led me into my house, then squatted in front of my fireplace and reached for the lighter I kept in a brass container on the hearth. "Here goes."

We watched as the pages caught fire and curled up, sending an unpleasant stench into the air. I wrinkled up my nose and backed away. "It even smells evil."

Once the cover caught fire, he rose, spun me around, and took hold of both my hands, his face filled with concern. "So, what's your take on Barbie, Valentine? You know her better than anyone."

"Diamond says she's doing these things for attention. Like the way she called you to come right away to fix her toilet rather than waiting until morning when she could call a plumber."

"But what do *you* believe?"

I paused and pondered my response. "I've seen her do bizarre things to get attention many times, but now? I'm not so sure. Usually, when she's lying, her face is a dead giveaway. But today it was different. Like she was desperate for me to believe her because she *was* telling the truth. Either that or I wanted to believe her so badly, I was imagining her sincerity."

"Your instincts rarely let you down."

"I hope they aren't letting me down this time. She needs someone in her corner."

"What about Diamond? Isn't she in her corner?"

"Oh, yes, definitely, but even Diamond's patience is wearing thin. Living with Barbie can't be a picnic. I'm convinced Diamond is doing everything she can. It's a real blessing she hasn't found a house yet. I don't know what would have happened if she hadn't been there."

"Barbie didn't look like herself in church Sunday."

"She's been on those high-powered diet pills for some time. Those worry me. She says she's not taking as many of them as she had been, but she's not eating. Diamond says she refuses everything healthy she fixes for her and lives mostly on low-fat, low-cal ice cream. Her bones look as though they are about to poke through her skin. She was thin when she moved back to Nashville, but she's lost more weight since she's been here. She even recited that silly quote to me, 'You can never be too rich or too thin.'"

"Maybe she should change doctors."

"That's exactly what I told her."

"Is she going to do it?"

"She said she would—when she gets to feeling better. But if that happens, she won't need to go."

Releasing his hold on me, Robert pulled his gloves from his pocket and tugged them onto his hands. "I'd better get back to work. I don't want Jake to think I've deserted him. How about having an early dinner with me at that Italian café down the street? I've got a board meeting at the church at seven."

"Sounds good. I love your company."

He bent and kissed my forehead. "Let's plan on going about five. If you don't mind, I'll come in about four thirty and wash up a bit. I put a clean shirt in my truck, hoping you'd say yes."

"I'll have a fresh towel and washcloth waiting for you."

Hovering tantalizingly close, he lifted my chin and gazed into my eyes. "We could make this a permanent arrangement, you know. I'm ready when you are."

"Time, dearest Robert. I need time."

He raised a brow. "Are you sure you'll ever be able to make that decision and do something about your house? I don't want to have to walk down the aisle when I'm old and my legs won't hold me up. I'll just bet—"

"You bet what?"

"Never mind."

"What?"

He squiggled up his face as if deciding if he should finish his sentence. "I don't think you want me to mention it again, and I don't have time to talk about it. I've got to go."

Suddenly, Reva's words came to me. *Robert loves you, but even though he's said he'll wait, he's a man. Many a man has been led astray by a beautiful woman.* Did he have someone else in mind in case we couldn't work out our difficulties? No. That couldn't possibly happen. Or could it? I could think of several women at our church, lovely widows who would jump at the chance to go to lunch with him or fix him a nice home-cooked meal. But if he loved me as he said he did, surely he would wait for me until we could work things out. But even Robert himself had warned me not to take too long.

Lord, I cried out, *if Robert and I belong together, why do I have these feelings for my dead husband? And why can't I face living somewhere other than here? Help me. Give me direction. Give me the peace that only You can give. I'm so confused.*

After he left, I ran a load of towels through the washer, dusted the living and dining room then, determined to look my best for him, hurried upstairs to freshen up my makeup and get dressed for our dinner date. Knowing Robert would be changing into a sports shirt, I opted for my salmon T-shirt, a cute pair of denim capris, and a colorful pair of flip-flops.

The cafe was crowded, but we managed to find a table for two in the corner. After we'd both ordered BLTs, we continued the discussion of Barbie we'd started earlier. We'd barely begun when the front door opened and in walked Reva with Chuck Clemson. They hurried to our table as soon as they spotted us. I was so happy for Reva I couldn't help grinning. "Hi, you two. What a nice surprise to see you."

Robert rose and shook Chuck's hand. "Good to see you, guy."

Dressed in a pink polo and a pair of stovepipe-leg jeans that looked great on her, Reva beamed, her cheeks as pink as her shirt. "Guess that's what happens when you eat in a neighborhood restaurant."

"Since there isn't room at our table," I gestured toward a table directly across from us, "why don't you sit there?"

Chuck nodded, then pulled out the chair for Reva.

"How did you manage to get away from your mother-in-law?" I asked Reva as soon as we'd all ordered.

She grinned. "Despite the way she treats him, my precious son offered to stay with her. She was none too happy about me leaving—"

"And would have been even more unhappy if she'd realized Reva was having dinner with me," Chuck inserted.

"I didn't lie to her," Reva said quickly. "I just told her I was having dinner with a friend, which was true."

Chuck gave Robert and me a shy grin. "I've had my eye on this pretty gal for sometime but only recently got up my courage to ask her out."

"You made a wise choice," I said. "Take it from me. They don't come any better than Reva." I had to chuckle when a slight blush tinted Reva's cheeks. I wondered how long it had been since she'd had occasion to blush. "So what are you two doing after dinner?"

Reva sent Chuck a glance before answering, "We're going to Sears to check out that power lopper tool by Black and Decker called the Alligator."

"That thing only weighs just slightly over six pounds and has a four-and-a-half-amp motor," Chuck added, his enthusiasm as high as Reva's. "It'll handle four-inch tree limbs without flinching."

Robert seemed impressed. "Guess I'd better check it out for my crew. Sure beats lugging around a heavy chain saw for the small stuff."

Reva nodded. "Be a lot safer than a chain saw, too. It grabs, holds, and cuts in one easy motion."

She was the only woman I knew who could get that excited over a tool, and it was nice to see she and Chuck shared the same interest. Though not the most handsome man in the world, Chuck was a great guy and had a heart as big as that of a giant. Everyone liked him.

We visited until our meal arrived, then turned our attention to our food. After a pleasant but hurried supper, Robert took me home. "You're such a sweet man," I told him as we lingered in my hallway. "Every woman should have a sweet, romantic man like you in her life. You're the godliest man I know, and—" I stopped midsentence. The sudden change of expression on his face frightened me, especially when he grabbed onto my wrist and narrowed his eyes.

"Don't call me that, please."

"Call you what? Romantic? Because you are. Or considerate? You're one of the most considerate men I know."

He relaxed his grip a bit. "Don't call me godly. I hate it when people call me that."

Silence hung in the air between us like a heavy, impenetrable fog. Even the clock on the wall seemed be mimic us with its incessant, loud *tick, tick, tick*. Though Robert's head hung low, I could tell by the quickened rise and fall of his chest that something was going on inside him that was not good.

Finally, when I could bear it no longer, I grabbed onto his arm and shook it. "What? Tell me what you're talking about. Why don't you want me to call you godly?" I couldn't hold them back. Tears began to flow down my cheeks, clouding my vision. "I thought you loved God!"

He pulled away from me and began to rub at his temples with both hands. "I do love God, but *I* am not godly!"

I'd never seen him shake like that. I wanted so much to wrap my arms around him and tell him everything was going to be okay. But was it? Were there things in Robert's life that could change my opinion of him? I quickly ran several possibilities through my mind. Pornography? Another woman? Financial problems? A few other thoughts too gruesome to even consider reared their ugly heads. I shook them off. "Why would you make a statement like that? Everyone thinks you're one of the finest, most honorable men they've ever met."

"Only because they don't know the real me, the man from my past."

Now I was frantic. "Then tell me, Robert! I have a right to know."

He lifted his face slowly and, avoiding my eyes, gestured toward the sofa. "You're right. You do have a right to know. I've wanted to tell you this for so long, but the time never seemed right. I may be late to the board meeting, but I have to get this thing off my chest."

With mixed emotions, I lowered myself onto the cushion, not sure if I wanted him to sit next to me or in the chair opposite me until I heard what he had to say. I was almost relieved when he moved to the chair. He sat for a moment, staring off into space. "My wife died because of me."

The blood seemed to drain from my veins, and I felt faint. *Wake up! Wake up!* I told myself. *This isn't really happening. He didn't mean it the way it sounded.* I swallowed hard. "Surely not. You weren't even there, were you?"

"Not when the accident happened, but I was with her earlier. I loved Lydia, honest I did, but like most couples, there were some negative times in our marriage. One of those incidents happened that very morning." He paused as if deciding what to say next. "I constantly got after her for letting her gas tank hit the empty peg before refilling it. I was in an important meeting with one of our key clients when she called me on her cell phone, telling me she'd run out of gas on her way to an antique store out on the highway north of town, and she wanted me to come and rescue her. At that moment, even though I was more concerned about taking care of our client than I was about my wife, I excused myself and, taking a gas can with me, I drove out to where she was stranded, fuming all the way. I was going to make sure she never pulled that trick again."

"That doesn't sound like you."

He gave his head a shake. "I had a pretty hot temper back then. I railed at her, reminding her how often I'd told her to keep that tank filled. And I said some other things I never should have said, which really upset her and made her cry. I fussed at her all the time I was adding the gas to her tank; then, as I drove off, I yelled at her and told her the next time she pulled a trick like that, to call someone else. I had better things to do with my time than rescue her because of her carelessness."

I gaped at him. The man he was describing was nothing like the thoughtful, caring man I thought I knew.

"I felt bad all the way back to town, so I tried to call her to apologize, but she didn't answer her cell phone."

"No wonder, after the way you'd talked to her. I wouldn't have wanted to talk to you, either. Running out of gas isn't exactly a crime. We've all done it at one time or another. You probably have, too. Did you keep trying to reach her?"

With his face cradled in his hands, he gave his head a slight shake. "Less than thirty minutes later, I got the call. My wife was dead. A dump truck had lost a lot of sand on the highway. A man who witnessed her accident said that when her car hit the sand, she hit the brakes, but she lost control and ran into the guardrail. She died instantly. All because of me and my out-of-control temper."

I ached for him. What a horrible weight to carry every day.

"That's when you moved back to Nashville?"

"No. Even though my son and I had buried Lydia in Nashville, I couldn't come back at that time. It took me months to muster up the courage to go through her things and even longer to decide to put our house on the market. Selling that house, the home she loved so much, made everything seem so final. With my son away from home in the Middle East, I had no idea where I wanted to settle down. I wasn't even sure I wanted to live after what I'd done to Lydia."

"You can't blame yourself for your wife's death, Robert. You said she hit the brakes. The loose sand on the highway is what caused her to lose control. That accident would have happened if you'd never said a cross word to her."

147

"I've tried to convince myself of that, but if you could have seen her face in the rearview mirror like I did as I drove off that morning, you'd understand why I feel responsible for her death. I'd never seen her look so sad."

I crossed the space between us and knelt in front of him, taking his hands in mine. "She loved you, Robert. She knew you didn't mean it. I'm sure if she would have lived long enough, she would have told you she'd forgiven you. There were probably times she said things to you that she didn't mean."

He lifted misty eyes. "I never had a chance to ask her forgiveness, but I did ask God for His. I begged Him to help me get over my quick temper. I never wanted to hurt another person like I'd hurt Lydia. It's been a struggle, but I think I've gotten victory over it."

"That must have been a horrible time for you."

"Yes, but my trouble didn't end there. Eight months later, two uniformed officers and an army chaplain came to my door, telling me my son had been killed in action by sniper fire. I tell you, Valentine, I'd never been at such a low. It was as if everything that mattered to me had been snatched away. The agony was unbearable."

"Did you blame God?"

"I would probably have gone through life blaming both God and myself, with that guilt eating at me and tearing me apart, if it hadn't been for my pastor. After I told him the whole sordid story, he took me under his wing and—through many months of counseling, scripture reading, and love—nursed me back to health. I became whole again, covered and absolved by God's forgiveness. God was faithful, Valentine, and reached out to me with a comfort only He can give, and made me realize I still had a life to live for Him. That's when I decided it was time to leave, start a new life in a new place, and try to put the past behind me. I didn't care where I went. I just had to get away from there."

"That's when you came here?"

"Yes. While searching for a landscape business I could buy, I stumbled onto—or should I say God led me to—the information that Mr. Miller's business was for sale. The idea of moving to Nashville, near my wife's and my son's graves, had great appeal to me. I truly loved my wife and wanted to be near her and near my son."

"What an ordeal that must have been for you."

"The whole thing was like the worst of nightmares. I shudder each time I think about it. So you see, Valentine, I'm not the godly man you and all the others think I am. I'm nothing more than a mortal man who, because of his out-of-control temper, lost the wife he dearly loved."

I tightened my grip on his hands and smiled up at him. "But you learned your lesson. You said you no longer have a problem with your temper. To me, you are godly because you love our Lord and want to serve him. No one is kinder or more thoughtful than you are."

He dabbed at his eyes with his sleeve. "I should have told you the first time you and I went to dinner. You may never have found out, but it still wouldn't have been right to hold it back from you. I believe in complete honesty between a man and the one he plans to marry."

He rose and backed away. "The only other people who know about this are Pastor Wyman and Jake, and now you. It's my prayer that you can forgive my foolishness, like God and my son have, and will become my wife. I love you, my sweet Valentine, more than words can express."

"Dearest Robert," I said rising to kiss his cheek. "I'm glad you told me, but let's never speak of it again. God forgave you, your son forgave you, and I forgive you for not telling me sooner. I love you, and I'll be praying that one day all these feelings of guilt you still bear will disappear. It's all in the past, my darling. It's time you concentrated on the future."

"Future? What future? It seems all I'm doing now is marking time, waiting until you decide to say yes and can move on with you life. I'm tired of standing still. I need to move ahead with things. I need you as my wife, sweetheart." He glanced at his watch and said, "I hate to leave you after dumping my story on you, but I promised to get some figures to Pastor Wyman before the board meeting adjourns."

I slipped my arms about his neck, pulled his head close to mine, then kissed him. "I know it was difficult, but I'm glad you told me."

He sighed. "Me, too."

After he moved out the door, I closed and locked it behind him. Like a robot, I walked into the kitchen, poured myself a glass of water, then sipped it slowly, my mind in a whir. In desperation, I cried out to the Lord, asking Him to be with Robert, to comfort his troubled soul and make him stronger in his faith than ever.

I hadn't even finished my water when the phone rang. It was Diamond.

"Barbie is feeling better now," she said, sounding both excited and hopeful. "I don't know if it was the nap she took or the bowl of potato soup she ate for supper, but she's more like her old self. She wanted me to call and let you know."

I glanced at the clock on the kitchen wall. It was barely seven thirty. Though I wasn't much in the mood for a visit, I did want to see Barbie. "I think I'll run over and tell her good night."

"Good idea. She always loves your visits."

I was surprised to find Barbie sitting in her solarium, clothed in one of her gorgeous colorful caftans, and wearing lipstick.

"Diamond fixed my hair," Barbie said proudly when I complimented her on her appearance. "I can't tell you how much better I feel. I haven't slept that soundly in days."

"And you ate a bowl of soup for supper?"

She gave me a smile. "Yes, a big bowl, and some melon balls, too."

I felt such a sense of relief as I gazed at her. She looked more like herself than the woman I'd left earlier that afternoon.

"Diamond and I are going shopping in the morning," she said as merrily as if there had never been a problem. She didn't even mention the loss of her jewelry, and I certainly wasn't going to bring it up.

"If you have the time, Valentine," Diamond said, "you could go with us."

I turned to her and thanked her but declined her invitation. I wasn't sure a shopping trip so soon after feeling so poorly was a good idea for Barbie, but I wasn't her keeper. If she felt like going, who was I to discourage her? I explained that Sally and I had planned to take coffee and rolls to Reva's house in the morning, but I'd take a rain check on the shopping trip.

As I stood to leave, her doorbell rang. Barbie rose to answer it, which surprised me since she'd been so weak that afternoon. From the trill in her voice, I knew she was glad to see whoever it was who had shown up at her door. Within seconds, she came back into the room, pulling Jake behind her. In his hand was a bouquet of red roses.

He gave her a shy grin as he handed them to her. "These are for you."

"Isn't Jake just the most wonderful, thoughtful man?" she cooed, smiling at him as she took the roses from his hand and tugged him toward the sofa. "Not many men would have thought to bring me flowers."

I wondered if Barbie realized how terrific Jake really was. Of all the men in our church, I would put Robert at the top of the "wonderful man list," with Ward and Jake tied for second place. All three men loved the Lord and weren't ashamed to admit it, and all three longed to serve Him in any way they could. In some ways I felt Jake was wasted on Barbie. There were so many women who would love to have a dedicated Christian man like him pursuing them. He was the kind of man women prayed for. Then I reminded myself that Jake had promised to keep his and Barbie's relationship on a platonic basis only. As strong in the Lord as he was, I doubted he would let that relationship cross the line, but the way he smiled at her and his gift of the lovely red roses did make me wonder. Could Jake be heading toward trouble? If David or Solomon could have had their heads turned away from God so easily, why not Jake?

I felt awkward staying. I'd come over to check on Barbie, and I'd already done that. With Diamond in the house to chaperone, I hoped Jake would be safe. "I'd better get on home." After the conversation I'd had with Robert, I really wanted to be by myself. He'd given me a lot to think about.

Barbie reached for my hand as I started to leave. "Thank you, Valentine, for being such a loyal friend and caring about me. I think I'm finally on the road to recovery."

"I'm glad to hear it. You really had me scared."

Diamond sidled up next to me and said quietly, "I'll walk you out."

I gave Barbie a wave, said good-bye to Jake, then, along with Diamond, made my way out onto the porch. "What a turnaround! I'm in awe of the change in her. She's not at all like the woman I left a few hours ago."

Diamond shrugged. "Just goes to show what happens when she eats nourishing food." Her expression turned serious. "When the two of us were sitting at the table having our soup, she mentioned hearing voices in the house last night."

"Maybe she'd left the radio turned down low. I know she leaves it on sometimes. She's said it helps her sleep."

"It was off when I checked it. But from what she said, the conversation she heard didn't sound like a radio station. She said it was two men using swear words and talking about filling a swimming pool with cement."

Her words frightened me. "That sounds more like a TV show than the radio. Maybe she dreamed it."

"She had to have dreamed it. No one was going to be talking about swimming pools during the middle of the night. Sometimes dreams can seem so real."

"Still no sign of her jewelry?"

"No. That officer came by again, but he didn't have anything to report. How could he? There's no evidence whatsoever that someone took it. We lock the house at night and every time we leave, and the alarm system is always on."

"For Barbie's sake, I almost hope there was a theft. I'd hate to think she could misplace such valuable jewelry."

Diamond sighed. "But a theft wouldn't explain all those charges on her credit card, the missing clothing, or the voices."

My ears perked up. "Missing clothing? More than what you'd already mentioned?"

"Like the jewelry, I'd hoped she'd simply hung things in one of the other closets in the house and then forgotten about them. But she swears she never puts her current season's clothing anywhere except her walk-in closet, which, as you know, is big enough to hold a dozen women's clothing. Besides the things I'd told you about, some of her favorite scarves are missing, too, some lingerie, and even several pairs of shoes."

Suddenly, my stomach felt queasy. Was Barbie having a breakdown? With all the difficulties with her divorces, her move to Nashville, and her propensity to starve herself, a breakdown seemed like a distinct possibility. And Diamond probably didn't even know about Barbie's increased stress from having Diamond living with her, when Barbie had expected her to be there for only a few weeks. But, as I'd said a number of times before, it was good to have Diamond there. Someone needed to keep a full-time watch on Barbie.

Diamond took hold of my arm. "I'm really worried about her, Valentine. Please continue to pray for her and for me, too, as I do my best to take care of her and encourage her to eat. She's such a beautiful woman, with so much to give. I can't stand the idea of her ending up in a mental institution."

I blanched at her words. "You really think that could happen?"

"I don't know, but if she keeps going downhill, who knows?"

"But she's so much better this evening."

"She has her ups and downs. This isn't the first time she's rallied and had one of her miraculous recoveries. Several times I've been ready to call you and ask if you thought I should take her to the hospital, but just as quickly as she did today, she recovers. Sometimes I wonder if she's taking other pills we don't know about. It's not normal for a person to bounce from high to low and back again like she does."

"What kind of pills are you talking about?"

"Maybe something like Ecstasy to give her those highs, and Valium to bring her down. I don't know much about drugs, but I have heard those two mentioned quite often on TV shows. I have no idea where a person would get Ecstasy, but Valium is quite easy to come by if you know the way to ask for it. A lot of women take it."

If her words had frightened me before, at that moment, they terrified me. As a person who rarely took even an aspirin, I knew absolutely nothing about drugs. I determined to get on the Internet as soon as I could and do some research.

Diamond gave my arm a squeeze, then moved away. "I'd better scoot. I don't want her to think we're discussing her behind her back. That would only add to her anxiety."

I watched her go, then slowly made my way home. *Lord*, I breathed out in an inaudible whisper, *be with Barbie and keep her safe. Make her realize drugs aren't what she needs. She needs You.*

CHAPTER 11

I had a rough time sleeping that night. In addition to my thoughts about Robert, I couldn't get Barbie off my mind. It seemed ever since that first day she'd moved into our neighborhood, her life had overshadowed mine in ways I could never imagine. I dozed on and off until about six, then, when I finally fell into a deep sleep, I didn't waken until nearly eight thirty. I hadn't slept that late in months.

Sally arrived right on time, a Starbucks sack in her hand. Rather than drive the short distance to Reva's house, we walked. Since I hadn't told Reva that we'd be coming when we'd run into her and Chuck at the diner, she met us at the door with an expression of both surprise and delight.

Sally dangled the sack in front of her face. "Look what we brought. Starbucks!"

Long before we could see her, we could tell by the *click, click, click* of her walker that Mrs. Billingham was making her way to Reva's foyer. "Oh, it's you two. Been to that expensive coffee shop again, eh? If it weren't for people like you who would rather spend money than cook your own breakfast, those fancy places would go out of business. You could probably feed a starving family in Nigeria for a month for what that stuff must have cost you. In my day," she went on with a scowl and pointing her finger at us, "we women were careful with our money and knew the value of a dollar. We spent it for things we needed, not the frivolous things you women buy these days. We made our own breakfast, and it tasted a lot better than that sugary, starchy stuff you girls buy. And our coffee tasted like real coffee and wasn't doctored up with those silly flavors."

Sally cast a questioning glance at me, then pulled out a single cup from the cardboard carrier and held it out to her. "We have hot tea for you, Mrs. Billingham. I hope you like Earl Grey."

Reva's mother-in-law snarled. "I hate Earl Grey tea."

Sally withdrew the cup. "I'm sorry. I guess I should have phoned to see what kind you like."

Reva grabbed it instead. "I love Earl Grey. If she doesn't want it, I'll drink it."

Sally wrinkled her face and added in an almost whisper, "We brought rolls for everyone, too."

Mrs. Billingham turned her face away in disgust. "No wonder you girls are getting so pudgy." As if she didn't load up on sugar calories every day!

Now she'd hit a nerve. Sally struggled with her weight, and Reva, being big boned, worked at keeping hers down, too. I forced a smile. "Let us know what you do like, and next time we'll make sure to bring the right kind."

Turning, Mrs. Billingham began shuffling her way back into

the living room. "Don't waste your money on me. I hate rolls, and if I want tea, I'll have Reva make me a cup."

Both Sally and I glanced at Reva. "She manages with the help of her walker to get herself into your foyer to chastise us for eating sweets, but she can't make herself a cup of tea?" I asked in an almost whisper.

Reva shrugged. "Not as long as she can get me to make it for her. But I don't mind. Actually, I don't like the idea of her messing around with boiling water. In fact, she has no business doing anything with food. Too many ways she can get hurt." She cocked her head toward the hallway. "Let's have our coffee in the kitchen. Her favorite soap opera will be on in a few minutes, so she won't be bothering us for an hour or so."

Once we seated ourselves at the table, Sally hiked her thumb toward the living room. "Girlfriend, I don't know how you put up with that woman. It's one thing to take care of someone who appreciates it, but her? She doesn't seem to appreciate anything anyone does for her, and from the sound of it, she never has."

Reva rotated her cup in her hands. "I have to admit it's pretty tough sometimes, but I do it for Manny."

I took a roll from the sack and handed it to Reva, then passed one to Sally before taking out my own. "Um, sticky pecan cinnamon rolls. Your mother-in-law may not like them, but they're my favorite."

Sally picked off a chunk of pecan and popped it into her mouth. "I don't think Manny would have had the patience you have, Reva. If he were here, I'll bet he'd put her in a nursing home rather than allow her to treat you like she does."

"You're probably right. But he wouldn't put her into a home

because of her mouthiness and her bad attitude. It would be because it would be the best place for her. And of course he would have confronted her for talking to me that way and put a stop to it. Her sense of balance is getting worse every day. I can't tell you how many times I've caught hold of her in the midst of a fall. And taking her medication? She fights me every time I try to give it to her. In a nursing home, they'd see that she gets it, or else. And it would do her good to be around people her own age. You know, someone to talk to and commiserate with."

Sally huffed. "They'd probably charge you extra for all the trouble she'd be."

Reva rolled her eyes. "And they'd be earning every penny." She sighed and gave a weary look toward the hallway.

"Does that mean you're considering putting her in a home?"

"Not unless it gets to the point I can't handle her. But I confess there are days when I think I've about reached my limit."

Feeling the need to change the subject for Reva's sake, I leaned toward Sally. "Guess who Robert and I saw at the diner last night."

Sally screwed up her face. "Um, the pastor and his wife?"

"No."

"You got me. Who?"

I gestured toward Reva. "Someone sitting right here at this table. And guess who she was with."

Sally gasped. "Reva? With Chuck?"

"Yep, Chuck."

Reva put a silencing finger to her lips. "Shh, you two. My mother-in-law says she can't hear very well, but she never seems to miss anything she's not supposed to hear. I sure don't want her to know about my outings with Chuck. At least not yet."

Sally pretended to zip her lips shut. "I won't mention his name again." She leaned close to Reva and asked in a whisper, "Do you like him? Did you have a good time together? Are you going to date him again?"

Reva laughed. "My answer is yes, yes, and yes."

Sally clapped her hands. "This is so exciting. Six months ago, the three of us were confirmed bachelorettes. Look at us now. Val has Robert, you're dating"—she glanced toward the living room with a snicker—"someone, and George and I are getting along really well. Isn't that amazing? I was beginning to think life had passed the three of us by."

I lightly pinched Sally's arm. "Enquiring minds want to know more about you and George. Come on, Sal, tell all."

"Well, I told you we were going to take the children to dinner and then to the Ryman Auditorium Thursday night, but what I didn't tell you was that George has sent me flowers. Twice! I was shocked the first time. The second time I was stunned speechless, which, as you know, is rare for me. Last night he showed up at my door with a new video game for Michael and a CD of some Jesus rap group he'd purchased at the Christian bookstore for Jessica. I wish you could have seen the look on Jessica's face. Turned out it was a CD she'd been wanting. Boy, did George score big brownie points with that one."

"And I'm sure that youngest son of yours was excited about getting the video game."

She nodded. "Was he ever. Took it right into his room and played it until I made him go to bed."

"George has kids, doesn't he?"

Sally wiped at her mouth with her napkin. "Yes, three sons, but they're all married and live out of state. He only gets to see his grandkids a couple of times a year. He said that's why he was enthusiastic about taking the three of us to dinner. He loves to be around kids. He told Jessica he'd always wanted a daughter. I'm amazed at the way she's accepting him. She even asked him to help her put up a shelf in her room."

"I would have put that up for her, Sally, if I'd known about it."

Sally laughed. "Reva, you have other things to do with your life than put up shelves for your friends. Besides, George said he liked doing it."

"So what are you going to wear?"

Sally fingered her new haircut. "I'd thought about wearing that red pantsuit I bought a few weeks ago, but after Mrs. Billingham's remark about me looking pudgy, I'm not so sure."

Reva grabbed onto her hand. "You don't look pudgy at all, Sally. You're adorable. I wish I looked like you."

"She's right," I chimed in. "You look terrific in that red pantsuit. That's what I'd wear if I were you."

"Are you sure? I wouldn't want to embarrass George."

"He'll love it on you. Red is your color, especially now that you have added those light highlights to your hair. That pantsuit, a pair of big gold hoop earrings, and you'll be a real knockout."

Sally let out a chuckle, "Me? A knockout? Hardly."

"Wear the red suit and the hoop earrings and see. I'll bet he'll be giving you compliments all evening."

She chuckled again. "It's worth a try. I'll do it. What have I got to lose?"

We paused to sip our coffees. "How's Barbie?" Reva asked, once we'd settled on what Sally should wear on her date. "She looked amazing at church Sunday, almost as amazing as Diamond."

I sighed. "Sunday seems like a long way off instead of just two days ago. She was really out of it yesterday. So weak she could barely lift her head. I was afraid she was going to end up in the hospital. But by the time I got back from having dinner with Robert, she'd made a miraculous recovery." Though I told my friends nearly everything, I wasn't about to tell them about Robert's and my conversation of the night before. I'd never betray his confidence.

Sally rolled her eyes. "She was probably weak from not eating. That woman is obsessed with her appearance, and having Diamond's gorgeous figure around all the time probably doesn't help. How much longer is that woman going to be with her?"

"Boy, Sally, I don't know. Barbie says Diamond isn't even look-ing for a house. She's still holding out for one here on Morning Glory Circle, and you know how few of these houses ever go on the market. But, I have to say, I'm glad she's still living there. Strange things have been going on with our Barbie."

For the next few minutes, I filled them in on the missing jewelry and other missing things, but I left out the part about the book on witchcraft. I didn't want to spread any stories that weren't true, and Barbie did deny she'd ever seen that book. "She needs our prayers" was all I said.

"It was nice to see her with Jake Sunday morning."

I turned to Reva. "Yeah, it was. He could be a really good influence on her. She seems to like him. Speaking of flowers, he brought her roses last night."

Sally let out a chuckle. "That was nice. Take it from me. A

girl loves to get flowers. Maybe, if she takes a shine to Jake, she'll leave Robert alone."

I laughed. "I can only hope."

Mrs. Billingham's voice rang out from the living room. "Reva, are you going to bring me that cup of tea, or am I going to have to get up and fix it myself?"

The three of us looked at one another, then burst out in laughter. Sally latched onto Reva's arm. "Just make sure it's not Earl Grey!"

I called Diamond a number of times to check on Barbie, but I didn't see my other friends the rest of the week, though we did have several lengthy gabfests on the phone. With the time it took to finalize my plans for the next Red Hat meeting; get the necessary information to Wendy so she could e-mail or call everyone on our new chapter's list with the necessary information; and work with Robert and his crew as they put the final touches on the arbors, pergola, fountain, and stone walkways, and added the few remaining trees, shrubs, and bushes I'd selected, as well as placed the concrete planters around the pool, and consider the possibility of giving up my home, I barely had a chance to catch my breath. By the time the workmen were ready to leave late Saturday afternoon, I was exhausted. But not too exhausted to stand in awe and gaze at the incredible Tuscany-style yard they had created.

"You like it?" a voice whispered over my shoulder as a pair of strong, muscular arms slid about my waist and pulled me close.

I swiveled around in Robert's arms and gazed up into his suntanned face, then gently pushed back an errant wisp of salt-and-pepper hair from his forehead. "I love it, but I have to admit I never dreamed you could complete it in the allotted time, or that it would be this lovely. You are truly amazing."

He grinned. "Good husband material?"

I grinned back. "Of course you are. Ask any of your groupies at church. You know they're all after you."

A chill coursed through me as his lips brushed my cheek.

"You know I'm only interested in one woman." His voice was low and raspy, and just hearing it sent a shiver down my spine.

"That one woman is in my arms right now, Valentine. The most beautiful woman I know, and I desperately want her to become my wife."

At that moment, especially knowing all he'd been through because of Lydia's death, if he'd asked me to run off to Las Vegas that very night and be married in one of those do-it-now wedding chapels, leaving my home and belongings behind, I think I would have been tempted to say yes. I wasn't sure if it was because of the romantic Italian atmosphere of the place where we were standing and the way he'd worked feverishly to complete the job, if the look of love in his eyes had cast a spell over me, or if I suddenly realized for the first time how much I truly wanted to be this precious man's wife, but I knew his love for me would last a lifetime. Acting on impulse, which was rare for me, I cupped his face with my hands, then kissed his sweet lips. "And *I* want to be your wife, my darling. More than anything, I want to become Mrs. Robert Chase."

For a moment, he stood staring at me as if afraid he'd misunderstood me. Finally, his gaze still locked with mine, he asked,

"Are you saying what I hope you're saying?"

I flattened my palms against his chest, then lightly pushed away. Smiling, but without a word, I held my left hand up between us and slowly removed my wedding and engagement rings.

CHAPTER 12

What I had expected as a reaction to my declaration was a kiss, a hug, shouts of happiness, applause—anything but the response he gave me.

Quickly turning me loose, he took a couple of steps away from me and pointed his finger in my face. "Don't move. Stay there. I'll be right back!"

Stunned and feeling disappointed, I stood there like a bumpkin—my rings cupped in my hand, my brows raised, and my jaw dropped—as he darted across my backyard and disappeared through the side gate. Next, I heard the sound of his truck starting and leaving.

I stood there not comprehending. Had I just been spurned? Rejected by the man I loved? I was sure he'd be so pleased to see me take those rings off that he'd shout for joy. But he hadn't. He'd simply walked away from me and driven off!

"Wait," he'd said. Wait for what? Time for him to think it over and maybe decide he really didn't want to marry me after all? Had he felt somehow *safe* dating a widow who refused to give up the husband she'd lost and move? Had his singleness been threatened by my saying yes? How could he just disappear like that? Without any explanation. Where was all the enthusiasm, the hoopla, I'd expected? Maybe he didn't want to marry me as much as I'd thought he did. I'd heard of men who were enthralled with women—until they began to feel their independence might be coming to an end—then they'd backed away. But hadn't Robert been the one who had constantly mentioned the *M* word? Begged me to marry him?

I felt like crying.

I trudged slowly into the house and, with a heavy, discouraged sigh, placed my rings on the coffee table, then plunked myself onto the sofa and kicked off my shoes. I was tired. My feet hurt from wearing those gardening shoes all day, and I was hungry. I wanted nothing more than to eat a bowl of soup, take a relaxing shower, climb into bed, and snuggle down under the comforter.

But Robert had said to wait.

I didn't want to wait. But hadn't *I* made *him* wait all this time?

His words had not only disappointed me, they'd confused me.

I stared at the clock as ten minutes ticked by. Then eleven. Twelve, and right on to eighteen. Maybe he *was* one of those men and wasn't coming back. Now, I was not only hurt and confused, I was embarrassed. I stared at the rings on the table. Should I put them back on? I gave my head a shake. No, even if Robert didn't want to marry me, it was time they came off my finger. The lifelong tie that had once held me to my husband had been severed the day the Lord had called him home.

Well, I told myself as the hands on the clock marked the twentieth minute since he'd left, *his time is up. I am not going to sit here and wait like some gullible schoolgirl. Life goes on, with or without Robert Chase.*

As I bent to pick up my shoes, I heard a truck screech to a halt in my driveway, followed by the sound of a slamming door. Surely it was Robert. Who else could it be?

My heart soared as he came bursting through my front door, dropped to one knee in front of me, and reached for my hand.

"Valentine, my dear one, my sweet one, love of my life—" He paused to catch his breath. "Will you marry me? Become my wife?"

With the anxious beat of my heart thudding against my ribs, I stared at him, excited that he was back but still bewildered as to why he'd left so abruptly. "When you left, I thought—"

"It was stupid of me to leave like that, with no explanation, especially after you'd taken those rings off, but I had to, sweetheart. It was important that I rush home and get something."

I watched with anticipation as he reached into his shirt pocket.

"This!"

My breath caught in my throat, and I found myself trembling. It was an engagement ring! A diamond solitaire even more beautiful than the one I had taken off. "That's why you left?" I finally managed to blurt out.

"Surely you didn't think I was running out on you, did you? I'd never do that."

I felt a weird fluttery sensation as his eyebrows angled upward with alarm. "I—I didn't know what you were doing, so—"

Embarrassed, I dipped my head. "I guess I panicked."

"Oh, Valentine, I am so sorry. But when I saw those rings come off your finger, all I could think about was rushing home as fast as I could and placing this ring on your finger before you changed your mind. I would have been back much sooner, but I got caught in one of those construction zones. It never occurred to me that you'd think I was running out on you. I love you!"

His words made me even more embarrassed. Robert had never given me a single reason to doubt him. So why had I then? "I'm the one who should apologize. I don't know what got into me. Maybe I was just tired. It has been a long day."

His grin was pure masculine charm. "Let's forget about it. It really doesn't matter. What does matter is how we feel about each other."

It was one of those magical moments I wanted to capture forever. One I could replay in my mind over and over as we spent the rest of our lives together.

"Valentine, would you do me the honor of accepting this ring as a symbol of our love for one another and of our commitment to spend the rest of our lives together?"

I had an "Oh, yes!" on the tip of my tongue, but before I could say it, I remembered the other problem that stood between us. "But we haven't settled on where we will live."

Apparently sensing my concern, Robert rose quickly and pulled me into his arms. "I'm hoping wearing this ring will help you make that decision. I don't care where we live, as long as it isn't this house and you're my wife. You can even bring Sprinkles," he tacked on with a mischievous smile.

He reached for my hand again, and this time I didn't pull

away. The tears that tumbled down my cheeks were tears of joy as I gazed into his eyes. The love reflected there filled me with a joy beyond any I'd ever known. Suddenly, consumed with love for this man, I extended the third finger of my left hand. "I would consider it an honor to marry you, Robert Chase. I know we can work things out. Today God impressed something upon my heart. If I lost you, I'd be giving up something I desperately wanted for something I could never have. I can't let that happen."

"I want us to grow old together."

"I want that, too, my darling." The expression of delight on his face as he slipped that beautiful ring on my finger sent a myriad of sensations rippling through me, and all I wanted was to hold on to this man forever and never let him go. "I love you, Robert."

"No language can describe my love for you, my sweet Valentine."

I could almost feel his words as they feathered my ear; then I shuddered as his lips trailed kisses down my cheek. The feel of his warm breath bathing my skin made me deliriously happy. When his lips reached mine, they lingered, teasing and tasting until I wanted to cry out. I'd never known a sweeter time. I wanted that kiss to last forever.

Finally, he pulled away and stood gazing into my eyes. "You do realize you're pledged to me now."

I stood on tiptoe and lovingly planted a kiss on his cheek. "And you're pledged to me." I felt giddy with love, and I adored the feeling. It was like walking on air with no fear of falling.

Taking a slight step backward, he captured both my hands in his and, pulling them to his lips, kissed them, one fingertip at a time. "I like the look of that ring on your finger."

I pulled my left hand from his and, for the first time, gazed at the magnificent ring. So caught up in the ecstasy of that special moment, I hadn't really seen it. I gasped as it caught the light from one of the lamps, sending out a myriad of reflections in every direction. "Oh, Robert. It's lovely. The most beautiful ring I've ever seen."

He grinned. "It's not the Hope Diamond, but I was hoping you'd like it."

I allowed my right index finger to trace its lovely marquise shape. "It's more than I should have. I'm afraid you've spent way too much."

"I would lay the world at your feet if I could."

I felt a smile dance at my lips. "I don't need the world. I need you."

He pulled me into his arms again, his hand cradling my head against his strong chest. "God, in His infinite wisdom, knew we needed each other."

As I lay in bed long after Robert had gone home, I couldn't help pinching myself. Had such a magical evening really happened? Was the ring on my finger truly an engagement ring? The symbol of the love that Robert and I had pledged to each other? Was I really going to marry this man of my dreams?

When Carter was taken from me, I'd felt my life had ended.

Now it was just beginning.

"Any regrets?" Robert asked when he picked me up for church the next morning.

Still reveling in the giddy feeling of the night before, I threw my head back with a laugh. "No way! I've caught you, and I have the ring to prove it. You can't get away from me, Mr. Chase. You're mine now."

Before I could stop him, he swooped me up in his arms and carried me to his truck. "You've got that backward, my love. That ring means you're mine."

I giggled like a schoolgirl as he placed me on the seat. What did I care if my newly pressed linen suit wrinkled? I was in love. That was all that mattered.

When we reached the church, Robert paraded me around, holding my hand and proudly pointing out my engagement ring to anyone who would take time to look at it. I knew I was blushing, and I didn't care. I was a woman in love, and I wanted the world to know it.

By the time Sunday school ended, nearly the entire congregation had heard of our engagement. Everyone congratulated us and wished us the best. And, as I knew they would be, Reva and Sally were ecstatic about our news and fawned all over both Robert and me.

"Guess who I'm going to ask to be my matron of honor?"

Both Sally and Reva looked from me to each other.

"Both of you! I'm going to have two matrons of honor!"

Sally's face fairly gleamed. "Both of us?"

"It's my wedding. I can do whatever I want."

Reva grinned. "Sounds like a good idea to me!"

Sally let out a giggle. "Atta girl, Valentine. Who knows? You may start a new trend."

I was surprised when Diamond and Ward came in late, without Barbie, and scooted into the pew next to us. Of course, Robert immediately grabbed onto my hand and showed them the ring. Ward sent me a congratulatory smile, but Diamond latched onto my hand for a better look, whispering, "It's beautiful, Valentine. I'm so happy for you."

I leaned toward her. "Where is Barbie?"

She responded with a shrug. "She refused to get out of bed. I told her I was going to leave without her, but she turned over and went back to sleep."

"Is she feeling okay?"

Again she shrugged. "Who knows? One day she's up. The next she's down."

Hating to have Barbie hear about our engagement from someone else, considering how adamant she'd been about catching Robert for herself, I determined, with his approval, that we should go by her house as soon as church was over and invite her to have lunch with us.

"So, when is this wedding going to take place?" Pastor Wyman asked as he shook Robert's hand at the end of the service.

Robert sent me an uncomfortable glance. "There are still a few details we have to work out before we can set a date." Taking on a smile, he added, "Since you're the one who will be performing our marriage ceremony, you'll be the first to know."

I couldn't keep my eyes off that ring as we drove toward Barbie's house. The sunlight caught it, fracturing its brilliance into a thousand colorful beams, making sparkling distorted ovals dance on the truck's ceiling.

We had to tap Barbie's doorbell three times before she finally answered. I gasped as the door opened. The woman standing before us looked nothing like the Barbie we knew. She was donned in a faded chenille bathrobe, her hair in total disarray, its roots desperately needing a color job, and she had mascara smudges around her eyes. With a countenance as white as alabaster, this woman looked much older and frailer than the woman who had moved in next door to me.

Without waiting for an invitation, I stepped inside and circled my arm around her. "What happened? You were doing so well the last time I saw you."

Wide-eyed, she leaned into me. "I've been sick again. I don't know what's wrong with me. I can't seem to stay on my feet. I'm weak, Valentine. I get light-headed so easily, and sometimes I can't get my eyes to focus."

Robert stepped forward and grasped her arm. "Let's put her on the couch."

After she'd settled, she leaned her head against the sofa's cushioned back and closed her eyes. "I'm so tired."

An empty coffee cup was on the table, but there was no sign of food. I knew from experience Barbie normally ate her meals while sitting on the sofa with a tray in her lap, and no tray was evident, either. "Have you eaten anything today?"

Her eyes still closed, she gave her head a nearly unnoticeable shake.

Bending over her, Robert took her hand and gave it a friendly pat. "We thought maybe you'd like to go to lunch with us."

"I can't. I don't have the strength."

I sat down beside her. "How long have you been like this?"

"Two days. Maybe three. I lose track."

Robert nodded toward her kitchen. "Stay with her. I'll see if I can find a can of soup or maybe some bread I can toast for her."

She opened one eye a slit and peeked out at me. "I'm cold. Could you get that rose-colored afghan from my room?"

"Of course I can." I stood and headed toward the staircase. "Anything else?"

"My hairbrush. It's on the bathroom counter, I think."

Knowing Robert was only a short distance away, I hurried up the stairs to her room. Clothing had been strewn everywhere, shoes lay scattered on the floor as if she'd kicked them off, unopened mail lay on her bed. The place looked like some teenager's room, not like the room of a sophisticated, mature woman who normally put everything in its place as soon as she'd used it.

I located the afghan, then headed into her bathroom to get her brush, but when I entered, all thoughts of the brush fled from my mind.

CHAPTER 13

There on Barbie's vanity lay all sorts of medicine bottles, each containing pills I'd heard discussed on TV or read about in magazines, most of which had numerous side effects. I knew instantly what they could do to Barbie, and it scared me. I scanned the labels and found, other than the over-the-counter pills, the other pills had been prescribed by a variety of doctors from Atlanta to Nashville. Why would she take such an array of medication? Or should I have said *drugs*, because that's what most of them were. Some of the bottles were nearly full, some empty. Some had no labels on them whatsoever. How would she know what she was taking or how often to take them? Or, even more important, *why* she was taking them.

From the frazzled way she'd looked when she'd opened that door, it appeared to me the woman had overdosed. On impulse, I stuck two of the unlabeled bottles into my jacket pocket, retrieved her brush, and headed back downstairs. I knew I'd have to choose my words carefully, otherwise she would accuse me of snooping and not answer the questions I intended to ask her.

Since Robert was still in the kitchen, I spread the afghan over Barbie, then sat down beside her and attempted to brush her hair. From the tangles and snarls, it appeared she hadn't brushed or combed it for some time, which was not at all like her. The Barbie I knew wanted to look her very best every minute of every day. Her appearance had been her number one priority in life. "Are you still taking those diet pills?" I prodded gently. "Maybe they are the cause of you feeling sick."

She moved her head slightly. "Is that all you think about? You're always asking me about those stupid pills." Her voice was curt.

"Only because I'm concerned about you."

She blanched me with an icy stare. "If you must know, I am still taking them, but I cut down on the dosage."

I worked diligently at a tangle with the brush, finally using my fingers to work it loose, rather than pulling her hair. "Good. How about other medication?"

"Only what my doctors prescribe."

With my free hand, I fingered the unlabeled bottles in my pocket. "Nothing else?"

"I'm a responsible, grown woman, Valentine. I think I know what is best for me."

With the tangle worked free, I continued brushing. "You know that I'm only asking because I'm worried about you, don't you?"

She released a deep sigh, then took the brush from my hand and placed it on the table. "I know. You and Diamond are the only ones who worry about me. I've found most of my so-called friends are fair-weather friends who disappear when things are going wrong."

"Not all of them," I countered. "I well remember when those nice ladies from your Red Hat group stepped in and took turns staying with you and helping you when you needed it."

"You're right. They did. I guess if they knew how sick I was, they'd be here now."

"You haven't told them?"

"No. To be honest, I didn't want any of them seeing me like this."

Then why aren't you taking action to get well? I wanted to ask. But knowing she'd be infuriated and probably order me out of her house, I kept my mouth shut. We both turned as the front door opened and Diamond appeared, looking more glamorous than a woman in her late twenties had a right to look. Well, maybe she was in her early thirties. I'd never asked. All I know was that she was one of the most beautiful women I'd ever met.

"Ward and I had a delightful lunch." She kicked off her shoes, then sat down in a chair opposite the sofa. "Lobster tails, steamed squash, and a wonderful green salad."

I was immediately miffed that she hadn't asked Barbie how she felt. Any sane person could tell the woman was ill. "That sounds lovely," I said through gritted teeth. But then I remembered how demanding and sassy Barbie could be and how many times she'd done things to get attention, and I felt sorry for Diamond. I'd never lived with Barbie 24/7. She had. I could only imagine what a chore it had been. "Barbie isn't feeling well," I said. "I'm worried about her."

Diamond hurried to the sofa and took hold of her hand. "Oh,

sweetie, I'm so sorry. If I'd known, I'd never have gone off and left you this morning. I just supposed you were overly tired when I tried to wake you, so I decided to let you sleep. You should have told me."

Barbie smiled up at her. "I didn't want to be a bother."

Diamond huffed. "A bother? You? Never. Don't ever think that. I'm here for you."

Robert came into the room carrying a tray with a mug of hot soup and a cup of tea. "Sorry it took me so long. I had a hard time finding a microwavable bowl." He placed the tray on the coffee table, then handed Barbie a napkin. "Better eat it while it's nice and hot."

She gazed at the soup for a moment, then turned her head away. "I don't want it. I'm not hungry."

I scooted closer and lifted the spoon. "Open up, please. You need some nourishment."

To my surprise, she opened her mouth and allowed me to feed her. "Isn't that good? There's nothing like chicken noodle soup when you're not feeling well." I offered it to her again. Then, again and again, until she'd consumed the entire bowl.

Frowning, she dabbed at her chin with the napkin Robert had placed on her tray. "I hate for anyone to see me this way. I must look a mess. I had to cancel my beauty appointments this week. My hair is like straw. I haven't put makeup on in days. My roots need touching up. My nail polish is worn off, and here I am sitting in this old, faded bathrobe."

What could I say? Though I'd never tell her, she was right. She did look a mess.

Robert, who always seemed to know the proper thing to say

or do, gave her a consoling smile. "It's you and your health we're interested in. Not your appearance."

Covering her mouth with her hand, she let out a gasp as I reached for the tray. "Surely that's not an engagement ring!"

I froze. I'd been so concerned about Barbie's physical appearance, her health, and her despondent state of mind, I'd temporarily forgotten about the sparkling diamond on my hand. Before I could decide how I should respond, I felt Robert's arm slip around me and pull me close.

"Yes, it's an engagement ring," he said proudly, smiling down at me. "Valentine has finally consented to marry me. I'm a happy man."

She stared at the two of us for a moment, then a frown creased her brow. "I—I knew you two were dating, but I'd had no idea either of you had even considered making it permanent."

Robert's face fairly glowed. "If I'd had my way, even though I didn't deserve her, this gorgeous lady would have said yes to my proposal months ago."

As her eyes zeroed in on me, her frown deepened. "But I thought you said you still loved Carter. Didn't you tell me you could never marry another man?"

"I do love Carter," I tried to explain, "and, yes, I said that I felt a lifelong allegiance to him, but that was before—"

She huffed, breaking into my sentence. "Before you met Robert!"

The woman was jealous. I didn't know where she got the energy, but her response was loud and almost angry, as if I'd done something spiteful to her by accepting his proposal. Surely she hadn't thought she still had a chance with Robert. Especially since she and Jake seemed to be getting very close.

I bit at the words I wanted to say and forced a smile. I certainly didn't want to add to her agitation. "Actually," I said, trying to sound calm and in control, "I did feel that lifelong allegiance until a few days ago, when, as I told Robert, I suddenly realized the life I'd had with Carter was over. It could never be again, but God intended that *my* life go on. When I fully came to accept that fact, I was finally able to acknowledge that I was now totally and wonderfully in love with someone else. A magnificent, sweet"—I sent a smile toward Robert—"godly man. One of whom I knew Carter would approve." I smiled up at him. "This man. Robert Chase. The man who has won my heart."

I could almost feel the glare of her eyes. I nearly shouted hallelujah when Diamond took the tray off Barbie's lap, placed it on the table, then reached for her hand.

"Now that you've had your lunch," Diamond said, "perhaps you'd like to go back to your bed, sweetie. You look worn-out."

Though Barbie gave her a leave-me-alone look, she allowed Diamond to pull her to her feet. "I am a bit weary," she said, leaning into Diamond. "And I need to take a Tylenol. For some reason"—she sent a cool glance my way—"I've developed a terrible headache."

"I'll check on you later," I called out as they moved toward the stairway.

Without turning, she answered back in that same angry tone, "You needn't bother; Diamond will take care of me," then continued on up the stairs.

I carried the tray into the kitchen and put the bowl and spoon in the dishwasher, then Robert and I let ourselves out.

He shook his head as we crossed the lawn to my house. "That woman is really something. She wasn't exactly happy for us, was she?"

"Pretty obvious, huh? Perhaps it was because she was feeling so poorly."

Though I was relishing our engagement, which should have been one of the happiest times of my life, I couldn't get Barbie off my mind. After spending the rest of an otherwise pleasant day with Robert, discussing our predicament, our plans for the future, and the Red Hat meeting at my house in my new Tuscany backyard, I spent a fitful night. I kept waking up thinking about her. If there was only something I could do to help her regain her zest for living and get her life back on track. But, as long as I'd known her, she'd always seemed to harbor such resentment of me. What could I do that I hadn't already done?

About ten that morning, I picked a few flowers from my yard, made my way to her house, and rang the doorbell. Diamond answered and, after taking the flowers from my hand, politely told me Barbie didn't want to see me. When I phoned later that afternoon, Diamond answered the phone. And although she was very kind and apologetic about it, she explained that Barbie had left explicit instructions that she didn't want to see me or talk to me or to Robert, that she could get along just fine without us, that she had no need for either of us in her life.

The same thing happened the next day and the next and the next, until an entire week had gone by. When Diamond wasn't at church on Sunday, I phoned again. She politely told me Barbie was doing somewhat better. I reminded her of my Red Hat meeting and that, as a widow, she was invited. She responded by saying that if she felt like Barbie could be left alone for a while, she'd try to make it. I hoped she could make it, not only because she was a widow and I thought she would enjoy it, but also because I was sure, after spending day in and day out with Barbie, she could use a pleasant evening out.

The next two days passed before I knew it. Wendy phoned early Wednesday morning with a final head count. Thirty-two women had signed up to attend our meeting, which was at least ten more than I had originally anticipated. How exciting. I wanted to shout for joy. If all of those women decided to attend on a regular basis, we might have to split off a second group before this first one even got off the ground. I'd had no idea so many widows would respond.

By late that afternoon, I had checked and rechecked and taken care of every last-minute detail I could think of but one—the final head-count call to the caterers. Morgan Childers, owner of the Katering King, answered on the first ring.

"Thirty-three will be no trouble at all. Let me assure you, Ms. Denay, everything is in readiness. I'm even sending more servers than usual to make sure all of your lovely ladies are taken care of in fine style."

I thanked him, but as I hung up, I rethought his words. More servers? Fine style? What did that mean? And had I detected an air of amusement in his voice, or had I imagined it?

I fluffed off my concern. Though I didn't know the man personally, I had met with him a number of times. Maybe I had just imagined his jovial attitude, but I still wondered about the *fine style* he'd mentioned. Didn't he take care of all his customers in fine style?

Robert, bless his heart for being so considerate, knowing I was exhausted from all my preparations and the added task of making sure my house shone, offered to pick up two carry-out dinners from one of our favorite restaurants on his way to my house that evening. It was a gorgeous night, so we ate out on the patio where we had full view of the spectacular landscaping job he had done on my yard. After we had consumed the last tasty morsel and the carryout boxes had been placed in the trash container, we cuddled on the swing, enjoying each other's company.

I snuggled up close to him, laid my head on his shoulder, then breathed a sigh of contentment. "Thank you for making my dream a reality. The yard looks fabulous. Even better than I had imagined."

"If only every day of our lives could be as satisfying and as peaceful as the one we're sharing tonight."

I stared up at him. "What do you mean?"

"I've been thinking a lot about life lately, and about Lydia. Life is so uncertain. We have no idea what God's plans are for us until they happen." His arm tightened about my shoulder. "I wish I would have told you about the circumstances of Lydia's death sooner, but I just couldn't. It—it was one of those things that—"

I pressed a finger to his lips. "Don't, Robert. It's over. We have to put it behind us and look forward to our future."

"*Our* future? *Together?* Sweetheart, don't you see? That's what I'm talking about. We have no idea what tomorrow, or next week, or even the next month holds for us. And we still aren't any closer to coming up with a solution to our housing problem than we were weeks ago."

After reaching up to gently stroke his face, I gazed into his eyes. The love and longing I saw there made my heart leap with joy. "We'll find an answer. And this marriage *will* happen."

"Val, I want you to know, if there is ever anything you desire, and it is within my power to give it to you, all you have to do is ask and it will be yours."

My gaze roved from his eyes to his handsome face. "Just promise you'll always be by my side. That's all I could ever want to make me happy."

He gave a slight chuckle. "By your side? Does that mean I'm invited to your meeting tomorrow night?"

I gave his arm a playful swat. "This is a Red Hat *ladies'* group. You're definitely a man."

"But I've worked so hard on this. I'd like to be here to listen to all the women ooh and aah over the transformation."

I grinned at him. "I'll pass all their compliments on to you when it's over."

He gave me an appreciative smile. "I love you, Valentine. I hope you know that."

"I do, and I love you, too."

We continued to gaze at one another for a moment, then he lifted my face to his and kissed me. His kisses had been sweet before. But once we became officially engaged, they became even sweeter. The delicious thought that I was going to have a lifetime of his kisses to enjoy sent my head reeling and my heart thundering. I was actually going to be Mrs. Robert Chase. If only I could bring myself to leave this house.

We said our good nights, then I watched until his lights disappeared down the street before closing the door and heading to bed. I was tired, but as I glanced at the ring on my left hand, I was also exhilarated. I had spent a wonderful, relaxing evening with the man I loved, and he loved me, and tomorrow I would be entertaining my friends.

But as I turned out the light, my mind went back to Barbie.

I couldn't have asked for a more perfect day for an outdoor party. The morning dawned absolutely gorgeous. There was hardly any wind, with the evening temperature predicted to be in the midseventies.

The florist arrived at four with the table centerpieces, huge clay pots filled with an assortment of colorful, long-stemmed foliage, fresh green bands of eucalyptus, statice, and all sorts of colorful flowers, including zinnias, roses, lavender and yellow mums, and even dried wheat stalks and oversized sunflowers. Each pot was so beautiful it took my breath away. He placed one in the center of each of the six tables I had rented and covered with burgundy linen tablecloths. Not even counting the landscaping bill I had requested from Robert, the party was costing me far more than I had intended, but it was worth it. Especially since Carter and I had planned a number of years ago to have our landscaping done by a professional. I had come out of the fog of despair that had engulfed me since I'd become a widow, and it felt good. I was starting a brand-new life. I had much for which to praise God.

The caterer arrived about the same time as the florist. "Don't be concerned, Ms. Denay," he said with a flourish of his hand as if reading my mind. "Most of the servers are coming later."

With everything under control, I hurried upstairs to take a

shower and get ready. I'd had a terrible time deciding what to wear and had visited a number of shops before making up my mind. But when I'd spotted a heavily embroidered and beaded purple, almost Bohemian-style, two-piece dress in one of them and it fit like it was made for me, I'd snatched it up without even looking at the price tag. The top was tunic length, and the skirt was long and gathered, with an uneven flounce set with godets at the hemline that made it swish to and fro as I walked. It reminded me of the dresses I'd seen on the Italian women in the Tuscany books I had checked out of the library. Though I normally didn't wear long, dangling earrings, I couldn't resist buying a pair with dozens of bright, shiny red discs that cascaded downward into a triangular shape that nearly touched my shoulders. A pair of red sandals, several gold bangles on each wrist, a heavy gold chain about my neck, and my outfit was complete. By the time I'd dressed and had done my hair in an upsweep with curly tendrils hanging freely around my face, I felt like a princess. Though I hated to smash my hair down after all the time I'd spent curling it with the curling iron, I added the requisite red hat—a cute, straw half-moon topped with a perky bow made of red netting. I smiled and gave myself a thumbs-up in the mirror, adding, "You go, girl! This is your night!"

I'd barely walked outside when Sally and Reva arrived, each wearing lavender pantsuits and pink wide-brimmed hats, and each grabbing hold of my hand to take another look at my ring.

Sally playfully covered her eyes as if being blinded by its brilliance. "You are one lucky woman, Valentine. That Robert of yours is a very special man."

Reva lightly jabbed her in the ribs with her elbow. "No luck about it, Sal. The Lord brought those two together."

Truer words were never spoken.

We three turned to find Wendy strolling in, dressed in a long purple sheath, elbow-length red satin gloves, and a red felt pillbox tipped jauntily over her gorgeous head of white hair. She shook a finger at us. "Don't you dare laugh. I decided if I was going to do this thing, I was going to do it right."

Though the three of us tried to keep straight faces, we couldn't help but laugh. We weren't laughing because she looked ridiculous; we were laughing because she looked so cute.

I wrapped my arm about her shoulders and gave her a loving squeeze. "You, my precious lady, are beautiful."

Sally gave her free arm a nudge. "Yeah, I want to be just like you when I grow up!"

Wendy grinned at her. "Just keep your eyes focused on God, and it will happen."

"Hi!" three voices called out simultaneously as the side gate opened and three women strolled in, clad from head to toe in purple and red. I didn't know them, but Sally did and motioned them to join us. She eagerly introduced each one by name, then explained, "These ladies are members of the exercise class I've joined at the YMCA. When they told me they were widows, I invited them to become a part of our group."

Reva, Wendy, and I made sure they felt welcome, then excused ourselves to greet other guests who were arriving. As each woman entered, she graciously complimented me on the lovely appearance of my yard and thanked me for hosting the evening. As I listened to them, I almost felt bad that I hadn't allowed Robert to come so he could have heard their praises firsthand.

By six o'clock, the starting time we'd announced, all thirty-two women, thirty-three including me, were enjoying the appetizer trays of munchies and good conversation. Though I hated to break up their fun and laughter, it was time to get started, so I loudly rapped on the table.

No response. None of them could hear me.

In desperation, I did something I rarely do in public. I stuck my two index fingers in my mouth and whistled loudly, something I'd learned as a child.

All sound stopped as thirty-two women stared at me, open-mouthed. I couldn't help it. I burst out laughing. I had forgotten all about the microphone and speakers Robert had installed for that very purpose. Rolling my eyes while giving everyone a shy grin, I moved to the mike, flipped the switch to the on position, then tapped the mike to make sure it was working. It was.

Still wearing my grin, I spoke into it. "Sorry, ladies. I hope my loud whistle didn't frighten you, but a girl has to do what a girl has to do, and I wanted to get your attention." I gestured to the speakers on the wall. "In my excitement of having all of you here, I forgot about the sound system that had been added by"—I tried to stifle a grin but it broke forth anyhow—"my fiancé." I knew my face was probably as red as my hat. That was the first time I'd used that term when referring to Robert. I held up my hand so they all could see that I was wearing an engagement ring.

Loud applause broke out, causing me to blush even more.

"I want to welcome you to my home. Some of you I've met, some I haven't, but I hope by the end of the evening, we'll all be friends. Let me introduce myself. I am your queen, the Queen of Hearts. My name is Valentine Denay." I felt myself blush again.

"Soon to be Valentine Chase."

A slight buzz circulated through the tables. I knew my announcement had come as a surprise to some, and others probably had no idea what I was talking about. So, for the sake of time, I chose to let the subject of my name change drop. Anyone who was interested could ask me about it later.

I gestured toward the tables set with the brightly colored Fiestaware plates the caterers had brought and the vast array of colorful linen napkins. "I've placed an information sheet by your plates. Take it home with you and post it on your refrigerator or some other conspicuous place where you can refer to it." I gave them a few seconds to scan the sheet before going on.

Laughter rumbled through the eager group.

"In a moment, I'm going to ask you to find yourself a seat so our servers may serve you, but first let's all bow our heads in prayer." Not wanting to overwhelm those who may not know and love the Lord as I did, I made it a simple prayer, thanking God for our food and asking Him to bless our fellowship.

After I'd said, "Amen," and lifted my head, I added, "Once you're seated, check under the seat cushion on your chair. One chair at each table has a bright pink sticker attached to it. If your chair has that sticker, you may take your table's centerpiece with you to enjoy in your home. But," I added quickly, "no fair peeking under any of the chairs until you have selected your seat and sat down. We want to be fair about this."

Instantly, before I could give them direction, thirty-two ladies scrambled to the tables, hoping to find seating with their friends. I nodded to our caterer, Mr. Childers, that we were ready to begin, then seated myself at the head table, took a sip of the fragrant peach iced tea from the glass that had already been filled, and settled back to enjoy the evening. I'd saved a place at my table for Diamond, but it looked as though she wasn't going to make it.

Then something happened that I hadn't planned, and I was almost angry with the caterer!

CHAPTER 14

Italian-type music with a bright tempo began playing loudly over the speakers. I had decided against playing the CD I had selected until later in the evening. Had the caterer overridden my instructions and decided to use it anyway? I was about ready to tell him to at least turn the volume down when Mr. Childers took the microphone from its place and gave it a light tap. What was the man doing?

"Ladies," he said, a smile lighting up his elfin face. "It is my privilege to be your caterer for tonight. I had told your host, Ms. Valentine Denay, that I would have a larger serving staff than usual tonight, so you may dine in fine style."

There were those words. *Fine style.*

"This evening, each of your tables will have two servers instead of one. If you need anything, don't hesitate to ask. Now, without further ado"—he gestured toward my garden gate—"your servers!"

I nearly fainted from surprise when a troop of men, each attired in either a purple or red short-sleeved shirt and tan Dockers and a white apron came marching in. Each one carried a tray in his hand, and each stepped to the beat of the music that Mr. Childers had turned up to top volume.

But the biggest surprise of all was who was leading them. Robert!

They ceremoniously circled the yard, then two by two, they stopped at a table, staking out their claim. Eventually, there were only two men left. Robert and Jake, who, grinning grins wide enough to distort their faces, stopped and took their places at my table.

The volume on the music lowered and faded away as once again Mr. Childers took the mike. "Red Hat ladies," he said with a chuckle, "tonight you are being invaded by the men who work for Chase Landscape and Garden, and who did the building and landscaping of this wonderful Italian yard. When Robert Chase called with the plan that these men act as your servers for the evening, I almost said no. But when he explained how hard each man had worked, how proud they were of what they had accomplished, and how willing they were to spend time with me to learn what they should do as successful servers"—he lifted his hands in surrender—"what could I say but yes?"

All the women applauded.

Mr. Childers motioned in my direction. "Their being here is a surprise to Ms. Denay, as well. She knew nothing about it." He gave another chuckle. "I just hope she doesn't fire me!"

Cornelia Higgins, a normally soft-spoken, quiet sort of person, stood to her feet, cupped her hands to her mouth, and yelled out, "Hey, we're a bunch of widows. Do we get to take one of them home with us?"

Those of us who knew her went into shock.

Mr. Childers gave us all a wave. "I don't think that will be possible. Time for me to get back to work. We have a wonderful meal planned for you, and it looks like you're going to have excellent service. Enjoy!"

Trying to keep a smile in tow, I lifted a brow and gazed up at Robert. "So our Red Hat Widows' Club has been invaded, huh? Why am I not surprised that this was all your idea?"

He responded with a shy grin. "I hope you're not upset with me. The men and I thought it would be fun to surprise you."

My smile broke loose. "Upset? How could I ever be upset with you? I think it's a wonderful idea." I reached around and gave him a playful swat. "Now get busy. We're hungry!"

I'd no more than said the words when Diamond slid into the chair beside me. "Sorry, I'm late. I wanted to make sure Barbie finished her dinner and was tucked into bed before I left."

I smiled at her. "I'm glad you made it. I know it's not easy caring for her. You deserve a break." She glanced up and laughed when she saw Jake standing by our table. "What are you doing here?"

Jake let out a belly laugh. "Serving you."

Knowing Diamond had missed the introduction of our servers, I quickly explained things to her. "Now aren't you glad you came?"

She nodded. "Very glad."

"I had invited Barbie to come as my guest," I said, "but I guess she didn't feel like it, or maybe she's still too angry with me to accept."

"She doesn't have much energy these days, but I think she is doing a bit better. She still refuses to see a doctor. I put her cell phone by her bed so she can call if she needs me."

I cupped my hand over her wrist. "Try to relax and enjoy yourself. She's probably sound asleep by now."

Diamond leaned back in her chair with a sigh. "You have no idea how I've looked forward to this evening. Being with you and your widow friends is exactly what I need."

I nodded in agreement. "We widows have to stick together."

Her grin was warm and friendly. "That we do."

As the string quartet I'd hired to play Italian music during our meal moved onto the area in front of the pergola, once more the ladies applauded. The music added just the touch of ambience I had envisioned. I smiled to myself. What a joy it was to bring this special evening into these ladies' lives. Though most were in good enough health to circulate among the community, a few rarely left their homes, except for church on Sunday morning, and then they had to rely on others to provide their transportation.

Sally, who was seated on my other side, nudged me with her elbow. "Valentine, have you tasted your salad yet? It's delicious! What is it?"

I was pleased she liked the salad since I had left the entire menu to Mr. Childers's discretion. "As I recall, our caterer said it was a combination of field greens, Havarti cheese, ripe olives, red onion, pine nuts, tomatoes, some sort of beans, and a dash of balsamic vinaigrette dressing."

Sally eyed her salad plate suspiciously. "Pine nuts and beans? I never would have thought to add those to a green salad, but I like it."

"The Havarti cheese is a nice touch, too," Reva added, spearing another cube with her fork.

"Typically Tuscan," I told her. "Healthy, too."

By the time we'd finished our salads, the sun had dropped below the horizon. I glanced up at the colorful strings of lights hanging over our tables and in the trees, casting a rosy glow that illuminated the whole area. Those lights had been Robert's idea.

I gave Jake a grateful nod as he removed our salad plates from the table.

"Madam Valentine, may I serve your entrée now?" Robert asked.

I smiled up into the sweetest face I knew, batted my lashes, and turned on my Southern charm. "Yes, sir, you certainly may."

My fiancé took on a serverlike stance. "Tonight, madam, we are serving Bistecchine di maiale"—he chuckled—"or however you pronounce it. It is flavored with thyme, marjoram, sage, rosemary, and fennel seeds, topped with a fine extra-virgin olive oil, and accompanied with carefully steamed vegetables. Our bread is pane toscano, Tuscany's famous saltless bread. I suggest you dip it into the sauce you'll find by your plate. The dipping sauce is a combination of olive oil, walnut oil, balsamic vinegar, and a few herbs. You'll find the bread extremely bland without it."

"Well, I do declare, sir," I said, still using my exaggerated version of a Southern twang. "You're a proverbial walking, talking information machine. I do thank you for explaining all of this to us."

He placed my plate on the table, then bowed low. "And I thank you, madam. I worked long and hard to memorize all of that list. I'm glad you appreciate my efforts."

All the women at our table laughed.

The conversation was stimulating and enjoyable. The food

was excellent. The ten dollars each lady had paid didn't begin to cover the cost of this extravagant meal, but to me, it was worth every penny. I was having the time of my life. And having Robert and his coworkers there to serve us was the best thing that could have happened. The women loved having the men fawn all over them and go out of their way to make them each feel special. As I listened to their laughter, I wondered how long it had been since some of these women, my fellow widows, had had extra attention from a man. Yes, Robert's idea of bringing his crew to invade our meeting was definitely one of the highlights of our evening.

By the time we'd finished our delicious salad and entrée, not to mention the bread dipped in that unusual olive oil concoction, we were all more than satisfied.

"What's for dessert?" Sally asked.

Almost everyone at the table groaned at the word.

"I hope you're still hungry. I have no idea what our caterer has come up with," I told them, "but I'm sure it will be as special as our meal."

I'd no sooner said it when Jake appeared, holding a large tray laden with some sort of cakelike dessert. With the usual flourish of his hand, Robert removed one plate at a time from the tray, dramatically placing it before each of us. "This beautiful Italian concoction, my lovely purple-and-red-clad ladies, is your dessert. Enjoy."

Again, we all laughed. I smiled at him with pride. I'd had no idea Robert could be such a chivalrous server.

By the time we'd all eagerly devoured our dessert and its decadent calories, we were almost too full to move. I groaned again as he removed my plate, reminding myself, as the Queen of

Hearts, I still had a meeting to conduct. I never should have eaten that last bite.

I allowed the ladies to linger over fresh cups of coffee as long as I dared, then rose and took the microphone. "Have you enjoyed your meal?"

My question was immediately met with enthusiastic applause and vigorous shouts of "Yes!"

I lifted my hand high in the air. "Have you enjoyed the service of this fine group of men?"

This question brought forth a loud outburst of appreciation.

"When are they going to dance on the tables?" a matronly woman at the same table as Cornelia Higgins shouted out.

Robert stepped up beside me and leaned toward the mike. "Sorry, ladies. This serving business is hard work. None of us has enough strength left to get up on a table, let alone dance, but thanks for asking." He gave the crowd an exaggerated wink. "Invite us back and maybe we'll do it the next time." With that, he turned to move away, but I grabbed onto his arm and pulled him back and spoke into the mike.

"My beautiful engagement ring was given to me by one of our humble servers, Robert Chase, this wonderful man standing next to me. It's official! We're going to be married!"

Every lady present rose to her feet and clapped her hands loudly as Robert pulled me into his arms and kissed me, right there in front of them! Normally, I would have been embarrassed, but not that time. That evening, I knew that every woman there, regardless of her personal circumstance, was happy for us.

I almost shuddered when Robert took the microphone from my hand again. "I want everyone to know how much I love this lady, this precious queen of yours. She has brought a happiness into my life I never expected to find again. We haven't set a date yet. We have a few things to work out, but," he added, thrusting his hand high into the air with exuberance, "she's committed herself to me, and you're all invited to the wedding!"

I found myself speechless. How was I ever going to conduct a meeting after all this frivolity? But I couldn't have said anything if I wanted, since Robert enveloped me in his arms and kissed me again, much to the ladies' delight.

"Now," he said into the mike, "my band of hearty men and I will take our leave. I'm sure I speak for each of them when I say it has been a pleasure to serve you. Farewell, lovely ladies, until we meet again!" With that, he and the rest of the men exited out the gate.

Though I felt a bit self-conscious about all the attention that had been lavished upon me during the evening, but recharged by Robert's sweet words, I took the mike and gazed at the sea of purple and red before me. Each woman wore a radiant smile. I once again welcomed them and began the meeting. There was a small amount of business that needed to be taken care of, but to make it an official meeting, it had to be done.

At the close of the meeting, I announced the date for our next get-together and mentioned that those who hadn't officially done so should meet with Sally and Reva to take care of the membership form before they left. Next, I offered everyone the hospitality of my home, should any desire to go inside. Then I turned the remainder of the evening over to our string quartet to entertain us with their romantic Tuscan music as we visited with one another and got better acquainted.

Diamond picked up her purse, then gave me a hug. "I'd better get back to Barbie. Thank you for inviting me, Valentine. I really needed this evening. You were a perfect hostess."

"You're more than welcome. I'm glad you came. Tell Barbie I'll be over to see her in the morning. I need to make amends with her. I can't stand having her angry with me, though I'm still not exactly sure why she's so upset."

Diamond's brow furrowed. "I'm not so sure that's a good idea. She's been adamant about not seeing you. You know her. It takes her a long time to get over one of her mad spells. Maybe you should wait a few more days. I'll give you a call when I think it's a good time. I'd hate to see her make another scene like that last one. You don't deserve it."

"But you will give her my love, won't you? Even if she doesn't want it?"

"Of course I will. Good night." After slinging her bag's strap over her shoulder, she moved away from the table and disappeared into the milling crowd of women. I couldn't help but wonder if Barbie realized how nice it was of Diamond to care for her, especially since Barbie rarely seemed grateful.

I had thought our time of visiting and getting acquainted would last maybe a half hour or so once I'd adjourned the meeting, but two hours later, I had to take the microphone and bid the ladies good night, since most of them were still there and still heavily engaged in joyful conversation, old friends and newly made friends with a common bond—widowhood.

Mortified that someone would be calling on me at such an early hour, I sat straight up in bed when the ringing of my doorbell awakened me the next morning. But a quick glance at the red numbers glaring at me on my nightstand clock told me I had slept way past my usual waking time. I yanked on my robe and hurried down the stairs, trying desperately to run my fingers through my tangled hair on the way. I knew I looked a mess. I'd been so tired after everyone had left, I'd simply pulled on my nightgown and gone straight to bed.

Don't get yourself in a tizzy. It's probably Reva or Sally wanting to hear more details about your upcoming wedding plans, I told myself as I braced my hands against my front door, closed one eye, and peeked through the peephole with the other.

But it wasn't my friends.

It was Robert!

He'd never seen me without makeup and my hair combed and sprayed into my normal style. Not only that, each time he'd seen me since we'd met, I'd either been dressed up for church or had known I would be seeing him and had attired myself in clean, well-planned clothing. I had no idea what I should do. If I opened the door, looking totally disheveled and unkempt, he might decide I wasn't the woman he wanted to wake up to every morning after all and ask for his ring back!

I couldn't decide if I should remain hidden behind the door until he got tired of standing there and decided perhaps I wasn't at home or throw caution to the wind and let him see me the way I was.

After three more rings, I decided, why not? No woman was perfect all the time, no matter how hard she tried to keep up her appearance. Though I didn't normally have dark raccoon circles around my eyes from sleeping in my eyeliner and mascara, and the robe I had on was comfy but not as pretty as the one I usually wore, I was still the same me. The woman he had asked to become his bride. He might as well see what he was getting.

Screwing up my face, I held my breath and threw the door open wide.

The sight of him made my hand fly to cover my mouth, and I let out a gasp.

Was this Robert? My Robert?

This man was wearing a faded, dirty shirt with paint smears all over it, a long tear on one sleeve, a pair of old jeans, also dirty and smeared with paint, and worn-out work boots covered with soil. There were even dirt smudges on his face, which was definitely in need of a shave!

"Sorry," he said apologetically while staring at my robe. "I didn't mean to waken you. I thought you'd be up by now."

I nervously fumbled with my hair. "I—I guess I overslept."

With a shy grin, he pulled his ball cap lower on his forehead with one hand and extended a McDonald's sack toward me with the other. "I know I'm filthy dirty and I need a shave—" He gestured toward his shirt and shoes. "I got up about five this morning and went directly outside to dig that dead stump out of my backyard. Before I finished, I got a hankering for an Egg McMuffin and a good hot cup of coffee. I thought maybe you could use one, too. So—" He paused and took hold of the storm door's handle. "If you'll let me in, I thought we could have a quick breakfast together." He glanced toward his feet. "You take the sack. I'll take off my boots."

I stood there in shock. The man hadn't even gone into cardiac arrest when he'd seen me looking like a reject from a homeless shelter. He hadn't even acknowledged that I had raccoon eyes. Still horror-struck about my slovenly appearance before this man who would one day become my husband, but seeing no way out of my dilemma, without a word, I unlocked the storm door and took the sack from his hand. I watched as he bent and removed his boots. It was then that the realization hit me that the man was even more handsome in his worn-out, paint-stained clothes and soiled boots, his ball cap pulled low over his uncombed hair, and wearing a scruffy beard than he was shaven, with his hair slicked back with gel, wearing his Armani suit.

Why couldn't we women be that appealing when we were in a bathrobes, our hair uncombed, and our makeup either missing or askew? I let out a groan of annoyance at the thought. That was one more proof that life wasn't fair!

Robert, now bootless, but wearing squeaky clean white socks, stepped inside, then stopped and gazed at me with mystification. "Why didn't you tell me you were this beautiful when you climbed out of bed in the morning?"

I couldn't help it. I let out a relieved boisterous laugh, threw my free arm about his neck, and kissed him fully on the mouth, without the least concern about morning breath. "You, Mr. Chase, have just proven your love for me. If you can love me looking like I do now, I know you can love me for a lifetime. And I love, love, love you!"

Grasping both my shoulders, he gave me a blank stare. "What do you mean, looking the way you do now? I think you're gorgeous." Taking on a mischievous smile, he touched a finger to my cheek. "You're kinda cute with sleepy eyes and your hair messed up like that. There for a while, I began to wonder if each day of our married life we were going to have to be dressed to perfection, with our hair combed just right, always looking our very best. Now—" After grasping both my hands in his, he stepped back and surveyed my unorthodox appearance, from the top of my messy hair to the soles of my bare feet and back up again. "Now I know we can live like normal people and not like the Cleaver family."

I gave him a shy grin. "You—you really think I'm beautiful like this?"

"Babe, you're a real knockout, with or without makeup. He jabbed at my chin playfully, then added with a sideways grin, "Well, maybe without the raccoon eyes."

As I nestled into that sweet man's arms, I knew life with him was going to be even better than I had envisioned, and my decision to accept his proposal had been the right thing to do. I could hardly wait to walk down the church aisle and become his wife.

After we settled ourselves at my breakfast table and he'd thanked the Lord for our food, he took a swig of orange juice, then set his glass on the table. "I almost hate to mention it, but I spotted a house not far from here that I thought you'd like. I was hoping you'd want to take a look at it."

I thought the whole idea a waste of time since I still hadn't convinced myself I'd even consider another house, but I didn't want to lose him, so I forced a smile and said, "If you think it might work for us, I'd love to take a look at it."

"Want me to set up an appointment with the Realtor?"

Still wearing my forced smile, I nodded. "Sure, go ahead."

We finished our breakfast, then Robert hurried home to take

his shower before going to check on his crews, and I headed upstairs to prepare myself for the day. But, as much as my mind focused on Robert, I couldn't forget Barbie. I wanted so much to go see her, but Diamond had said I should wait. *Umm,* I thought to myself as I pulled the curtain aside and stared at her house. It was Friday, the day Diamond usually went to the beauty shop to have her hair and nails done. I glanced at my watch. Nine forty. Her standing appointment was at ten. I wondered if she'd canceled it or would try to make it.

A few minutes later, Barbie's garage door opened and Diamond's convertible backed out of the driveway and headed down the street. I had no idea what I might be getting myself into, but I had to see Barbie. If she was still angry, she might throw something at me or order me out of her house or, worse yet, not open the door when she realized I was the one ringing her bell, but I had to take that chance. I still felt God had placed the two of us together, right next door to each other, for His purpose.

Remembering the information sheet I had printed and placed at each table setting the night before, I grabbed up one of the spare copies from my kitchen counter, pulled a couple of colorful zinnias from the leftover centerpiece, and hurried across the lawn to her house. Swallowing back the hurt feelings I'd suffered the last time I'd seen her, I lifted my head high and pressed her doorbell.

No answer.

Okay, I decided, *you may not want to see me, but I want to see you.* I rang it again. A minute later, a third time. And a second minute later, the fourth. It was obvious she either wasn't going to answer or was asleep. Now what?

An idea occurred to me. When Barbie had gone to visit one of her ex-husbands, she had given me the code to her garage door so I could water her plants. Surely she hadn't changed it since then.

Feeling like a criminal, I hurried down her porch steps to the pad of buttons beside her garage door and entered the numbers as I remembered them. Almost instantly, the door began to rise. I was sure it was noisy, but to me, an intruder, it sounded like a machine shop on overtime. A horrible thought hit me. What if Barbie heard it and called the police, thinking someone was breaking in?

No, she'd probably think it was Diamond coming back early.

I slipped into her garage, leaving the door open, rather than have it make its eerie closing noise a second time, then reached for the knob on the door that led into her back entry hall, hoping she hadn't locked it from the inside. The knob turned freely in my hand, so I stepped inside and softy called out her name.

CHAPTER 15

No answer.

After a hurried, tiptoed walk through most of the downstairs rooms, I silently crept up the stairs toward her bedroom. Finding the door closed, I rapped on it gently with my knuckles. "Barbie? It's me. Valentine. Can I come in?"

I wasn't sure, but I thought I heard a faint moan. I put my ear to the door and rapped again. "Are you okay?"

A noise sounded inside, like something dropping to the floor. Without taking time to think how upset she might be at my entering her house, I pushed the door open and stepped inside. Other than the light coming in through the doorway, the room was dark. Gloomy and dark. Depressing. I could see Barbie lying as still as death on the bed. Why hadn't she answered me?

I moved cautiously toward her, half prepared for the tirade I'd expected, the other half fearing she had overdosed and really hadn't heard me at all. When I reached the side of the bed, I whispered her name again, then sat down beside her and gently touched her arm. I didn't want to alarm her, but I had to make sure she was all right.

She shifted her body slightly and stared up at me through swollen, glassy eyes. "Valentine?" Her voice was nothing more than a whisper, and she looked awful. Her normally voluminous hair lay flat against her head, mascara smudges ringed her eyes, and her lips appeared dry and cracked. This was a far cry from the woman whose first concern was normally her appearance.

"Yeah, honey, it's me. I brought you some pretty zinnias to brighten your room."

With great effort, she rolled over onto her side and grabbed hold of my arm. "I've wanted you to come. I've needed you."

I stared at her in amazement. "You've wanted me to come? Diamond said you made it perfectly clear you never wanted to see me again. She told me to stay away."

She laboriously rotated her head from side to side. "No. I—I told her to call you and ask you to come. She said she did but you wouldn't." Her voice was so weak I could barely understand her.

"Why would Diamond say such a thing?"

"I don't know. Sometimes she scares me, Valentine."

My heartbeat quickened. "Scares you? How?"

"She's so bossy. Drink this, eat that, take your medicine, it's time for your nap."

"I'm sure it's because she wants you to get well." Her comment about Diamond being bossy really irritated me. She had no right to upset Barbie by ordering her around, even if it was for her own good. As many pills as Barbie was taking, I just hoped Diamond was being careful with her dosage.

"She makes me eat food I don't like."

"Sweetie, you have to eat. You're nothing but skin and bones. You're lucky to have someone like Diamond who is willing to stay with you and care for you, even if she does get impatient with you."

She closed her eyes, then pulled the quilt up beneath her chin like a naughty child who had just been scolded. "You're against me, too. Everyone is against me."

I leaned over her and kissed her forehead. "I'm not against you, honey, but I am concerned about you. Aren't you feeling any better at all?"

An almost undetectable shake of her head was her only response.

"Why don't you let me take you to my doctor? Maybe he could run some tests to find out what's causing you to feel like this and to be so weak." I wanted so much to help her, but how? Since Diamond was living with her and caring for her around the clock, why did she need me?

"No. Too many doctors all ready. None have done any good, and I don't want to have to take more pills."

Her comment reminded me of the unlabeled pill bottles I'd stuffed into my jacket pocket. With everything going on and my excitement about my Red Hat meeting, I hadn't taken time to take them to the pharmacist. Perhaps the best thing I could do for Barbie was to get them there as soon as possible, to see if he could tell what they were. Maybe they were totally harmless, but then again. . ."

"Valentine."

"What, sweetie? I'm right here."

"Would—would you pray for me?"

I wanted to slap myself up the side of my head. Why hadn't *I* offered to pray for her? That was the absolute best thing I could have done to help her. I gently took her free hand and enfolded it in mine, then bowed my head and asked God to touch her and heal her. When I said, "Amen," her fingers gave mine a slight squeeze.

"Thank you, Valentine. This probably sounds silly. *I* know who God is, but I don't think *He* knows me." The poor thing's lips were dried and cracked.

"He knows who you are, Barbie. He created you."

"Sometime you'll have to tell me more about God, but right now, I'm tired. I just want to go to sleep."

My heart sank. I had so hoped her comment meant she was ready to talk about her relationship with God, but it was obvious she didn't feel up to it. "Go to sleep, sweetie. I promise I'll be back. We'll talk later." Thankful she had at least expressed interest in the things of God, I rose, smoothed the covers over her, filled her water glass, then stood gazing at her, a question niggling at my mind. Why would Diamond tell me Barbie didn't want to see me when Barbie said she'd been asking for me?

As soon as I reached home, I went directly to the phone and called Wendy, who was the head of the church prayer chain, and asked her to put out an emergency call for prayer for Barbie's healing and her salvation. Next, I phoned Della Gentry, the person in charge of the card ministry, and gave her Barbie's address so the members of her committee could send her get-well cards and cheerful notes. Last, I contacted one of her Red Hatters and alerted them to her illness but told the woman it would be best if they sent cards and notes, rather than call her or go see her, since she was so weak. After that, I grabbed the pill bottles from the pocket of the jacket I'd hung in my hall closet and headed toward the pharmacy. Barbie was my friend, and I was going to do all I could to help her, even if it meant locking horns with Diamond.

The expression on Thad Bailey's face frightened me when he looked up from the pills he held in his hand. "Where did you get these?"

"From a friend," I replied quickly, not wanting to mention Barbie's name in case she did her pharmaceutical business there.

He gave me an intense frown. "I hope whoever you got these from isn't a close friend. These things are dangerous."

"What are they?"

"They're a highly potent form of hydrocodone. I hope your friend hasn't been taking them with other drugs or using alcohol. Those definitely don't mix well."

A wave of fear surged though me. I knew Diamond had been making sure Barbie regularly took her medication, but I had no idea what those medicines were or the dosages she'd taken. "I'm not sure, but I know she has a lot of other prescription bottles on her nightstand."

"Hopefully, none of those pill bottles contain antidepressants, pain relievers, anxiety or seizure medicine, or muscle relaxers. Hydrocodone can actually increase the effect of drugs like those and cause dangerous sedation, dizziness, or drowsiness." He gave his head a shake. "The side effects of taking hydrocodone alone can be just as serious as mixing them with drugs."

"What kind of side effects?" My heart raced. What had Barbie gotten herself into?

He stared at me through his thick glasses. "Severe weakness, dizziness, cold clammy skin. Unusual fatigue, bleeding, bruising. Difficulty breathing, closing of the throat, swelling of the lips and tongue and face, hives, yellowing of the skin. Sometimes even unconsciousness. Has your friend displayed any of these symptoms?"

"Yes, Mr. Bailey, I'm afraid she has."

His frown deepening, he pointed his finger at me. "No one, for any reason whatsoever, should keep dangerous drugs like this in an unlabeled bottle. If I were you, and the person you got these from was a good friend, I would go to her immediately and demand she remove any unlabeled pill bottles she has in her house and flush those pills down the toilet. Seeing them in unmarked bottles like this leads me to believe she didn't come by them honestly. No decent pharmacist would ever give these to a client in an unlabeled bottle. Getting rid of them would be my best advice."

I was so stunned I could barely speak. "Can—can you tell me what's in this second bottle?"

He poured a few into his hand, then stared up at me again. "I'm sure you've heard of these. They're illegal to produce in North America but easy to come by if you have the right source. They're from the Rohypnol family of drugs, commonly called on the street by names like Roffies, Roche, sometimes even Mexican Valium, but they're better known as the date rape drug."

Those words struck horror. "You can tell what they are just by looking?"

He picked up one of the pills and held it up before me. "See the split-pill line on one side and the word ROCHE with the number in a circle stamped on the other? You'll see a 1 or a 2 in the circle. These babies are quickly dissolved in water when crushed and can be added to any liquid without detection."

"What happens when you take them?" I asked, dreading his answer.

"Disinhibition and amnesia, excitability or aggressive behavior, decreased blood pressure, memory impairment, among other things. None of them good for a person. If your friend is taking both of these, and who knows what else, that person is in desperate trouble. I suggest you leave these here and let me destroy them for you."

"I can't. She doesn't know I took them. Besides, I want to confront her with them. Maybe if she knows she's been found out, I can get her to seek help."

He slid the date rape pills back into the bottle and screwed on the lid. "Your choice, but it's not a good idea for you to be carrying these things around. If you'd get stopped for a driving violation or have an accident, you'd have a lot of explaining to do."

"I'll be careful," I assured him. The last thing I wanted was to be found with someone else's drugs, especially ones in unmarked containers. I thanked him for his help and hurriedly walked out to my car with my knees feeling like freshly poured cement. Had Diamond been lying to me? Did she have anything to do with this? Or was Barbie the liar and using Diamond as the scapegoat? I had no idea which of those two women to confront, but I had to do something—but what?

I started to call Robert for advice, but then I remembered he'd mentioned he had to drive to Memphis to pick up a piece of machinery and wouldn't be back until early evening. I slipped the bottles into my purse and took the shortest route home. I didn't care if either Diamond or Barbie suspected I was the one who had taken them. I was not about to return those dangerous things to Barbie's house. Since there were no names or instructions on them, in her disoriented and weakened condition, it would be very easy for her to overdose. No, as her friend, I owed it to her to keep them away from her.

I'd no more than pulled my car into the driveway when Diamond came flying across the lawn, her face in a scowl. *Oh, oh,* I said to myself. *Here comes trouble.*

"I thought I told you Barbie didn't want to see you."

I climbed out of the car and met her nose to nose. "And she told me she'd asked you to call and invite me over, and you told her you I wouldn't come. One of you is lying, Diamond. Which one is it?"

Her hand went to her hip. "It certainly isn't me!"

"Why would Barbie lie about it? What reason would she have?"

Her face reddened. "Let me ask you the same question. Why would *I* lie about it? What reason could I have? I've given up my own life to stay here and take care of her. Do you honestly think it's any fun to be locked up all day in a house with a crazy woman?"

"You think she's crazy?" I shot back. "Maybe the medication you're giving her has something to do with her lapses in memory and her strange behavior." My words slipped out before I could stop them.

She lifted her chin defiantly. "Exactly what are you accusing me of, Valentine? I'd like to know."

I had spoken without thinking. Now I remembered what my mother had taught me when I was little—I bit back the snappy retort tickling at my tongue, held my breath, and counted to ten. "I'm not accusing you of anything. Like you, I'm concerned about Barbie and want only the best for her. Now tell me, what can I do to help?"

I guessed my calm demeanor and gentle words helped, because she immediately came down from her high horse and let out a long, slow sigh.

"I'm sorry, Valentine. I had no right to tear into you like that. I should have known Barbie would lie to you. Lying comes more easily to her than anyone I've ever met. I'm sure this isn't the first lie she's told you about me, and it won't be the last."

I reached out and patted her arm. I figured if she was on the up and up, I should support her. If she wasn't, I should take another piece of my mother's advice and keep my enemies close at hand. How could I know which one was telling the truth if I wasn't on good terms with them and banned from entering their house? "Look, Diamond, I know from experience how difficult Barbie can be. Why don't you let me help you lighten your load? Any time you feel you need a break, call me and I'll come running. You can go jogging, to the country club, shopping—whatever you like—and I'll stay with Barbie."

"You'd do that?"

The smile I gave her wasn't exactly genuine, but close. I still wasn't sure I could trust her. "Absolutely. Just make sure you leave me a list of the medications she needs to take and when to take them."

I was half afraid the mention of Barbie's medication might

cause Diamond to ask about the missing pill bottles, but she never so much as batted an eye at my words.

She smiled back. "You're a good friend, Valentine. I'm sorry I came at you like that. By the way, how did you get in? I thought sure I'd locked the house up tight, and since Barbie was asleep when I left for the beauty shop, I'd pulled her bedroom door shut so the ringing of the doorbell wouldn't waken her."

Yikes! I sure didn't want to tell her I knew the garage door code. She might be tempted to lock the door leading from the garage to the front hall, and I'd never be able to get in. "Barbie had given me a key in case of an emergency," I said, trying to appear nonchalant. I wasn't lying. At one time she had given me a key, but I'd given it back when she'd returned from her trip.

Fortunately, Diamond accepted my answer without further question. Of course that wouldn't prevent her from changing the locks or putting on the front door chain.

"I'd better get back to her. I fixed a casserole of macaroni, cheese, and ham, one of her favorites, and it's time for it to come out of the oven. I'm hoping she'll eat a good supper."

"Tell her hello for me."

"I will, and thanks, Valentine, for being there for me. For both of us."

I gave her a wave as she turned to leave. "Remember, just call if you need me."

When Robert stopped by on his way back from Memphis, I dumped the whole day's happenings in his lap. How good it felt to have someone to share my concerns and burdens with. He listened carefully, then paused, pondering my words.

"Which one do you think is lying?" he finally asked.

I shrugged. "One minute I think it's Diamond, the next minute, Barbie. I honestly don't know."

"The pharmacist was sure that's what those pills were?"

I nodded. "Yes, he even showed me the identification markings on the date rape drugs. Why would anyone have such drugs in their home? Do you think I should confront Barbie about them? I doubt she'd confess to buying them, but I could at least see if she acts guilty."

"You think they're Diamond's?"

I rubbed at my temples. This entire distasteful situation was giving me a headache. "I'm not sure about anything. I'd make a lousy detective."

Robert sat down on my sofa and extended his hand. "Come here, sweetheart. You look exhausted."

Without hesitation, I hurried to his side and snuggled up close to him. He felt warm and safe, and I needed that feeling.

"Better now?"

I smiled up at him with a sigh of contentment. "Much better."

"I called Mrs. Stebbins, the Realtor, on my cell phone on the way to Memphis. She said we can see the house anytime tomorrow."

"Tomorrow?" He certainly hadn't wasted any time.

"Would two o'clock work for you?"

"I'll have to let you know in the morning after I check on Barbie."

For a long time, we sat in silence. It wasn't necessary that we have a conversation. Just being together was enough.

Finally, Robert spoke, "Are you sure it's safe for you to go over there by yourself? People under the influence of drugs can do some strange things, even hallucinate. What if she gets spacey and sees you as a threat? I'm not so sure it's wise for you to go at all."

"I have to go. Ever since the day I learned my new neighbor was Barbie, I've felt God brought our lives together for a purpose. What could that purpose be, other than for me to befriend her and help her understand that God loves her? I can't just walk out on her, especially now. It would be like turning my back on a job God specifically gave me to do. I owe it to Him to be faithful."

His shoulders rose in a shrug. "I can't argue with that. But you will be careful, won't you?"

I tapped the cute indentation in his chin with the tip of my finger. "Yes, my love and protector, I'll be careful. But you will pray for me, won't you?"

"Every minute, until I know you're safely back home. Keep your cell phone with you. If you need me, call, and I'll come running."

We stayed on the sofa, snuggling in each other's arms until it was dark outside; then Robert kissed me good night and headed for home. I shut and locked the door, then stood surveying my room. I loved this house. I'd never thought I could leave it. But spending the evening with Robert, simply sitting on the sofa and enjoying each other's company like old married folks, made me wonder at my priorities. Which did I love most—Robert or this house?

As I reached to turn off the lamp on the end table, my attention fell on Carter's picture, one of the dozens I had placed around the house. Something compelled me to pick it up and gaze upon his sweet face. He was smiling that thin-lipped smile that was so characteristic of him, and his eyes were directly on my face. For an instant, the old weighty feeling of dedication and obligation fell over me like a heavy blanket, blotting out the love I felt for Robert. But this time when the guilt engulfed me as it had in the past, the feeling lasted for only a moment. And in my mind's eye, Robert's face appeared in Carter's place. I stared at the picture, then turned it face down on the table. Not that I planned to forget about my husband, because I didn't. But the time had come to look forward to a new and bright future instead of backward to the love I'd shared in the past.

I reached again for the lamp switch but stopped midway. My hand moving slowly, I picked up the photograph and held it to my breast, then opened the table's drawer and slid it inside.

I woke up early the next morning feeling rested, refreshed, and ready for whatever the day would bring. I'd thought a lot about seeing the house Robert had mentioned. He was trying to meet me halfway. The least I could do was take a look at it. Knowing he was an early riser, I phoned his house.

"Really? You can make it about two?" he said, seeming pleased when I told him I would like to take a look at it. "I'll call the Realtor and confirm our appointment."

After we decided what time he'd pick me up, I hung up the phone and wandered into my kitchen. I missed my usual morning coffee and conversation with my friends. Hopefully, the things in our lives that were keeping us so busy would begin to settle down and we could convene again on a regular basis.

Why wait until then? There's nothing preventing you from going to see them. Within minutes, I'd walked to Sally's house and stood knocking at her door. But the vibrant, happy-because-George-had-come-into-her-life Sally I'd expected to find when the door opened up a crack didn't look like that Sally at all.

Before I could say hello, she threw her arms around my neck and began to sob as though her heart was broken. "It's over, Val. George and I are through. He just told me."

Holding on to her arms, I took a step back and stared at her. "Over? What happened? I thought you two were getting along so well."

"We were, but after our last date, when he didn't phone me like he said he would, I called him. A woman answered."

I felt my eyes bug out. "Maybe it was his sister or a neighbor."

"I wish it had been," she said between sobs. "When she put him on the phone, he explained she was the woman he'd been dating before he asked me out. They'd broken up, and he hadn't thought there was any chance they'd get back together, so he'd taken me out, but things had worked out between them after all. He was really nice about it and said he'd had a wonderful time with me, but he really felt she was the right woman for him."

I racked my brain for a way to console her. Poor Sally had purposely kept her guard up so she wouldn't get hurt, but she had gotten hurt anyway. "You wouldn't want to get seriously involved with the wrong man, would you? Perhaps, even now, God has the right man warming up in the wings."

She motioned me inside, then crawled into the corner of her sofa with a look of despondency. "George was so—so right, Val. A gentleman, liked my kids, and really seemed to like me. Why did that woman have to come back into his life and mess things up?"

"Maybe because she *is* the right woman for him. Maybe God

brought George into your life to make you see it was time to date again," I countered, wanting so much to encourage my friend.

She lifted watery eyes. "Then why didn't He send the right man into my life in the first place, rather than let me end up hurt like this?"

Since I didn't have an answer, I simply sat down beside her and patted her hand.

"God sent Robert into your life. Why couldn't He have done the same thing in mine?"

"I wish I could tell you, Sally, but I'm clueless. But I have learned by experience, all we can do is trust God and lean on Him. He knows what is best for us."

"That's easy for you to say. You have Robert, Reva has Chuck, but I have no one."

"Have you told your kids?"

"Yeah, I had to tell them when they found me crying." She sniffled. "They said the same thing you just did, that they'd hate to see me with the wrong man." She paused and drew in a heavy breath. "George said he and that woman are talking about getting married right away. I guess I was just a fill-in until they got things worked out."

I wrapped my arm about her shoulder and gave her a hug. "Oh, sweetie, how awful for you."

She leaned into me. "I was such a fool. I was so happy being with George. I pictured us moving from dating to engagement to marriage."

"Oh, Sally, I'm sure George never saw you as a fool. If you're a fool, then I'm an even bigger fool. You're a woman who loved your husband and loved being married just like I did. There's nothing wrong with that. In fact, it's honorable. Being a good wife and mother, like you are, is a calling from God. If He wants you to have another husband, He'll bring the right one into your life. You just have to be patient."

"What if He doesn't?"

I shrugged. "Then I guess you'll have to accept it as His will."

"But I'm not meant to live alone, Valentine. In a few years, my three kids will be out of school and on their own. I need someone in my life. I don't want to grow old alone."

How well I knew that feeling. "I wish I had some magical answer for you, my dear, dear friend. I don't. But I do know the person who does. God. All we can do is ask Him for His perfect will for our lives. If it includes a husband for you, and for Reva, then it will happen."

She pulled away from me and pressed back into the sofa. "I know you're right, Val, but I seem to question God a lot lately. First, when Eric died and I missed him so much I felt life wasn't worth living, then when I had trouble selling our business and had to move into another house, and, next, when Jessica was causing me so much trouble. Now this. I need answers."

"I know."

"Am I being a big baby?"

I cuffed her arm playfully. "Maybe a little bit."

She wiped at her tears with her sleeve, then smiled at me and said, "I think God sent you here because He knew I needed you."

Even though my friend was hurting, a joy came into my heart at her words. "That's what friends are for, to comfort and encourage one another. I can't count the times you've encouraged me. You just have to hang on, sweetie. This too shall pass. In fact, you may be glad some day, when God brings the man of His own choosing into your life, that you and George never got together."

We shared coffee and the only doughnut she had in the house while we changed to the subject of my engagement and then to Barbie's health. Although I answered in general terms, since I had no real evidence about the drugs or who they belonged to, I told her what I could of what was happening. "I'm going to go see Barbie later this afternoon. I'll tell her hello for you." I reached for her hand and gave it a squeeze. "Sure you'll be okay?"

Sally walked me to the door, then kissed my cheek. "Don't worry about me, Val. I'll be fine. I just needed to vent. Like you said, I don't want to have a man in my life who isn't God's first choice, no matter how nice he is. I guess I should be grateful for the time George and I did have together. At least, he's made me see there *can* be life after the death of my husband."

Though I knew her heart was still breaking, it was good to see her smile again. I mentally moved her to the number two spot on my prayer list. With all her problems, Barbie still held the top-priority position.

Robert arrived right on time, and we headed toward the house he'd seen. I liked the neighborhood right away, which was a plus I hadn't counted on.

"Here it is!" He turned into the circle drive in front of a large two-story home that reminded me of one of the old antebellum homes I'd seen on one of our trips to Louisiana. If the inside was anything like the outside, I knew I'd love it. The place fairly dripped with charm.

"Nice to see you folks," Mrs. Stebbins said as she opened the door and stood back to allow us entrance. "I always love showing prospective homes to engaged couples."

After we exchanged greetings and we answered a few of her questions about our likes and dislikes, she led us from the foyer into the huge living room with its high arched ceilings and elegant moldings. I couldn't help but be impressed. From there, she walked us through the dining room, which was perfect for hosting the large dinner parties I knew Robert and I would want to have, then into the kitchen.

"Whatcha think?" Robert asked, motioning to the deep cherry wood cabinetry and the built-in stainless steel barbeque. "We could cook up some great dinners in here."

I grinned at him. "We?"

He grinned back. "Sure, we. I'd want to help. Though I don't get many opportunities to try out my talents, I'm a pretty good cook."

The rest of the house proved to be every bit as spectacular as the living room, dining room, and kitchen. It included four huge bedrooms, four baths, all beautifully decorated, an office, a laundry room, and an oversized family room with a stone fireplace.

"This house has a three-car garage," Robert reminded me as we moved back into the foyer.

"Do you think this home might be what you're looking for?" Mrs. Stebbins asked when we'd finished our tour.

Robert nodded. "I like it."

I liked it, too, but did I like it enough to leave the home I loved? That was the question.

She walked us out onto the porch. "I know you need time to think it over, but if this one suits your needs, I wouldn't wait too long. Homes like this, in this neighborhood, move pretty fast. I'd hate to see you lose it."

We thanked her, then headed back to Robert's truck. "I could live in that house just the way it is, without changing a thing. How about you?" he asked as he opened my door.

"I liked it, too."

"Enough to consider living in it?"

"Maybe."

He waited until I was seated, then hurried around and climbed into the driver's seat. "We can look at as many houses as you like. We don't have to settle on this one."

"I doubt we'd find another house that has as much going for it as this place. *If* I did decided to sell my house, this is the kind of house I'd want."

"Remember, I said we could build whatever kind of home you'd like. But"—he took his eyes off the road long enough to send me a slight smile—"it takes time to build a house. If we bought this house, the owners would probably give us possession in a month or so. We could be married and move right in. After we did any painting or remodeling you wanted to do."

I smiled back. "I'll think about it."

"That's all I ask."

When we reached my home, Robert walked me to the door. "I don't trust Diamond. Promise you'll be careful when you go see Barbie, okay?"

I promised I would, kissed him good-bye, then stood in my doorway waving until he'd turned out onto the street. I was dreading the possibility of having to fight Diamond to get in to see Barbie and hoped she'd be off to the store or on one of the many errands she seemed to run so I wouldn't have to confront her. I crossed the lawn and rang the bell once. Then, when she didn't respond, I decided to enter through the garage. Maybe, if she was in the house and she didn't see me enter, she would assume I'd used the key to get inside. I wanted so much to help Barbie take a sponge bath and fix her hair. Maybe even assist her in applying a little makeup, since I knew how she liked to look her best. The woman had dozens of beautiful silky nightgowns and robes. Just getting into one of those should make her feel better and help her attitude about herself. When I entered the garage, I felt a great relief. Diamond's car was gone.

Not wanting to bop into her room unannounced, in case she was asleep, I cheerfully called out Barbie's name. No answer. I moved into the kitchen and fixed a tray with a nice hot cup of her favorite tea and a couple of the shortbread cookies I found in the cabinets and headed toward the stairs.

But as I passed through the living room and into the front hall, the tray fell to my feet and I screamed out in horror!

CHAPTER 16

B arbie!"
 My feet felt like they were in lead boots as I rushed toward her twisted body as it lay askew at the bottom of the curved stairway. She was unconscious, maybe even dead, her head surrounded by a pool of blood.

All I could think about was dialing 911 on my cell phone. "She's bleeding! There's blood everywhere. Send somebody!" I blurted out when a woman's voice answered.

"Calm down, ma'am. I need more information. Where are you and who is bleeding?"

"My neighbor. She fell down her stairs. She's bleeding badly! Please get someone here right away!"

"Are you with her now?"

"Yes. I'm the one who found her!"

"Is she breathing?"

"Yes. I think so."

"Give me your neighbor's address."

"It's. . .ah. . .ah—" *Why couldn't I remember Barbie's address?* "Ah. . .1618, I think. Morning Glory Circle."

"Help is on the way, ma'am. Are you alone or is there someone to help you?"

"I'm alone."

"Here's what I want you to do. Take a clean towel or a clean tissue—either will do—and press it as tightly as you can to her head wound to slow down the bleeding. Can you do that?"

"Yes."

"Do it now. I'll stay on the line until you're back."

I glanced toward the kitchen. *Towel. I needed to get a clean towel.* But then I remembered the fresh tissues I'd folded and put into my jacket pocket. I pulled them out and, stooping over Barbie's limp body, pressed them to the horrible gash on her head. "Okay," I said, still trying to calm myself down. "I've done it. Now what?"

"I need her name and approximate age."

"Barbie Baxter. She's fifty—my age—fifty-three." I was so concerned about my friend, I wasn't sure my words made sense.

She instructed me to stay on the line and continued to talk to me, for which I was grateful. I'd never felt so all alone, except that last night Carter had been with me. I cried out to God from the depths of my heart, "Please give me another chance to lead my friend to You before it's too late."

"You're doing fine, Ms. Denay. Keep the pressure on that wound."

"Shouldn't the EMTs be here by now?"

"They're nearly there. Release the pressure long enough to go to the front door and make sure it is unlocked and standing open so they can get in."

Though I hated to leave Barbie even for a moment, I did as I was told, then quickly returned to her side. Suddenly, out of the silence, a siren sounded, and within seconds, three men in white uniforms came rushing through the door, one of them holding a medical kit, the other two carrying a gurney. "Stand aside, ma'am," they told me.

With thankfulness they had arrived, I stepped back out of their way. "Is she going to be okay?"

"Ma'am, you were here when this happened?" one of them asked me without answering my question, his eyes going from me to the long, curved stairway. "When she fell?"

I gave my head a shake, "No. I live next door. I came to check on her. She was like this when I found her."

"She lives alone?"

"A friend lives with her, but she's not at home."

"I don't like the way she's bleeding," the man hovering over her, taking her vitals, said with concern as another EMT pressed a cloth to her head. "Let's get her into the ambulance."

Instantly, the legs of the gurney snapped into place and the three carefully lifted Barbie onto its bed and covered her with a sheet.

"Can I go with her?"

The man who had been taking her vitals nodded. "I'm sure she'd like to have you with her."

I followed them to the door, then checked to make sure the front door of her house was locked before climbing into the ambulance and onto the small seat one of the men directed me toward.

It seemed to take forever before we reached the hospital. I

wanted to go into the emergency room cubicle with her, but they wouldn't let me and told me to wait in the waiting room, assuring me someone would come and talk to me after one of the doctors on duty had a chance to examine her. I hadn't realized how badly I was shaking until I sat down in one of the chairs along the wall and tried to speed dial Robert's number.

He answered on the first ring. "Everything okay? Did Diamond let you in?"

As best I could with chattering teeth, I told him all that had happened.

The words "I'll be right there" gave me the comfort I desperately needed.

As promised, Robert appeared in the doorway in no time.

"You're here!" I rushed to him, threw my arms around his neck, and for the first time since I'd found Barbie in that frightful situation, I began to weep. Robert held me tightly, his chin resting in my hair. No questions. No words. He just held me close, in the security of his arms.

When I finally felt like it, I told him everything that had happened in detail, and he prayed for Barbie. Not in the hurried, confused way I'd screamed out to God, but quietly, to God as the Great Physician, asking Him to touch not only Barbie's body but her soul. At that moment, this man, whom I was pledged to marry, was truly my hero. Not because he'd done anything amazing or heroic, but because he knew the God of the universe and was confident that He would hear his prayer.

"Are you Mrs. Baxter's friends?"

Both Robert and I turned as a man in blue scrubs approached.

"I'm Dr. Danner. Considering the amount of blood she lost,

Ms. Baxter is indeed fortunate you found her when you did. She's conscious now but dazed and confused from both the loss of blood and what happened to her. I've examined her, and from all appearances, her fall must have been a nasty one. In addition to that rather severe cut on her head, which is going to require stitches, her body has sustained some deep bruising that's going to make her uncomfortable for quite some time. There may be broken bones, too, but right now I'm more concerned about her head. We'll know more after a few tests." His brow furrowed. "Do you happen to know what medications she's taking?"

"I have seen a number of pill bottles on her nightstand."

"Did you, by any chance, read any of the labels?"

"Yes, I did." I went on to name the ones I remembered, as well as the ones the pharmacist had identified.

"She was taking all those medications at the same time?"

"I don't know. The lady who is staying with her was helping her with her medication."

"No Coumadin?" the doctor asked, seeming surprised I hadn't mentioned it.

"Maybe. I don't know."

Robert leaned toward him. "Do you think she's been taking Coumadin?"

The doctor paused before answering, "It would certainly explain the excessive bleeding. The woman has lost a lot of blood, more than would normally be caused by a wound of that size."

"But isn't Coumadin given to people who need to have their blood thinned? Usually someone at risk for a blood clot? Or has a heart problem?"

He nodded. "Usually."

Robert glanced toward me. "Did Barbie ever mention having a heart problem?"

"Not to me."

The doctor rubbed at his chin thoughtfully. "I'm having her blood tested. If Coumadin, or anything else threatening, is in her system, we'll know it. We'll be taking care of her head wound, then keeping her here for observation. There's no reason for you to stay. Why don't you go on home and check back on her tomorrow?"

I decided, since I wouldn't be able to see her until they'd done whatever was necessary to care for her injuries and run the tests, I might as well leave and come back in the morning as he'd said. "Don't you need me to sign some papers or something?"

He shook his head. "You might stop by the desk on your way out, in case they have any questions, but I understand from the nurse, she's been a patient here before."

I thanked the doctor, told him I'd be back in the morning, left my phone number at the desk in case they needed to reach me, then walked with Robert, arm in arm, out into the late afternoon air. But, inside, I felt bad for leaving Barbie there by herself. Maybe I should have stayed in the waiting room. At least, I'd have been nearby.

My thoughts returned to the vision of her lying at the foot of the stairs. How could something like that have happened? And why had she been out of her room and near the stairs? Had she been dizzy or light-headed from the drugs she'd been taking? Maybe disoriented or hallucinating?

By the time we got back to her house, I'd made up my mind. If Diamond still wasn't home, I was going back into Barbie's house to search for Coumadin or any other drugs I might have missed. If either Diamond or Barbie became angry with me for the intrusion of their space, so be it. I had to do what I could to ensure Barbie's safe recovery.

"You want me to go in with you?" Robert asked as I exited his truck.

I shook my head. "No, I have to do this by myself. Call me later, and I'll tell you if I find anything."

I crossed the yard and let myself in through her garage, relieved that Diamond's car wasn't there.

The pool of blood at the foot of the stairs sent shivers down my spine. How helpless Barbie had looked when I'd found her, like a rag doll who had been thrown away by a disgruntled child. Would she ever be the same again? I thought about cleaning up the blood but decided against it. *If* Diamond had been the one giving drugs to Barbie, it might be good for her to see what they had done to her.

Pressing myself against the wall, I tiptoed around the spot and on up the stairs to Barbie's room, which gave me an eerie feeling as I entered. Her sheets lay crumpled on the bed as she'd left them, her glass of water still full on her nightstand, her pill bottles scattered across its surface. I could almost feel Barbie's presence.

I crossed the room and checked the labels on the bottles for any that might be marked Coumadin. Not one. Next, I pulled open the drawer. The only bottles it contained were the ones I'd already seen. Undaunted, I moved to her bathroom and searched the medicine cabinet. It was full of all sorts of over-the-counter things but no additional prescription medication. If she had any drugs in her possession, other than the ones I'd already found, where would she hide them?

Maybe in her dresser? Or the two chests of drawers that lined the wall opposite her bed? My search through those turned out to be a complete waste of time. I felt like a thief going through her things like that, but if I wanted to help her, I knew it was necessary.

I moved into her walk-in closet, which had originally been another bedroom until she had the carpenters cut a door to link the two together. One look and I realized I had my work cut out for me. Clothing on hangers covered three entire walls. The fourth wall had cabinets from floor to ceiling.

Okay, I thought, *if I'm going to get through all this stuff, I'd better get moving. Who knows when Diamond may come bursting in through the front door and throw a fit because I'm here uninvited. Maybe, when she learns what happened to Barbie, she'll realize the severity of her situation and why it's necessary that the doctor know what Barbie has been taking.*

Horror struck my thoughts.

Unless Diamond was the one who caused her fall!

Again, the same question entered my mind. *Why? Why would she do such a thing?*

I decided to go through the cabinets first. No success there. Next, I leafed through the hangers, taking time to check for anything that may have been in the pockets. When I finished and took time out to sit down for a moment to regroup, I wasn't sure if I should be elated that I'd found nothing or sad because of the wasted effort.

Now what? And where is Diamond?

Another thought occurred to me. If she was the one responsible, wouldn't the most likely place she would keep any drugs she was giving Barbie be her own room?

After making sure I hadn't left any lights on in the closet, I moved into the hallway. Did I dare go into Diamond's room, too? I could always explain I had been in Barbie's room picking up a nightgown to take to her at the hospital. But how would I ever explain going into Diamond's room if she caught me?

I padded my way the short distance down the hall to the room I knew that woman had claimed as her own, pushed open the door, and after taking a deep breath, entered.

Fortunately, her room contained only one dresser, one chest, the bed, and two nightstands. However, none of them contained anything that I was looking for. Next, I checked her bathroom. Other than a few bottles of vitamins and supplements and things like Tylenol, antacids, and sleep aids, everything else was makeup, skin care, or hair related. I felt total frustration and wondered if I should simply give up the whole snooping-through-other-people's-things mission I'd assigned myself and let the police take care of it. I was getting nowhere.

That thought disappeared quickly. I'd gone this far; I couldn't give up now. So I moved into her closet, which wasn't nearly as large as Barbie's, but was lined with equally gorgeous suits, dresses, blouses, and too many other things to list, and turned on the light. It, too, had a wall of cabinets and shelves. Deciding it would be easier to go through the cabinets than the clothing, I opened one of the drawers.

In it, I found something that startled me.

Something I hadn't expected to find.

CHAPTER 17

The drawer was filled with scarves in every color. That part didn't surprise me. But at the bottom of the pile were at least a dozen scarves Barbie had said were missing from her room. I knew, because I had personally given her three of them as gifts! The only conclusion I could draw was that Diamond had taken them. But what upset me most was that she claimed to be a Christian! Had she only said that and talked about the Bible so she could get into our good graces? I suddenly felt betrayed.

That discovery made me forge ahead with my search. The next two drawers contained lovely, lacy lingerie. The third drawer contained the same thing, but each of the items still had their price tags attached. Clotheshorse that she was, why hadn't Diamond worn them?

I moved to the second set of drawers. The top two boasted an array of neatly folded, either filmy or lacy nightgowns any woman would be proud to wear. The bottom drawer, too, contained night-gowns, but those had their price tags still attached. Why would

Diamond buy so many nice things and never wear them?

I shrugged and moved on. There were no surprises in the third set of built-in drawers—until I reached the bottom one. But it wasn't the many neatly folded T-shirts and tank tops that caught my eye and set my heart racing. It was the large manila envelope that lay beneath them.

I pulled it from the drawer and carefully slid open the flap. Inside were dozens of receipts from department stores, shops, and boutiques. Each receipt listed a number of clothing items that had been purchased, and the signature on the bottom of each one was *not* Diamond Jenson.

It was Barbie Baxter!

Why would Diamond have receipts for Barbie's purchases hidden in a manila envelope in the bottom drawer of her closet?

My blood ran cold as I read the description of some of the items listed. They sounded to me like the very items Barbie had claimed she hadn't charged. I gave my head a shake. Surely Diamond hadn't charged them and signed Barbie's name. Had she?

That discovery sent me rushing to the hundreds of clothing items hanging in the closet. As I hurriedly leafed through them, I found dozens of items still containing tags, and many of them fit the exact description and stock numbers as listed on the receipts I'd found.

Those items had been charged to Barbie's credit card. If they were hers, why had they been hanging in Diamond's closet? And why did Diamond have the receipts?

Panic struck as I heard the front door open. The last thing I wanted, especially after the items I had discovered, was for Diamond to find me in the house. I quickly turned off the closet light, rushed out of her room into the hall, and darted into one of the spare bedrooms. I figured, since the first thing she would see would be the drying pool of Barbie's blood at the foot of the stairs, she'd be so shocked she'd either try calling the hospital or rush over to my house to see if I knew anything about what had happened, where Barbie was, or if she was even alive.

I could hear her moving about downstairs. Why hadn't she screamed out when she saw the blood like I had? Next, I heard her talking on the phone, and I assumed she had called the hospital. I couldn't make out her words, but a few minutes later, I heard the front door close, the sound of her car starting, then silence. I waited a moment, then quickly moved into Diamond's room, took several receipts out of the manila envelope along with the pieces of clothing that bore the same item numbers, and hurriedly exited the house, relieved I hadn't been caught. My legs were so weak they would barely carry me across the lawn, but with the amount of adrenaline flowing through my system, I barely noticed. All I wanted was to get inside where I felt safe.

"You what?" Robert barked into the phone, interrupting my news before I could get it all out when I called him a few minutes later. "Do you have any idea the kind of charges that could be pressed against you for entering someone's home and rummaging through their things? Especially Diamond's! You might have conjured up a reasonable explanation for being in Barbie's room, but not hers. What were you thinking, Valentine?"

"Robert! Forget about that and listen to me. I didn't find any drugs other than the ones we already knew about, but I found dozens of receipts for the things Barbie said she never charged and the items to match them. There may have been drugs in her closet, too, but I didn't take time to look for them."

"Those items and receipts were in Barbie's room?"

"No! Diamond's!"

I heard him sigh. "I don't get it. Why were they in Diamond's room?"

"I think she's the one who charged them and signed Barbie's name. Living in her house, she certainly had access to Barbie's credit cards."

"Isn't that a little far-fetched? Diamond isn't lacking for money. Why would she charge those things to Barbie? It doesn't make sense."

In frustration, I plunked myself down on the sofa. Maybe my idea was too far-fetched, but what other explanation could there be? "Look, I have no idea why Diamond would do such a thing or what she could gain by it, but it looks to me like she purchased those items, used Barbie's credit card, then hid them away so that when the end-of-the-month statement arrived and Barbie made a big issue with the credit card company and anyone who would listen, like you and me, it would appear she was losing her mind or had become extremely forgetful."

"Umm, that would explain the discrepancy, I guess."

"There's more. Some of the scarves in Diamond's drawer were the very scarves Barbie claimed were missing from her room. I knew, because I gave her three of those scarves. What were they doing in Diamond's room? Tell me that!"

Before he could answer, I went on, "Then there's the problem of the drugs. The drugs on her nightstand were both uppers and downers. What would happen if a person took an upper one time and a downer the next?"

"Extreme mood swings?"

"My point exactly."

"You do realize the seriousness of your implications, don't you?"

"Yes, Robert, I do, but my intuition tells me I'm on the right track. I don't know why, but I'm sure Diamond is responsible for these awful things that have been happening to Barbie."

"Maybe it's time you went to the police. Let them handle it."

My landline phone rang. "Hang on a sec."

It was the emergency room doctor. "Ms. Baxter is doing as well as can be expected, but I have some alarming news. The tests show an inordinate amount of Coumadin in her blood, and she claims she has never taken Coumadin. Though she has that injury to her head, she is alert and her thinking seems fairly clear. Since you are a close friend, do you have any idea why she would lie about taking it?"

How could I answer such a question? I certainly couldn't accuse Diamond without proof that she was the one who had given Barbie the Coumadin. "I don't know, Doctor, but I'll ask her about it when I see her. Maybe she'll open up to me. How soon can I come?"

"Visiting hours will soon be over, but you can come if you like. A friend of hers is here now. A Ms. Jenson, I think her name is. When I told Ms. Baxter I was calling you, she asked me to tell you to bring her a few nightgowns. She hates our hospital garb."

"Tell her I'm on my way."

I grabbed up my cell phone. "Robert, it was the doctor. He said they found Coumadin in Barbie's system, but she claims she's never taken it."

"She must have if it's there."

"I'm going back into her house and look for it again before I go back to the hospital."

"Valentine, no! Not again."

"I have to, Robert. I owe it to Barbie. Besides, he said Diamond was at the hospital, so I'll be safe. And now I have an excuse for entering. The doctor told me Barbie wants me to bring her some gowns."

"Just be careful."

"I will. I'll call you later."

The house had that same eerie feeling when I entered the second time. I hurried up the stairs to Diamond's room and into her closet. I stood there for a few moments, surveying it from top to bottom. If I wanted to hide some sort of incriminating evidence, like a drug I'd been giving to someone without her knowledge, where would I hide it? A drawer? Too obvious. The shelves? Maybe. I checked all the shelving units. Nothing.

Shoe boxes? There were literally dozens of them on her shelves. Maybe that was where she hid things. I started at one end, carefully opened each box and examined its contents, finding nothing until I reached a hatbox on the upper row. As I pulled it from the shelf, I noticed it was heavier than the others. Cradling it to my chest with my free hand, I lifted the lid.

Bingo!

Coumadin! Not just one pill bottle containing that prescription, but three, sealed in a zip-type plastic bag. Each bearing a man's name I'd never heard of and labels from a pharmacy in Atlanta.

Diamond was giving Barbie Coumadin!

That had to be the answer! How could Barbie not realize it? I was beginning to wonder if I searched other places in her room

I'd find the missing jewelry, but there was no time for that. I had to get to the hospital.

I stuck the bag with the three bottles into my jacket pocket, placed the box on the shelf where I'd found it, checked to make sure I was leaving everything in order, then rushed into Barbie's room to grab several of her nightgowns from her closet. My heart was pounding so hard I could hear its beat thundering in my ears as I raced down the stairs toward the front door.

But as I reached for the knob, the door opened.

CHAPTER 18

Diamond stared at me. "What are you doing here?"

I held out the gowns. "The doctor said Barbie wanted these. I–I'm going to take them to her." I hoped my voice wasn't quavering.

Her face took on a sympathetic expression. "She looked so pitiful it made me want to cry. I went into shock when I came into the house and found that pool of blood. I can't believe she fell down those stairs. I'd told her to stay in her room until I got back. I'm so thankful she wasn't hurt any worse than she was."

"Yeah, me, too." I wanted to ask her where she'd been and why she'd left Barbie alone all that time and why she hadn't screamed out, like I had, when she'd seen that pool of blood, but I didn't. My goal was to get out of there before my guilty face gave me away. I hurried past her. "I told them I'd be there right away."

"Tell her I'll see her in the morning, okay?"

I nodded. "Sure, I'll tell her." I couldn't close that door fast enough.

Now that I'd found the Coumadin, what should I do? Take it to the doctor at the hospital? Call the police? Or call Robert? I'd lived a sheltered life and had never been involved in something this heinous before.

I opted to call Robert. In turn, he called a Nashville police detective he'd met who agreed to meet us at the hospital. I was glad when Robert offered to drive me. I was in such a state of nerves I wasn't sure I had any business being behind the wheel. Wanting to make sure he knew every little detail after he'd picked me up, I chattered on endlessly as we made our way to the hospital. Detective Lopez met us at the emergency room door and guided us to one of the small empty waiting rooms where we could talk.

"And these are the bottles you found in her friend's room?"

"Yes, hidden in a hatbox."

"You didn't take them out of the bag?"

I shook my head. "No, I could read them quite clearly through the plastic."

"Then you haven't actually touched them."

"No, I brought the bag just as it was."

He seemed relieved. "Good. You did the right thing."

I didn't want to ask, but I was reasonably sure it was because of the fingerprints they might find on the bottles.

He asked a few more questions, then I explained about finding the scarves, the receipts, and the clothing still containing the tags.

"And you went in through the garage, even though no one had given you permission?"

Feeling like a criminal, I lowered my eyes. "Not permission exactly. I used the garage door code Barbie had given me earlier.

244

The doctor said she wanted me to bring her some of her gowns so I had a reason for going in—this time."

A smile tilted at his lips. "Good thing you did. You may have saved your friend's life. From what Robert told me, if you or someone hadn't found her, she may have bled to death."

Just the thought of it took my breath away.

He extended his hand. "I'll take it from here, but I suggest you don't mention any of this to your friend or anyone else. Just put on a smile and take the gowns in to Ms. Baxter and cheer her up, as I'm sure you can do."

Robert put his arm around me protectively. "You think Valentine is safe?"

"For now, probably, but I wouldn't take any chances. She should avoid all contact with Ms. Jenson. Although that woman knows Mrs. Denay has been in the house, she also knows Ms. Baxter had asked for her nightgowns. Since no one has mentioned the Coumadin to her, which is the way we want to keep it, she has no reason to be suspicious unless she notices the bottles are gone. I've already asked the judge for a search warrant as well as a warrant for her arrest. If she goes back to Ms. Baxter's home, we'll get her. Hopefully a thorough search of the house's contents will bring up even more evidence."

After our conversation with Detective Lopez ended, we made our way to Barbie's room. She looked so frail and helpless. I couldn't believe how upset I was at seeing her that way, with her head all bandaged up, bruises on her cheek and arms. Even her lips appeared to be bruised. I rushed to her and gave her a careful hug. "You'll be as good as new in no time," I said, hoping to cheer her up. With all the drugs that had been pumped into her, it was a wonder the woman had been able to move at all.

"I don't know what happened," she said in a mere whisper when we began to talk. "Diamond had left to go shopping, and I thought I heard a noise downstairs, so I got out of bed and went to the landing to look. The next thing I knew, I was in the hospital. The doctor said I had fallen down the stairs." A tear rolled down her cheek. "He also said I might have died if you hadn't found me when you did."

I carefully took hold of her hand. "But I did find you, and you're going to be just fine. We'll soon be taking you home." There was so much I wanted to ask her, but I knew I shouldn't. Not now anyway. Any questioning needed to be done by the detective. Wanting to change the subject, I held up her gown. "Maybe in the morning, if you feel like it, I can help you into this. The doctor said you hated the hospital garb."

The tiniest semblance of a smile appeared on her lips. "That would be nice."

Robert wished her well, then, not wanting to tire her, we left.

"I think you should stay away from your house," he told me as we moved out into the parking lot. "Maybe you ought to stay with Sally for a few days."

I stared at him. "You really think that's necessary?"

"I'd prefer you be on the safe side. We only think we know Diamond. If she is guilty and she feels trapped, no telling what she might do."

"I am a bit afraid," I admitted. "Especially since I found the Coumadin."

"Better safe than sorry. I know Sally's place is only a couple of houses away, but I'd feel better if I knew you were there. Why don't

I wait until you give Sally a call and pack a bag, then I'll follow you to her house. Since she has a two-car garage, maybe she'll let you park in one side so your car won't be obvious if Diamond drives down the street." He gave me a shy grin. "I'd invite you to stay at my place, but I know you'd refuse."

Although I hadn't given Sally any more information than necessary, twenty minutes later I found myself in her house, in the psychedelic-decorated bedroom Jessica had vacated for me. Sally grinned at me as she tugged the clean pink-and-lime striped sheets onto the bed. "I sure like having you here."

"I'm glad to be here." I reached out and patted her arm. "How you doing, Sally? I mean really doing?"

She bit at her lip. "I still hurt."

"It had nothing to do with you, Sally. I hope you realize that. He knew that woman and had a relationship with her before you even came along. George isn't the only nice man out there."

"I know. I keep telling myself about all those other fish in the sea, but I'm not sure I'll have the courage to cast my line out again. Or even want to."

"You will. It just takes time. You're still young."

"So when do you plan to see Barbie again?"

"In the morning. I know you'd like to see her, too, but maybe you'd better wait. She's in such a weakened condition, it would probably be best if she didn't have company for a day or two."

I had a hard time going to sleep that night. It was nearly two before I drifted off.

The house was empty when I finally woke up. There was a note on the kitchen table from Sally, explaining that she'd taken the kids to McDonald's for breakfast so they wouldn't disturb me.

By the time I was dressed and ready to go to the hospital, she was back.

"I hate to rush off," I told her, giving her cheek a quick peck. "But I promised Barbie I'd be there early."

"Tell her I'm praying for her."

I assured her I would and left.

Barbie was sitting propped up against pillows when I entered her room, her bruises even more evident than they had been the day before. Despite her sore lips, she smiled at me.

"You're looking better." I pulled a gown from the drawer where I'd placed it along with her others and held it up before her. "And you'll look even better when we get you into this turquoise gown. You look terrific in turquoise. Are you ready?"

She sighed. "I guess so. The nurse's assistant has already given me my bath."

I helped her, and even with the pain each movement caused, eventually we got it on her. She leaned breathlessly back onto the pillow, totally spent. I wished there was something I could do with her hair, but with that bandage wrapped around her head, it was impossible.

"They had to shave some of the hair on the back of my head. Can you imagine what I'm going to look like?"

"But you're alive, Barbie. That's the important part. Your hair will grow back."

"I still don't know how I fell down those stairs."

"You must have lost your balance."

"Maybe, but I don't remember any of it. What's happening to me, Val? I feel like an old woman."

"They've run some tests on you. Maybe they'll find out when

the results are in. At least you're in the hospital where you're getting excellent care."

I turned when Barbie glanced toward the door. Surely it wasn't Diamond.

"Well, well, look at Queen Barbie."

It *was* Diamond! Why hadn't the police apprehended her? I was not only afraid of her, but I hated having to face her and fake a smile so she wouldn't be suspicious and run, when what I wanted to do was pull her hair out by its dark roots for what she had done to Barbie.

Her smile widening, she sat down on the side of the bed and rubbed Barbie's hand. "My, sweetie, you sure look pretty. Are you feeling better?"

"Some, I guess."

I glanced toward the door. I needed to phone the police and let them know she was here. "I'll step outside and let you two visit," I said, trying to sound casual, though inside I was a bundle of nerves.

Diamond reached for my hand. "No, stay. I want you here, and I'm sure Barbie wants you here, too." Turning to her, she added, "Don't you, sweetie?"

Barbie nodded. "Yes, Valentine. Please stay."

Not sure what else to do, I moved back toward the bed. To my dismay, Diamond grabbed onto my hand and held it. I had to get out of there, but how could I do it without alerting her that the police were looking for her? What if she decided to leave and got away before I could let them know? I had to find a way to excuse myself.

Still holding onto me, she turned her attention back to Barbie.

"How did you ever manage to fall down those stairs? You promised me you'd stay in bed until I got back."

Barbie sighed. "I heard a noise in the hall." From the exhausted expression on her face, I was sure getting into that nightgown had tired her.

"You shouldn't have gotten out of bed, Barbie. If you'd listened to me, you probably wouldn't have had that fall. Don't you know I love you?"

I wanted to puke. Love her? You don't do the things she'd done to those you love. I had to reach the detective. I tugged my hand from her grasp. "You ladies will have to excuse me. I need to go to the restroom."

Diamond motioned toward the door along the wall. "Why don't you use Barbie's?"

I gave my head a quick shake. "I don't think they want visitors using the patient's restroom." Before she could give me another argument, I grabbed up my purse and hurried into the hall. As soon as I rounded the corner, where I would have some privacy, I dialed Detective Lopez's number. "Diamond's here—at the hospital—in Barbie's room."

"Keep her there if you can, but don't alarm her. We're on the way."

I put the phone back into my purse, took a deep breath, and headed back toward the room, hoping Diamond would stay until they arrived. But as I entered Barbie's room, my heart sank.

Diamond was gone.

I gaped at Barbie. "Where is she?"

"She said she had to go and asked me to tell you good-bye for her."

Diamond had gotten away. I could only hope the police arrived before she got to her car.

Without explanation, I hurried back out into the hall and dialed the detective again. "She's gone."

"I was afraid of that. Did she say anything that would make you think she knew we were on to her?"

"No, nothing. She was like her usual self."

"I wonder if Ms. Baxter said anything that would arouse her suspicions."

"I doubt it since she really knows nothing herself."

"We'll get her. Robert told me you aren't staying at your house. I'm glad to hear that. No sense inviting trouble. At this point, you should avoid all contact with her until we know more. Call me if you need me or if she makes any attempt to get in touch with you."

"I—I will."

I pasted on a smile as I moved back into Barbie's room. "Sorry about that. I needed to make a phone call." Before she could respond, I sat down on the side of her bed and linked my fingers through hers. "A number of people are concerned about you. I called and let one of your Red Hat ladies know about your fall so she could tell the others, but I asked her to tell them you weren't up to having company yet. Our church's prayer chain is praying for you, as well as our pastor and Sally and Reva, and Robert and me, too."

A feeble smile curled at her tender lips. "Am I ever going to be well? I'm so tired of feeling bad."

I so much wanted to tell her what I knew about the drugs, but now wasn't the time. "I know you are. Hopefully, all the tests they're running on you will give them the answer."

When she turned her head and closed her eyes, I figured she was sleepy, so I sat quietly, still holding her hand.

Finally, she turned back to face me. "Valentine, if I'd died falling down those stairs, where would I have gone?"

I gasped inwardly. This was the very thing I'd wanted to discuss with her. But now? When she was so weak, should I tell her what God's Word said? That the only people who could enter His kingdom were those who acknowledged that they were sinners, confessed their sin, repented, and accepted Him as their eternal Savior? She'd been furious with me for even suggesting that she could be a sinner. I struggled for words. "Where do *you* think you would have gone?" I finally asked.

She appeared thoughtful. "If God thinks I'm a sinner, He probably wouldn't let me into heaven, so I guess I'd go—" She paused as if she couldn't bear to say the word.

"No one *has* to go to—that place. The choice is up to us."

"I've thought about it some since I've been sick. I guess I could be called a sinner. Sometimes, anyway. But I'm also a good person."

"Your description of yourself sounds like most of us, but God isn't interested in how good we are or what wonderful deeds we've done. He's interested in having a personal relationship with us. But He wants us to come to Him by admitting we are sinners and letting Him, by His forgiving love, wipe the slate clean. The worst thing we can do is turn our back on Him and refuse His offer of salvation." How I wished I was more eloquent. I felt as if I had bungled the words and done the poorest job possible of explaining the most important thing in life. Not sure exactly what else I should say to clarify, I just sat awkwardly staring at her.

"I *am* a sinner."

Her voice was so soft, I wasn't sure I had heard her correctly.

"I know that now. I guess I've always known it, but I didn't want to admit it."

My breathing quickened. This was what I'd prayed for since that first day Barbie had appeared at my door.

"I have to know. Are there any sins He won't forgive?"

I placed a reassuring hand on her shoulder. "There's nothing He won't forgive. You just have to ask Him."

She stared at me for a moment. "Do—do I have to tell Him my sins out loud?"

I had to smile. "No, you can say them in your heart and He'll hear every word."

She smiled back. My answer seemed to have pleased her.

"Then I want to know God like you do, Valentine."

Without thinking what a hug would do to her injured muscles and flesh, I wrapped her in my arms, turning her loose quickly when she flinched and cried out in pain. "I'm so sorry," I told her, backing away, "I forgot, but I was so excited. You have no idea how happy it makes me that you want to have a personal relationship with God."

She lifted misty eyes. "Can I do it now, or do I have to be in church?"

I smiled. I'd never seen her look more beautiful. Her wide-eyed expression showed an openness to the things of God I'd never seen before. "Now is the perfect time. You can accept God anywhere. He's always waiting to hear from you. If you meant what you said, repeat after me." Joy rippled through my soul as I led Barbie in a prayer of repentance. I had always thought God had moved her into the home next to mine for a purpose. Now, as I praised Him, I was sure of it.

When she opened her eyes, despite the swelling and the bruising, her face shone with a look of peace and contentment. I felt that same peace and contentment, for I knew that she and I were now sisters in Christ. That didn't mean we'd get along perfectly from now on, because we wouldn't. Like sisters, we would occasionally have our differences, but the bond between us would never be broken. I bent and placed a gentle kiss on her cheek. "I love you, Barbie." She began to weep, and I wondered if I'd upset her.

"No one has said they love me in a long time. My three husbands said it occasionally, but I doubt they meant it. Do you really love me? After all the mean things I've said to you?"

I grabbed a tissue from the box on her bedside table and carefully dabbed at her eyes. "I love you more than words can express."

A nurse came into the room and, upon seeing Barbie in tears, gave me a frown. "Maybe we should give Ms. Baxter time to rest."

I nodded, then bent and kissed her again. "She's right, sweetie. It's important that you get your rest. I'll come back later."

Barbie gave me a sweet smile. "I love you, Valentine."

I backed away and blew her a kiss. "I love you, too."

God had answered prayer.

Barbie was now a Christian.

I could hardly wait to tell Robert and my friends.

Sally was gone when I got back to her house, which was no problem, because I knew where she kept a spare key. I dialed Robert's number the minute I walked through the door and was disappointed when I got his voice mail saying he was out for the remainder of the day and to leave a message. I didn't want to leave a message. I wanted to tell him in person. But I was able to reach Reva. Like me, she was ecstatic. Not only ecstatic, but encouraged to continue to pray for others on her prayer list.

I seated myself in a chair at one of Sally's windows and watched for Diamond's car to enter the cul-de-sac, but when she didn't show up by six, I began to wonder where she was. Surely if the police had arrested her, Detective Lopez would have let me know. And even if she'd gone back to see Barbie, which was doubtful, she wouldn't have stayed that long.

When Sally and her family came home, we all enjoyed a quick-fix supper of sandwiches and soup while I filled her in on my suspicions about Diamond, at least the things I felt I could safely share.

Robert finally phoned about seven. "Barbie is a Christian!" I blurted without preamble. "Our prayers have been answered."

"Hey! That's the best news I've heard in a long time." He chortled. "Except when you finally consented to marry me and accepted my engagement ring. You think it was for real? She has a lot of drugs in her system."

I couldn't contain my smile. "I'm sure it was real. If you'd been there, you would have thought so, too. Isn't it wonderful?" My smile left. "But I'm convinced Diamond lied to us about *her* being a Christian. I think she did it to push all our buttons and get us to trust her. Just the thought of her deception, makes me sick to my stomach."

"Well, we can take solace in the fact that she can't fool God. Hopefully, she'll come to a true knowledge of Him before it's too late and not just fake her Christianity. We'll have to pray she will. But let me tell you what I've learned about Diamond. Detective Lopez left a message on my phone. They still haven't found her. I told him I was afraid she might try to go back to the house and remove any other evidence that might exist. He considered that already and has the beat cop keeping an eye on her house."

Still seated where I could see out the window, I gave my head a shake. "I've been listening for her car and watching the house, but there's been no sign of her. Where do you suppose she is?"

"Beats me, but I don't want you confronting her. Stay away from her, and don't let her know you're staying with Sally. You do have your car parked in Sally's garage, don't you?"

"Yes, but who knows what she might take if she gets back into that house by herself. Maybe I should go over there and try to—"

"No, sweetheart, it's too risky. If Diamond would fill Barbie full of the medications we think she has, after Barbie befriended her and opened up her home, what do you think she would do to you if she found you intruding on her space? No, it's not safe. You have to stay away."

"But—"

"Please, dearest, for me, promise you won't go."

I hated to make a promise like that, but what could I say? I knew Robert had my best interest at heart. And to be honest, I, too, was afraid of what might happen if she caught me going through her things.

"And get away from that window. Even if she does come home, there's nothing you could do about it. The best thing is to let the police handle it."

"But what if they—"

"Valentine." His voice was stern, sterner than I'd ever heard it. "The matter is out of your hands. All you can do is pray."

I knew he was right, so I agreed. We visited a little longer, then said good night after deciding to go together to visit Barbie the next day.

I'd no more than hit the disconnect button and walked away from the window when I heard a car coming down the street, then Sally, who had just arrived home, calling out, "Two cars just pulled into Barbie's driveway. One of them is a police car."

Well, I figured if the police were there, looking out the window wouldn't hurt anything, so I joined her as she pulled aside the drapery. We watched as the officers and Detective Lopez stepped up onto the porch and rang the doorbell. When no one answered, one of the uniformed officers gave the door two hard kicks, and it opened. It was all I could do to keep from running over there.

I didn't.

But I sure wanted to.

Sally and I hung around the window, with Jessica looking over our shoulders, until the men emerged nearly an hour later carrying several black bags that looked like trash sacks, secured the front door, then entered the cars and drove away.

Whoever said women were more curious than men knew what they were talking about. Our curiosity was as high as Mount Everest.

But one question remained.

Where was Diamond?

I phoned Robert, told him about the police arriving, and made him promise to call Detective Lopez, then call me if they had any news.

Though I was tired, sleep didn't come easily that night for me or Sally. It seemed at least once or twice an hour, one of us, or both, ventured into the living room and peeked through the sheers to see if there was any sign of Diamond's return. But there never was. No car in the driveway. No lights in the house. Nothing.

Where was she? Had the police found her?

I got up again about six and ventured to the window and was surprised to see a light on in one of Barbie's upstairs windows. It had to be Diamond. My heart banging against my chest, I hurried into Sally's room and woke her up. By the time we got back to the window, the light had gone out.

"Are you sure you didn't imagine it? Or it wasn't a reflection on the window from the yard light?" Sally asked me, turning loose of the curtain. "There sure isn't a light on now."

I shrugged. Maybe it was my imagination. Maybe I wanted to believe she was there. I glanced in that direction one more time. No light. I was ready to turn away and go back to bed when Barbie's garage door went up and Diamond's car backed out. "It's her!" I called out to Sally, who was already on her way back to bed. "She's leaving!"

CHAPTER 19

Sally rushed to my side and spread the curtain open a crack. "How'd she get in there without us seeing her?"

"I'd better call the police." I picked up the phone and dialed 911. The operator immediately transferred me to Detective Lopez's cell phone.

"She was there?" he said.

"Just drove out," I told him, my hands shaking as I gripped the phone.

"We've been watching for her car most of the night. She's a slick one. She must have waited until one of our patrol cars did a run past the house, then drove into the garage. Thanks for calling. We'll get right on it. If you see her again, call us immediately but don't approach her."

I swallowed hard. "You don't have to worry about that."

I phoned Robert as soon as I hung up, and he said nearly the same thing. "Maybe you should leave Sally's and stay at my place. It may not be proper, but it would be safer than where you are now."

Though I considered his offer, I decided to stay with Sally. With her there with me, and each of us having cell phones, I didn't feel I was in any immediate danger.

By nine o'clock, Robert and I were standing beside Barbie's hospital bed, telling her how much better she looked. Even though her head was still wrapped with a huge covering of gauze, her right eye swollen and watery, and her face and arms covered with bruises, she did look better. Her eyes had a brightness they hadn't had for weeks, and her cheeks were pink instead of the pale, chalky color that had made her look like warmed-over death.

She gave us a half smile. "You really think so? Even though I still hurt, I am feeling slightly better. But I'm still so weak I can barely get out of bed, even with the nurse's assistance. I could use another gown. I got blood on a couple of the ones you brought."

"I'll bring one to you this afternoon." *Or at least, one of mine since they don't want me going into your house.*

"Maybe you can send one up with Diamond. I'm sure she'll be here later."

I didn't want to worry her with the truth, or what I knew of the truth. "I haven't talked to her since she left here yesterday, so I don't know." She seemed to accept my answer and went on to point out all the lovely flowers the church, Jake, Robert and I, and her Barbie's Red Hat Babes had sent to her. It was good to see her smiling again and sounding more like herself.

"Did Valentine tell you I'm a Christian now?" she asked Robert proudly when we'd finished oohing and aahing over her flowers.

He reached for her hand and gave it a pat. "Yes, she did, and I can't tell you how happy I am for you. God is very real, and He loves to hear from His children."

Her smile widened. "I know. I've already talked to Him. Just like you and Valentine do, like He's my friend."

"He is your friend, and He's your Father, too. As His children, we can come boldly before Him at any time. He's always ready to listen."

"And He's your protector, too," I told her, thinking how close she had come to dying in that fall. Surely God's arm of protection had been about her.

"I know, and I'm so grateful."

Robert glanced toward the door, then bobbed his head in that direction. "I'd like a cup of coffee from the hospital cafeteria, and I'll bet Valentine would, too. You get some rest, and we'll be back in a little while."

"You promise you'll come back?"

"Absolutely."

Though I couldn't understand why he'd gotten a sudden yen for coffee, I followed him into the hall. Detective Lopez was standing outside the door. "Have you found Diamond?" I asked, hoping his answer would be yes.

"No, but we did find a few interesting things in her room, in addition to the items you found." He paused, as if deciding how much he should reveal, then continued. "One of the most important discoveries was a locked box containing at least a dozen driver's licenses bearing Ms. Jenson's picture with other names and identities, two of them issued to a Barbara Fielding. Did you ever hear her mention that name?"

I shook my head. "No, never."

"It appears your Ms. Jenson isn't exactly who or what she claimed to be." Detective Lopez sent a glance my way. "So far, she's eluded us. If you see her or hear from her, don't confront her. Get to a phone and call 911. After what it appears she's done to Ms. Baxter, there's no telling what she might do if she felt she was cornered."

Robert rubbed at his forehead. "This beats all. To think a beautiful, sophisticated woman like Diamond could waltz into our community and charm her way into Barbie's home and into our lives really upsets me."

"Don't feel bad. Criminals like her are pros at this sort of thing. I'm sure you're not the first ones she's taken advantage of."

I finally found my voice. "You *are* going to catch her, aren't you?"

"Oh, yes. She's crafty, so it may take awhile, but we'll get her. What she did to Ms. Baxter could have taken her life. That may have been her intent."

"But why? Why would she want to endanger Barbie's life? If robbery was her motive, she could have taken the missing pieces of jewelry and moved on. Why go to all the trouble to hurt Barbie when she'd been so good to her?"

"I don't know. That puzzles me, too. In most cases like this, the perpetrator gets in, pulls off their theft or scam, and gets out. The longer they stick around, the greater chance they have at being caught." He motioned toward the hospital room. "Now if you'll excuse me, I need to talk to Ms. Baxter."

"Poor Ward," I told Robert when we were alone again. "He really seemed to care for Diamond. He'll be devastated when he finds out what has happened."

Robert sighed. "You're right about that."

I shrugged. "What else did she lie about? I wonder if she was even a widow."

He took my hand and pressed it tightly in his. "Promise me

you'll be careful. Diamond is probably miles from here by now, but we can't be sure. I want you to be on guard every minute until she's found and arrested."

"You think she'd come after me?" A chill ran through me.

"It's a possibility. Besides her, you were the only other person with easy access to Barbie's house. If she discovered some of the drugs were missing and someone had rummaged through her drawers and clothing, who else would she suspect? I mean it, Valentine—you must be careful."

"I can't stay with Sally forever. If Diamond is as crafty as Detective Lopez said, it might be months before she is caught."

"I know. That's what worries me. Why don't you stay with Sally for another night? Maybe by tomorrow they'll know more. If they don't, we'll get you a hotel room, or maybe you can stay with one of the women at the church."

Though I wanted to go home, inwardly I was terrified. I'd led a pretty quiet life. I'd never dealt with anyone like Diamond. The woman we'd all trusted and looked upon as a fellow Christian had not only deceived us and tried to destroy the woman who had befriended her, she may even have had a criminal record. How many other people had she hurt? Just the thought made me queasy.

Robert lifted my face to meet his. "I'm glad you'll be staying at Sally's house tonight."

I nodded. "Me, too."

"Do you think she was trying to kill Barbie?" Reva asked me later as the three of us sat in Sally's kitchen, idly munching on the freshly baked cookies Jessica had helped her make that afternoon.

I lifted my shoulders in response. "Either that or get her hooked on drugs so she could hurt herself. I still can't figure out why."

Sally poured more iced tea into my glass. "What I don't understand is why she chose Barbie as her victim. Why not someone else? And how did she know her? Diamond came here from Georgia, didn't she?"

"Remember? Barbie moved here from Atlanta. Some former friend of hers told Diamond about her."

Reva huffed. "I hope the police are checking on that friend. Maybe she knows something that will lead them to her."

"Smart thinking, Reva." I had forgotten about that friend suggesting Diamond pay Barbie a visit. I hurried to the phone and called Detective Lopez so he could get that friend's name from Barbie. It could be a valuable lead.

"And ever since we met her, we believed she was a Christian." Sally took a slow sip of tea, then stared off into space. "She sure duped all of us."

Reva huffed again. "She might have fooled us, Sal, but she didn't fool God. She'll have a lot to answer for."

"Life sure deals some surprising blows. I'm wondering if I'll ever get over George."

I turned to Sally. "Try not to let it get you down. I know losing George hurt, but you're adorable and you're such a good catch. There will be other men in your life. Maybe several before that right man comes along. You don't want anything other than God's best, do you?"

She absently fingered the sugar bowl. "No, you know better than that."

"I sure never expected to be dating Chuck. Now the highlight of my day is getting to see him or talking to him on the phone."

I gave Reva's arm a playful jab. "Actually, this Chuck-thing of yours is kinda funny. Here you are a grown woman with a grown son, and you're sneaking off to meet your boyfriend like some teenage girl whose parents have forbidden her to even have a boyfriend."

"Can't help it. That's exactly the way my life is going. I hate sneaking around, but if my mother-in-law knew about him, she'd make my life even more miserable than she does already."

Sally giggled. "You could give him up. Then I could go after him!"

Reva rolled her eyes. "No way. He's mine. Not many men around like Chuck. You have to find your own fella."

Sally's face puckered up as she shrugged. "I thought I had, but George belongs to someone else."

A heavy sigh came from deep within Reva's chest. "Chuck hates this clandestine arrangement. If I don't find some way to spend more time with him, our relationship may end. He thinks I should just come right out and tell her."

"Maybe you should," Sally said.

Reva grabbed onto the table's edge and leaned forward. "Sally, the tirades you and Val have seen are nothing like the way she behaves when she's really mad at me. You have no idea how hateful she can be."

"Maybe, for her own good, it's time for her to go into that nursing home," I interjected, giving my friend's shoulder a pat. I hated to say it, but I felt I had to for Reva's sake. Even if she wanted to care for Mrs. Billingham, it was an impossible situation. She needed help.

Reva leaned back in her chair and rubbed at her eyes. "I'd never put her in that home just so I could meet with my boyfriend. I owe her more than that for giving birth to Manny."

"Oh, honey, we know that." I gave her hand an affectionate pat.

"But I'm finally coming to the realization, even as strong as I am, that I can't handle her anymore. She's way overweight, which makes walking difficult. She refuses to give up her six portions a day ice cream habit. She has almost no sense of balance. Her eyesight is getting weaker by the day, and she refuses to have the cataract surgery her doctor says she needs. Her blood pressure is sky high and extremely hard to regulate. Her hands are so crippled with arthritis she can barely grip her cane, and those are just a few of her problems. Even her doctor insists she belongs in a home where she can have twenty-four-hour care. To top it off, he thinks she is in the beginning stage of Alzheimer's. I'm about at my wit's end."

We three sat silently for a moment. I ached for her. Complaining was not something Reva did. Normally she held her personal feelings inside and only opened up when we prodded. Finally, I asked, "What can we do to help? I'm sure I'm speaking for Sally, too, when I say we'll do whatever we can."

She responded immediately. "Pray. Pray that I will do the right thing and for the right reasons. I never want to put my needs or wants ahead of hers. If putting her in a home is what is best for her, I want God to send me a very clear message. This is a big decision. I need more than the doctor's recommendation."

Sally sighed. "That's a tall request."

"I know, but it can happen. God is able. Just promise you'll pray with me about it."

"You know we will."

Suddenly, Reva brightened. "David has volunteered to stay with his grandmother tonight, so Chuck is taking me to dinner at that barbecue place in the mall. Why don't you two come with us?"

Sally leaned toward Reva and grinned. "Reva, haven't you heard that two is company, four is a crowd? Enjoy your time with Chuck. Val and I have plans to order in pizza and watch a sappy, romantic movie." She gave her a playful shrug. "Or—you could cancel your date with Chuck and join us for pizza."

Reva huffed. "Dreamer!"

That night, Sally and I pigged out on pizza, cried over the movie, then, with a friendly hug, told each other good night.

Mentally exhausted from the day's happenings, I went right to bed. Though I had half expected to lay awake for hours, I didn't. I awakened about four, slipped my feet into my slippers, and tiptoed downstairs to get a glass of water. But as I pressed the water button on the refrigerator's door, I suddenly remembered Sprinkles. My cat had plenty of food, but he hadn't had fresh water for two days. His water bowl had to be bone dry. I had to give him water.

I walked to the front door and, not wanting to wake up Sally or her children, quietly pulled it open. I was wearing a pair of dark-colored pajamas, which looked quite similar to a lightweight pantsuit, so I wasn't concerned that someone might see me. Most folks were in bed anyway, sleeping like I should have been. And it was doubtful Diamond would be around. Like Robert had said, she was probably miles away by then.

Besides the streetlights lighting up our cul-de-sac, there was a full moon, so what could it hurt if I hurried across the two lawns between Sally's house and mine and filled his water bowl.

I would have brought him with me, but two of Sally's children were allergic to cats.

Convinced I would be safe, I checked to make sure the door wouldn't lock behind me and stepped off the porch and into the damp grass.

I was not at all prepared for what happened next.

$\mathcal{C}$HAPTER 20

$\mathcal{C}$oming slowly down the street was a car that looked exactly like Diamond's.

No, it couldn't be, I told myself, stepping back into the shadows. Though I was some distance away, I had to admit I was scared. *It only looks like her car,* I told myself, trying to sound convincing. *You're letting your imagination run wild.*

I continued to watch, the beat of my heart nervously booming like the beating of a marching band's bass drum. As the convertible slowed to a near stop, its headlights went black, and the driver maneuvered it into Barbie's driveway.

It had to be Diamond!

The woman had the gall to come back? After all she'd done? Why? Why would she take a chance like that?

I stood there, mesmerized, my mouth hanging open, my palms sweaty, as the garage door lifted and the car rolled silently inside. I don't know what was the matter with me. I guess I still thought it was all a dream and I'd awaken any minute and find myself in the bed in Sally's house. But once that door lowered and I realized I was indeed awake, I hurried inside, and in the darkness of Sally's living room, located the phone, grabbed it up from the end table, dialed 911, and totally forgetting about the four people sleeping upstairs, screamed into the phone, "She's back! Send someone quick before she gets away!"

The operator who took my call asked me who was back and why they should send someone. I felt like a dork. Poor thing. She had no idea what I was talking about. After sucking in a breath, I calmed myself down, gave her the proper information, and asked her to call Detective Lopez.

Sally came rushing into the room, followed by her half-asleep children, and flipped on a light. "It's after four in the morning. What's going on? Who are you talking to?"

"Turn that light off! It's Diamond. She's back!"

She flipped the switch. Then, after she, in drill-sergeant fashion ordered her troop to go back to bed, we two crept out onto the yard and hid ourselves behind a tall shrub. I didn't know why we crept, but it seemed the right thing to do. We kept watching for a light in Barbie's house to go on, but none did.

"She must be using a flashlight," I told Sally, my eyes glued on the darkened house.

"Why do you suppose she came back? She must have known the police had already searched the house."

I shrugged. "Maybe she left something of sentimental value. Something the police wouldn't care about."

"She's sure taking an awful chance by coming back to get some knickknack."

Maybe because that was the way they did it in the movies,

but I fully expected police cars to come roaring down the street and uniformed officers to leap out, each pointing a gun at the house as one man with a megaphone ordered her to come out with her hands up, but it didn't happen. Instead, two unmarked cars entered our cul-de-sac with their lights out and rolled quietly to a stop alongside the curb a little distance away.

No one got out. No one yelled into a megaphone.

I craned my neck for a better view and, in the process, scratched my hand on a wiry branch. "Surely they're going in after her." I winced as I blotted a drop of blood onto my sleeve.

Sally nodded. "I wish they'd hurry."

We stood behind that bush waiting, but nothing happened. Maybe those cars weren't police cars after all. But if they weren't, who were they? And where were the police? "Keep an eye on things," I told Sally. "I'm going back inside and call them again."

When I questioned the dispatcher as to why nothing was being done, the woman, who sounded like the same person I had spoken with earlier, told me that the police were on the scene, that I should go back in the house where I would be safe, and that they would take care of things.

How simple she'd made it sound. I couldn't help but wonder if she'd be content to go back in the house and wait if the same thing were happening to her or her family. I didn't know about Sally, but I wasn't about to stay in the house. When I told Sally what the woman had said, she laughed and said she didn't want to leave, either.

After thirty minutes of no activity, we got tired of standing and sat down on the porch steps hoping, with the distance between the two houses, that we wouldn't be seen.

Another thirty minutes passed. By then, a few lights had come on in some of the homes as people prepared to leave to go to work.

"Are they just going to sit there?" Sally asked with a grunt as her hand went to her backside. "My bottom is getting tired."

Mine was, too. I wasn't used to sitting on concrete steps. "They must be waiting for her to come out."

"Wouldn't it be better to go inside and get her?"

She had no more than asked the question when the garage door lifted and Diamond's car backed out. What happened next happened so fast, Sally and I could barely take it in. The two cars lunged forward, blocking her exit. Then four officers jumped out with guns drawn and rushed her car. Apparently, she hadn't locked her door, because one of them jerked it open and simply reached in and pulled her out. We could hear her cursing at them, using vulgarities that sent both of us into shock, as she screamed and kicked, trying to get away from them. Within seconds, they placed Diamond in the backseat of one of the unmarked police cars, and it disappeared down the street. The other men remained behind to close the garage door and make sure the house was locked up tight, and then they left.

I turned to Sally. "Whew, did that all just happen?"

She nodded. "I think so."

I breathed a heavy sigh. "I guess it's safe to go give Sprinkles some water now."

"Give your cat water?" Sally gave me a blank stare. "After what just happened, you're worrying about him having fresh water?"

I gestured toward my house. "That's what I was on my way to do when I saw Diamond's car coming down the street."

Sally gave me a once-over, then snickered. "Most of our neighbors are probably up by now and ready to leave for work. Are you sure you want to walk down the street in your pajamas?"

I glanced down at my attire. In the beginning light of day, they did look more like pajamas than a pantsuit. "Maybe I should change first."

Of course, the first thing I did when I got to my house was call Robert. Sprinkles's water could wait. I had news to tell him.

"Valentine, I thought I asked you to stay away from that house," he said in a slightly irritated manner when I stopped talking long enough for him to get a word in. "With her warped state of mind, no telling what she would have done if she'd seen you."

"It was four in the morning. I never expected her to come back at that time. You yourself said she was probably miles away by then. I felt perfectly safe."

"But you weren't, were you? For all you knew, she could have had a gun with her."

His words frightened me. "I thought of that later."

"Any idea why she came back?" he asked.

"No, but Sally thought maybe she came back for some memento, something of sentimental value to her."

"Maybe. The police were pretty thorough in their search. I doubt they left anything important behind."

"What do you think will happen to her?" I shuddered to even speculate, after what she'd done.

"They'll be able to hold her while they wait for the test results on Barbie and some of the substances they found in the house. I guess what happens next depends on those results, as well as on what a search of her background turns up. Who knows? She may even be wanted elsewhere on other charges. We'll just have to wait and see."

"I've always thought I was a pretty good judge of character," I said, "but she sure had me fooled. I feel partially responsible for what happened to Barbie. Thinking Diamond was exactly what she needed, I actually encouraged her to stay."

"She fooled all of us, Ward included. He's sick about this whole thing. He'd really grown fond of Diamond. I'll call you later. I want to phone Detective Lopez and get the scoop."

"I'm going to give some water to Sprinkles, eat a little breakfast, take a shower, then go see Barbie. I guess I shouldn't say anything about what happened. I don't want to upset her. I'll leave that job up to Detective Lopez."

"Good idea. What she needs right now is you, especially since she asked you to lead her to Christ."

"I'm taking my Bible with me. I thought I'd read some of its wonderful encouraging verses to her. She needs a couple of fresh gowns, but I doubt the police would want me in her house. I'll take some of mine instead."

"Good idea. You know, if Barbie is doing well, they may let her go home soon."

"I hope so. When you're not feeling well, there's no place like your own bed."

After we'd said good-bye, I gazed around my home. I had so much, far more than I needed. I'd thought Diamond had, too, but I guess I'd been wrong. From the sound of things, everything she had told us about her world travels and her wonderful social life in Atlanta had been a lie. A story made up to impress us and worm her way into our good graces. She always seemed to have plenty of money. If she lied to us about her wealthy husband, their big homes, and their investments, where had the expensive clothes and car come from? Had she stolen from other unsuspecting people? Was that the reason she never bought a house in Nashville like she told Barbie she was going to do? She didn't actually have the money, so she'd sponged off Barbie?

Though she didn't deserve it, in some ways I felt sorry for her. What would drive a beautiful woman, who seemed to have everything going for her, to spend her life lying about her identity and fleecing others? As gorgeous as Diamond was, and as well educated and well mannered, she could easily have risen to the top of some profession on her own without taking from others. What a waste of both beauty and talent.

Barbie was propped up in bed when I entered her room, looking better than I'd dared hope. But even though she looked so much better physically, her face bore a sad expression.

"That detective just left," she said the minute I walked through her door. "The doctor came in with him. They told me how Diamond had pumped me full of drugs. No wonder I felt so bad all the time."

Not sure exactly how much they had told her, I simply nodded.

"The doctor said if she'd given me a few more doses, I could have died." Her eyes saddened even more. "Why, Valentine? Why would she do this to me? I trusted her. I'd never done anything to her but treat her with kindness."

"I don't know, honey. I just wish I would have been savvy enough to notice." I lowered my head in shame. "I actually encouraged her to stay when you began to feel bad. Maybe if I hadn't—"

"It wouldn't have made any difference. I wouldn't have believed

275

you if you'd told me you didn't trust her. I thought she was my friend. Even when she did things I didn't understand, I fooled myself into thinking it was my imagination. How could I have been so stupid?"

"I thought she was my friend, too, until she began trying to keep me away from you by telling me you didn't want to see me. I should have insisted you tell me yourself, face-to-face, rather than listening to her."

She reached out her hand. "I should have known you'd never desert me. You've always been there for me, even when I treated you badly, apologizing when I should have been apologizing to you."

I took hold of her hand, then sat down on the edge of her bed. "You were so sick, sometimes even talking out of your head. I should have ignored Diamond and dragged you out of that bed and taken you to a specialist."

"She was giving me both uppers and downers, Val. That's why I felt terrible one day and like I was recovering the next. But the doctor said the Coumadin was the biggest problem. With the drugs causing my constant dizziness and the massive amount of Coumadin she was giving me, it was inevitable that sometime I would sustain a terrible fall and possibly even bleed to death." She gripped my hand so tightly, it was all I could do to keep from flinching.

"Diamond made me fall, Valentine. I didn't remember it at first, but now that my mind is clearing, I do. The day I fell, Diamond and I had been arguing. I had asked her to bring my purse from the front hall table where I'd left it days ago. When she refused, I told her if she didn't, I was going to get out of bed and go after it. She glared at me and told me to go ahead, that she was getting tired of having to wait on me like she was my servant. I was furious. I vaguely remember getting out of bed and reaching for my cane, but it wasn't there. So, bracing myself against the wall, I hobbled into the hallway and toward the stairs. When I reached the landing, I realized I didn't have the strength to continue and turned around to go back, but Diamond was blocking my way." Her frail shoulders lifted in a shrug. "That's the last thing I remember until I woke up in the hospital."

"You remember all that? Maybe you just supposed it happened that way."

"No. I admit bits and pieces of that morning are either unclear or missing, but I distinctly remember the parts I've told you."

For a moment, her eyes closed and her hand went to cover her mouth. Finally, she said in a shaky, hushed tone, "I'm sure she pushed me."

"You really think she did?"

She gave her head a positive bob. "Yes, I'm almost certain of it. But whether she pushed me or just watched me, Diamond had to have been with me when I fell down those stairs."

"She told the police you fell after she left."

"That was a lie. She left me all right, Valentine, but not until after I had fallen. She had to know my blood was thin from the Coumadin, and all it would take was a bad fall down those stairs to make me bleed to death. She pushed me, then went about her merry way and left me to die. I know she did."

I had no response. Her words hit me like a car whose brakes had failed, leaving me stunned and trembling. "Did you tell that to the police?" I finally was able to mumble.

"Yes, to Detective Lopez, just before you came. He had suspected as much."

I gave my head a shake. "I can't believe she would go off and leave you like that. How could she be that heartless?"

"All I know is, if you hadn't found me when you did, I wouldn't be here now. I owe you my life, Valentine."

"You owe me nothing! If I'd been more perceptive and less gullible, I would have realized you weren't behaving like your normal self and come to your rescue long ago. Instead, I let Diamond deceive me like she deceived you."

"Detective Lopez said, in most cases, there's a reason behind every dreadful act, but I can't think of a single one. All I've done is be her friend. Sure, we've had a few disagreements, but nothing of any importance. Why would she want to harm me?"

"She may have fooled us earthly mortals, but she hasn't fooled God. He's known her heart from the beginning and won't let this go unpunished." I had to ask her the question I'd wanted to ask ever since I'd found her in that pool of blood. "Do you think she's lied about everything else? Did she ever ask you for money?"

Barbie appeared thoughtful. "Funny thing is, she never asked me for anything. In fact, many times she offered to pay rent and even took me out to dinner. She was always buying groceries, especially the things she knew I liked. Money never seemed to be a problem with her. She even showed me one of her bank statements one day. I was amazed at the significant balance it showed."

"None of this makes any sense. But, of course, she could have created those bank statements. It'd be pretty easy to accomplish with a computer and a scanner."

"I know. That's what worries me. I need answers."

"Answers to what?" Robert asked as he strolled into the room, a bouquet of red roses in his hand. He reached them toward Barbie.

"Answers to why Diamond would want to harm Barbie." I slipped my hand into the crook of his arm and smiled up at him. "Pretty roses."

Despite her swollen cheek and sore lip, Barbie smiled at him, too. "Thank you, Robert. How thoughtful of you to bring them. I love flowers, especially roses."

He gave her a gracious bow. "Pretty flowers for a pretty lady."

Her smile narrowed. "Not so pretty now. After the nurse bathed me, she gave me a hand mirror. But keep the compliments coming. A girl, even one who looks as bad as I do, can never hear too many compliments."

"Has the doctor said when you're going to be released?"

"Probably tomorrow. Now that Diamond is in custody, I'll feel safe going home. The doctor has already arranged for a home health nurse to stay with me for as long as I need her."

Her news surprised me. "That soon? Are you sure you feel up to it?"

"The hospital staff has been wonderful to me, but I'm anxious to get back into my own bed. I'm sure, with the nurse staying with me, I'll be fine. I'll just have to take it easy and give my body time to heal. I'm fortunate there were no broken bones. The doctor said it was because I was relaxed when I fell. My head is doing well, but I guess I'll be feeling my bruises for some time to come."

"I could have stayed with you," I offered.

Barbie reached out her hand. "I know, but you've done enough already. Anyway, I'll probably feel better knowing a registered nurse will be with me. The doctor also said it is going to take awhile for all the drugs to get out of my system. He didn't actually use the word *withdrawal*, but I think that's what he meant. I may have some rough times ahead."

I took her hand and gave it a squeeze. "I'm here for you whenever you need me."

"I know, and I love you for it."

"And I'll be there, too," Robert offered.

She grinned up at Robert. "At one time, I had hoped you'd end up being with me on a full-time basis, but I guess Valentine won you over. I never had a chance."

Robert pulled me close. "This precious lady captured my heart that first day I took her out for a business luncheon, and I've been her captive ever since."

Barbie shrugged. "I should be so lucky." She nodded toward me. "Valentine, I hope you realize what a fine man you've got."

I leaned into him, relishing his manly scent. "I do, and I appreciate him more every day. I can hardly wait to become his wife."

He bobbed his head toward me. "I offered to take her to one of those wedding chapels in Las Vegas, but she wouldn't go."

"And she shouldn't! You two need to be married right here in Nashville, where all of your friends are. So when is this big event going to take place?"

He gestured toward me. "Ask her. She's the one holding up the works. I'm ready now."

"We're getting close to setting a date. We have a few more things to work out first, but we're getting there. I'm sure we'll be making an announcement very soon."

Barbie actually seemed pleased. "I'm your friend. Promise I'll be one of the first to be told."

I smiled at her. We truly were friends now. "I promise."

"Okay," Robert said, grinning as we settled onto the sofa beside each other after enjoying our take-out Chinese dinners in my family room that evening. "What exactly did you mean when you said we 'were getting there'? Did I interpret it right? That you're ready to become my bride? What about this house?"

"The house *was* a problem."

"Was? What does that mean?"

"I've decided where *I* think we should live, but the final decision has to be satisfactory to both of us."

He slipped his arm around me and drew me close. I loved the feeling of being near him. "You know how I feel about that. I'd live with you most anywhere, just so I could be with you! You name it."

"Would you consent to living in this house?"

He glanced around at the pictures of Carter that I kept on the mantel and on the wall. "I think I've already stated my position on that one. No."

"Would you be happier if I moved into your house with you?"

"I'd like that, but I'd never ask you to do it if you didn't want to."

"Would you be happy if I said I was ready to have you build a house for us, but it would have to be completed before our wedding?"

He took on a scowl. "You know I want to build a house for you just the way you'd like it, but I wouldn't want to wait that long."

I gave a shrug. "Well then, it looks like there is only one other choice. If it is still available, it looks like we'll have to purchase that home you found for us and get married right away!"

The startled expression on his face was everything I'd hoped it would be.

"Don't joke with me, sweetheart. This isn't funny."

I threw back my head with a laugh. "You think this is a joke?"

A smile broke out across his face. "It isn't? You're serious?"

"Absolutely." I lifted my face to his and nuzzled his cheek. "I want us to buy that house and get married as soon as possible. I love you, Robert. I want to be your wife so bad I can hardly stand it."

He smothered my face with kisses before his lips claimed mine in a long, slow kiss that made me weak with love for the man. Finally, he drew back and gazed into my eyes. "But I don't get it. What happened? You've had a hard time even talking about leaving this home that you and Carter shared."

"The other evening, after you'd left and I was alone in this house and already missing you, for the first time I asked myself an honest question. Was leaving this house and all its memories really that important? Important enough to give up the man I dearly loved and wanted to be with? Without someone to love, wasn't a house just a house? That's when I knew, with the love we had for each other, we should be together. Nothing, especially something as material as a house, should keep us apart." I reached up and stroked his face. "How could I have let such a foolish thing bother me? Where we live is no longer important to me. I just want to be with you."

"And I want to be with you." He leaped to his feet, pulling me up with him, then swirling me around with his strong arms before crushing me to him so tightly it made me gasp for breath. "I can't tell you how happy this makes me. I was beginning to wonder if we'd ever get married!"

When he finally stopped whirling, I was so dizzy and breathless the room kept spinning long after we'd stopped. "I love you more than you'll ever know, and I intend to spend the rest of my life proving it. Can we go check on that house tomorrow?"

Another kiss, a hug we would never forget, and an enthusiastic, "Uh-huh!" was my answer. After that, we just held each other.

Robert and I were finally going to tie the knot.

I was going to be Mrs. Robert Chase.

I could hardly wait to tell my friends.

Though I had a hard time keeping my news to myself when Sally and Reva joined me for coffee the next morning, I filled them in on Barbie's happenings first, explaining that I had already gone over to her house, cleaned up the blood as best I could, and straightened things up. I'd also put fresh linens on the bed and did a thorough cleaning of her bathroom, making sure to put anything out of sight that might remind her of Diamond.

"You really think she pushed Barbie down the stairs?" Sally asked, caught up in the mystery of my story.

"She had to have been there when Barbie's mishap occurred."

Reva stared into her coffee cup. "I can't imagine hurting anyone like that, especially leaving them to die like she did."

I agreed with Reva. "You should have heard how many times she used God's name in vain when they tried to put her in that patrol car."

"Well, I'm just glad they caught her. Sometimes you hear about people doing awful things, then disappearing and never getting caught. No one should get away with hurting anyone. If Diamond gave her those drugs, it would be attempted murder, and so would pushing her down the stairs and leaving her to bleed to death."

"You're right about that. The whole thing makes me sick." I leaned back and folded my hands on the table. "Enough of this bad news. Wanna hear some good news?"

Two heads nodded.

I nearly burst with my news. "Robert and I will soon be announcing our wedding date!"

Both Sally and Reva spun in my direction. "I thought since you couldn't bring yourself to move out of this house, you were going to—"

"I'm going to sell it!"

Sally's eyes bugged out. "You're kidding. You're actually going to leave this house?"

My insides were churning with excitement at the thought. Just saying I was going to sell it made my decision seem so real. "Yep, I sure am. Know anyone who might want to buy it?"

Sally grabbed onto my wrist. "You're serious!"

"Never been more serious."

Reva grinned. "I wish I could say Chuck and I might want to buy it, but we're far from ready to talk marriage. But, I tell you, Valentine, if we do ever get to that point, I'm not going to let the house Manny and I shared keep us apart. I've seen what that decision has done to you."

Sally nodded in agreement. "I think all three of us have put more value on *things* than we should. I had a terrible time convincing myself it was time to sell our last house. Isn't it amazing how attached we women can become to our homes?"

"I guess it's our built-in desire for nesting." With a mischievous laugh, Reva gestured toward me. "Diamond was holding out for a house on Morning Glory Circle. You might sell yours to her."

I laughed back. "After what she's done, I doubt she'll be available to live in it for a long time, if ever."

Sally waved her hand through the air. "Enough talk about that horrible Diamond person. I want to know about you, Val. When did you make this horrendous decision about selling your house? And why? What happened to make you change your mind"

I told them what I had told Robert—that a house meant nothing without the one I loved to share it with me. "I can't believe it took me so long to figure it out. You're right, Reva. None of us should ever let a house come between us and our true love. Take it from a woman who should have realized it long ago—it's not worth it."

"I agree. Though George and I never got beyond the friendship state, if we had, like Valentine, I think I would have decided to sell my home." Sally grabbed the last donut from the plate. "You two were destined to be together right from the start. Everyone knew it. I'm glad it's working out for you."

"But, Valentine, you just spent a fortune on that amazing backyard of yours. Surely you're not going to go off and just leave it. You've wanted to do that beautiful landscaping job for as long as I can remember."

"I'll be honest, Reva. Had I known I'd be accepting Robert's proposal and deciding to leave this house this soon, I probably wouldn't have done nearly as much as I did, but I look at it this way. That wonderful Tuscany-type yard is going to be a major selling point when my house goes on the market." I grinned. "But remember, I'm marrying the landscaper! I'm sure he'll be redoing our yard wherever we live. Maybe, at my next house, we might decide to do the yard in the style of an old Southern plantation, or maybe some other wonderful theme."

"So? When is the big day?"

"The moving day?"

Reva swatted at me. "No, silly, your wedding day."

"We're going to go check on a house we looked at earlier. We both liked it, and it's not far from here. If it is still for sale, we're going to buy it. Then, depending on when we can move in, we'll set the date."

Reva's eyes widened. "What if it's already sold?"

I gave her a blank stare. "I don't know. I guess I just supposed God was keeping it for us until I came to my senses."

Sally reached over and patted my hand. "God is so good at miracles, I'm sure He's been keeping it for you."

"But what if He hasn't?"

I mustered up a smile. "Then I guess we'll live in a tent until we find another house."

Sally roared with laughter. "You? Live in a tent? That I've got to see."

"Don't laugh. If I had to choose between living in this house alone for the rest of my life and living with Robert in a tent, I'd choose the tent in a heartbeat. I love that man!"

Sally thrust her fist into the air. "Hip, hip, hooray for Queen Valentine! May she and Robert live a long and happy life. And may she never have to live in a tent."

Joining in the hilarity of the moment, Reva lifted her juice glass and gestured for us to do the same. "I propose a toast. To us. Husbands are great, and we need them in our lives, but may the friendship we three share last into eternity."

I clanged my glass against hers, then Sally's. "To our friendship. May it never wane."

Sally clinked her glass against ours. "And may God always be at the center of that friendship."

I smiled at the two of them, then setting down my glass, I reached out, took their hands in mine, and began singing a precious song Sally and I had learned at Brownie Scout camp when we were little girls: "Make new friends but keep the old. One is silver, the other gold." Silver friends are wonderful, but these two friends sitting beside me were definitely worth gold.

By the time Robert and I took Barbie home from the hospital the next day, the home health nurse had already arrived, and she welcomed us at the door. We stayed long enough to make sure Barbie was settled and ready for a nap before we left, with the promise that we'd be back to check on her later.

"Are you sure you should be taking this much time away from your business?" I asked Robert as we headed toward the house we hoped was still on the market.

Without taking his eyes off the oncoming traffic, he reached across the console and took hold of my hand. "Don't worry your pretty little head about it. Jake's keeping an eye on things for me."

I let out a squeal as his truck turned the corner and headed up the street toward the house we'd agreed would be perfect for us. There, much to my relief, in the well-maintained front yard, was the FOR SALE sign!

"Want to go in and take another look around?"

"Don't we have to call the Realtor first?"

I could tell by his grin, as he hurried around to open my door, something was up. "She's inside waiting for us."

My heart did a flip-flop with joy. "You called her?"

"First thing this morning."

"So you already knew it was still on the market. Why didn't you tell me?"

" 'Cause I wanted to see the look on your face when you caught sight of the FOR SALE sign. You have no idea how cute you looked. I want to remember that expression the rest of my life."

I playfully poked at his ribs. "And here all the time we were picking Barbie up from the hospital, taking her home, and getting her settled, I was worrying that someone had already snatched up our dream home."

He grabbed onto my hand and tucked it into the crook of his arm as we hurried up the lovely brick sidewalk that led to the front door. "*Our* dream home? Is that really the way you think of it? I want you to be happy with our selection. Don't just say that because you think it's what I want to hear. This is going to be *our* home, yours and mine. I want it to be right for both of us, but especially you."

Before he could reach for the doorbell, I grabbed onto his

arms and spun him around. "I love this house, but any house the two of us live in will be my dream home simply because you're there."

As his lips claimed mine, I knew, by deciding to marry Robert and give up the home I'd loved, I had made the right choice. I was filled with so much happiness I thought my heart would explode.

We quickly parted when we heard the front door open. Mrs. Stebbins, the Realtor, who seemed almost as embarrassed as I felt, gave us a silly grin. "From the looks of things"—her smile broadened—"I'd say you two are really looking forward to your wedding day. Am I right?"

Robert slipped his arm around me possessively, which only heightened my joy. I *was* his!

"Absolutely. The sooner the better." He nudged me toward the door. "If you don't mind, we'd like to take another look around."

"Of course." The woman gestured toward the grand foyer. "As I'm sure you've noticed, the owners have moved all their things out, and the workmen have been here most of the week touching up anything that was needed, including putting in a new hot water tank and a new dishwasher. The place is ready for you. Since you've already given me your offer to purchase and your earnest money check, and the owners have already accepted your offer—"

My jaw dropped. "You've already given them your offer?"

A wide smile blanketed Robert's face. "On the condition of your final approval."

Mrs. Stebbins nodded. "So—if you approve, Ms. Denay, all the two of you need to do is sign the contract so I can take it to the title company along with your earnest money. If everything goes well, which I have no doubt it will, since you've already been prequalified, you should be able to close by the end of next week and the house will be yours."

Words failed me. Although I had hoped the house would still be on the market and, if everything was agreeable, we could sign an offer and get the ball rolling, I'd had no idea Robert had already taken care of those details and we could close that soon, but I was pleased he'd gone ahead and secured it for us.

"Give us time to take another walk-through, and if Valentine is still agreeable, we'll sign the contract before we leave." With that he ushered me into the living room.

The house had looked big with the owner's furniture and personal items in it, but now that it was empty, it looked massive, much larger than the house Carter and I had built. I grabbed onto Robert's sleeve and tugged him to the center of the room. "I really don't need such a fine house. Maybe we should look for something less—not so large."

Smiling down at me, he cuffed my chin. "What you're really saying is, 'Can we afford it?' Right?"

"I don't want you to do something—"

He pressed a finger to my lips. "God has been good to me, dearest. I made a nice profit on the house Lydia and I shared all those years, and all that money has been invested in CDs ever since. My business has done far better than my expectations, and I still have most of the money my parents left me."

"And we'll have the money from the sale of my—"

"No. We can put that money aside for a rainy day, if you like, but I want to provide a home for you. It's important to me, Valentine. I hope you understand."

I touched the cute little dent in his chin with the tip of my finger and gave him a coy smile. "Like—me, Tarzan; you, Jane?"

He chuckled. "I guess that'd be a good way to put it. Providing a beautiful, spacious home for you is one of my greatest desires. Besides, I'm sure we'll want to do lots of entertaining."

My love for Robert grew with his every word. "I do understand, my sweet husband-to-be, and I love you for it."

We wandered aimlessly through the house, opening cupboard and closet doors, staring out the windows at the various views, sometimes stopping long enough to kiss each other or simply stand wrapped in each other's arms. "So? Are you ready to sign the contract?" he asked me as we prepared to leave the family room, the final room on our tour.

I couldn't contain a giggle of both satisfaction and joy. "Yes! Where's the pen?"

Within less than twenty minutes, we bade farewell to Mrs. Stebbins, our copy of the contract in hand, and walked out into the bright, sunny day. It could have been pouring down rain, but to me, it would have seemed like the most beautiful day of my life. I was so happy I felt as if I were floating down the front steps as I clung to Robert's arm. Suddenly, he pulled away from me and moved in the opposite direction of his truck. "Where are you going?" I called out, confused by his action.

"To get this!" He hurriedly crossed the yard to the FOR SALE sign and, after a couple of tugs, pulled it out of the ground. "We don't want anyone else looking at this house. It's no longer for sale! It's going to be ours!"

CHAPTER 21

"You actually bought a house?" Sally asked.

"Sure did. Robert and I signed the papers a little over an hour ago. We should be able to close in a week or so."

She motioned me inside, then closed the door behind us. "Boy, you and Robert didn't waste any time. I'm really happy for you."

"I can't stay. I promised Barbie I'd look in on her when I got back."

Sally's smile disappeared. "What am I going to do without you? Walking over to your house each morning, sharing coffee and doughnuts with you and our other friends—" She threw her hands up in frustration. "I really am going to miss you, Valentine. Life isn't going to be the same here on Morning Glory Circle without you."

I squeezed her arm and said, "I'm not moving that far away. We can still have our morning coffees. We'll just do it in another kitchen."

"I thought Robert wanted to build you a house."

"He did, but then we considered the time it would take. Neither of us wanted to wait, and we'd both fallen in love with the house we just bought, so we decided to go for it."

"You're being honest with me—it doesn't bother you to leave the house you and Carter shared?"

I bit at my emotions. Though I'd made up my mind and had no intention of changing it, I did wonder if it was going to be as easy to leave as I hoped it would. "A little, I guess, but I know I'm doing the right thing."

"Where is this dream house?"

I moved toward the door, anxious to see if Barbie was getting along okay with her new caretaker. "It's over on Windmill Road. The old Garvey—"

"The Garvey house? I used to babysit their children when I was a teenager. Oh, Val, I love that house!"

Sally's enthusiastic reaction pleased me. "Robert and I both fell in love with it the minute we walked through the front door. I'm sure we'll want to redecorate eventually, but the house is in amazing condition." I laughed aloud. "Surprisingly, the walls on the main floor are all burgundy. *If* we decide to use any of my furniture, it will fit into the decor perfectly." I grabbed hold of the knob and opened the door. "I really must be going, but I wanted you to be one of the first to know about our new home."

I said good-bye, then hurried to Barbie's house. She was sitting on her chaise lounge reading a new fashion magazine when I entered her room, and she looked amazing.

"My hairdresser was sweet enough to come by and spruce up my hair with the curling iron," she explained, carefully fingering what was left of her locks. "She suggested I might want to have my hair cropped short, into an almost pixy cut when this bandage comes off, so it won't be so obvious where the doctor had to shave the hair off. She even helped me with my makeup."

"You look beautiful, and I think you'd look like an absolute doll with a short haircut." I sat down beside her and took the magazine from her hands. "I have something to tell you."

She frowned. "Something good, I hope. I'm tired of bad news."

"Robert and I bought a house."

She looked surprised. "You're moving away from Morning Glory Circle?"

"Yes, but not far. The house we bought is over on Windmill Road."

"The big one with the tall columns out front that looks like an old Southern mansion?"

"Yes, that one. You know it?"

"Diamond and I looked at it that Sunday we visited several other open houses. I love that house. If I hadn't already bought this one, I might have bought it. Oh, Valentine, it's gorgeous!" She took on a frown. "But that means you won't be my next-door neighbor any more."

"But I'll still be your friend."

"But I need you close to me."

I placed her magazine on the table, then scooted over to sit on the edge of her lounge chair. "We girls will still be gathering for coffee and chitchat every morning. You're part of our group. I do hope you'll come. My new house is less than a ten-minute drive from here. Besides, you'll still have Reva and Sally as close neighbors. They're your friends, too."

She took on a warm glow. "They are, aren't they?"

"Yes, and you have many friends at Cooperville Community Church. And don't forget your Red Hat ladies. You know they love you. You're their queen."

She tilted her head contemplatively. "I've been thinking about my Barbie's Babes Red Hat chapter. When I get over all of this, I'd like to throw a big party for them, similar to the one you had for the Widows' Club. Would you help me with it? You're so good at that sort of thing."

"I'd love to."

"We'll always be friends, won't we, Valentine?"

I grinned. "Till death do us part."

That night, Robert and I, after spending a lovely, lazy evening together, set our wedding date for August 1, which gave us four weeks to plan our wedding.

When Barbie phoned me the next morning saying she had made arrangements with Detective Lopez to talk to Diamond and that she wanted me to go with her, I immediately said yes.

"I have to find out why she did those awful things to me," she told me as we followed him down the long corridor to the interrogation room where Diamond was waiting under the watchful eye of one of the officers. "I can't believe she just picked my name out of the phone book to terrorize."

I did a double take. "I thought a friend of yours told her to contact you."

"So did I, but when she mentioned that friend's name and I couldn't place her, I let on like I remembered her rather than admit I'd forgotten her. I'm not sure I ever knew her."

Detective Lopez let out a snort. "I checked that woman's name out and couldn't find any evidence of anyone by that name ever having lived in Atlanta. It was all a part of her scam. But Ms. Jenson still hasn't told us why she selected Ms. Baxter as her victim."

Diamond gave us a haughty tilt of her head when we entered. Barbie and I sat down at the table opposite her, but the detective remained standing. "So why did you want to see me?" Diamond's voice had a hard edge to it.

Barbie sat staring at her for a moment. "I have to know, Diamond. Why me? Why would you try to hurt me like you did?"

Diamond let out a huff. "You're a stupid woman, Barbie. I would think you would have figured that out by now. I'm amazed you couldn't connect the dots. I certainly gave you enough clues. Does the name James Morgan ring any bells with you?"

Terror traced its way across Barbie's face. "How did you know him?"

A sneering smile crept across Diamond's face. "The question is—how did *you* know him?"

Barbie moaned as her hand flew to cover her mouth, and she turned an ashen white. For a moment, I thought she was going to faint. What was going on between these two women?

"Who are you?" Barbie finally managed to mumble.

"I'm surprised you never guessed. You have to know who I am." Diamond gestured around the room with a swoop of her hand. "James Morgan was the man who took me as his daughter when I was an infant. Tell them, Mommy. Tell them—"

Barbie let out a shriek. "You're my daughter?"

I gasped. "Barbie's your mother?"

Diamond gave her head an exaggerated nod. "Mother? That word is too good for her. *Whore* would be a better word. I'm the daughter she threw away like yesterday's newspaper."

Barbie's hand flew to cover her face, and she began to bawl like a baby so loudly the ear-splitting sound filled the small room and ricocheted off the walls. "I didn't want to give you away," she said between sobs. "It wasn't my fault."

Diamond sneered, then pointed her finger in Barbie's face. "Not your fault? Tell them how you dumped me off at that children's home, with no concern of what my life might be like as I was passed from one family to another, being spat upon like trailer trash, abused by the man of the house, and treated like a slave by his wife and children. It was your fault all right. You never cared one whit for the baby you deserted."

Barbie's shrieks sounded like the cry of a wounded animal. "I couldn't keep you!" she screamed, wildly flailing her arms at Diamond. "My father made me give you away. I had no choice. Besides, I knew nothing about taking care of a baby. He convinced me you'd be better off with someone else!"

"You could have stood up to him, but you didn't. You left me and never looked back. All those years, even though I didn't know your name, I hated you and swore I would get even with you. Now I have!"

Her eyes narrowed and her face took on an intense look of hatred I'd never seen on a human being. It was an evil look, which made me wonder if Diamond *had* gotten into witchcraft and had planted that book in Barbie's bedroom, hoping Barbie would read it. I looked from mother to daughter, for the first time seeing a distinct resemblance. How could I have been so blind? Why hadn't I noticed it before? If Barbie had dumped Diamond off, discarding her like a piece of trash, with no concern for her well-being, it was no wonder Diamond had such hatred for her. Things that had confused me before began to make sense.

Diamond leaned forward as far as her restraints would allow and gave Barbie a menacing stare. "Thanks to you, my life was a living hell."

Barbie wiped at her eyes as she floundered for words. "I never meant to hurt you. I thought people would be good to you. Mr. Morgan assured me he and his wife would be good to you."

"Why should anyone be good to me? When my own mother didn't care enough about me to keep me? I could tell you stories of what happened to me that would make you want to vomit. I ran away from my last foster home on my fifteenth birthday and lived on the streets of Las Vegas. Anything was better than staying with that family and having that man do what he did to me. Guess what I had to do to support myself?"

My blood ran cold at the thought of a child that young being at the mercy of anyone who would give her money.

"I learned to play the game early in life, and it paid off for me. I could con my way into anything. Fortunately, I inherited my mother's beauty, and I used it to the maximum. There was always a man just around the corner waiting to be taken advantage of. Las Vegas was my playground. And where was my mommy all this time? Fleecing three husbands out of their fortunes." She flipped her hand at Barbie. "Like mother, like daughter."

"How—how did you find me? James Morgan didn't know where I was."

"At first I had trouble locating you, but after I conned the man at the children's home to open the records for me, I was able to find James Morgan. By using my charms on him and convincing him I loved you and wanted to be reunited with you, the sucker bought my line and helped me locate the next foster family I'd stayed with. Little did he know it wasn't love that motivated me to find you, but hatred. Hatred for what you had done to me, hatred for never knowing who my father was, hatred that you never came looking for me. It took me nearly three years to run you down, but I never stopped looking. All these years, my goal in life has been to make you pay. Getting you to take me in was so easy I nearly laughed in your face."

I ached for Barbie. "She took you in out of the goodness of her heart. She didn't deserve what you did to her."

"Oh, shut up, Valentine. You were as gullible as she was. You and your ditsy friends. What a bunch of losers."

Barbie's tear-filled eyes narrowed. "You're the loser—"

Diamond gave her another sneer. "What's the matter, Mommy? Don't you know my real name? Call me Diamond. I like it better than the one you put on the birth certificate."

"You nearly killed her!" I shouted out at her. I couldn't help it. I felt the need to defend my friend, despite what she had done by giving up her baby.

"You made it easy, Valentine. You actually encouraged my mommy to take the medication I was giving her."

I had nothing to say. She was right.

Diamond turned her wrath back on Barbie. "Pumping you full of drugs and watching you suffer made all my efforts worthwhile. I'm just sorry you didn't die when you fell down those steps."

I glared at Diamond. "You mean when you pushed her down those steps, don't you?"

She let out a shrill laugh, then stuck out her chin defiantly. "I guess no one will ever know the answer to that but me. Mommy was so drugged up, she couldn't put one foot in front of her without falling, so she's no witness. I guess we'll just have to say she fell on her own. Ah, revenge is sweet. I never realized it would taste so good."

Detective Lopez motioned to the officer. "Take her away. I think we've heard enough."

Diamond extended her cheek toward Barbie. "Don't you want to kiss your little baby good-bye, Mommy?"

Poor Barbie just sat there motionless, as if in a trance.

In some ways I almost felt sorry for Diamond. It sounded as though her entire life had been consumed with nothing but hatred and sorrow.

I slipped my arm protectively about Barbie's shoulders. "Leave her alone, Diamond. She thought she was doing the best thing for you. Are you so cruel that you have no feelings of pity for her?"

Her eyes narrowed. "You mean the best thing for *her*, don't you? What did she ever do for me except throw me away? I hate her. I'll always hate her. I just wish I could make her suffer more than she has already."

"You'll probably get your wish. I'm sure Barbie will suffer the rest of her life because of what you've done to her."

"Good! That was my intent. If I couldn't have her dead, at least I wanted her to be miserable." Diamond let out a raucous laugh. "I guess that means she won't come and visit me in prison."

"No, but God will. He's ever watching you. You lied to us

when you made us believe you were a Christian."

"You were easy to fool, Valentine. I guess I'm a better actress than I'd thought. Lying is one of my talents."

I couldn't resist pointing my finger at her. "You'd better think long and hard about what you've done and ask God's forgiveness. Unless you make your peace with Him, you'll spend eternity in a place far worse than any prison."

"Forget it, Valentine. If there is a God, I doubt He's interested in me. He's too busy taking care of goody-goody fools like you and those pious friends of yours."

"He loves us all equally, Diamond. He loves you as much as anyone. What you have done is horrible, but God can forgive even that. When you think you're all alone in that cell, remember He is there, too. All your life, others may have failed you, but God never fails. You can always count on Him."

She glared at me. "Yeah? Then where was He when I needed Him?"

Detective Lopez nodded to the officer. "Take her."

As they passed by us, Barbie reached out her hand and grabbed onto Diamond's sleeve. "I wish I'd kept you."

Diamond jerked her sleeve away. "Too late, Mommy. Little Diamond, whom *you* named Carolyn, is all grown up and bound for hell."

Barbie collapsed into my arms and sobbed her heart out. All I could think about was how much Carter and I had wanted a baby and hadn't been able to conceive. My heart cried out to God. *Why?*

I was relieved to find Robert waiting in the hall when we came out of the meeting room. I desperately needed his strength.

301

I'd never felt so drained. I could only imagine how Barbie felt.

"I thought you ladies might need some help getting home." With a tender smile, he reached out his hand toward Barbie. She took it and allowed him to help her stand.

At that moment, I was filled with pity for Barbie. I had no right to judge her. As her sister in Christ, it was my duty to hold her up in any way I could, and to be there for her. "Come on, sweetie, let's get you home. You're safe now. Diamond won't bother you again."

She was quiet all the way across town and said very little when we reached her house. Although the nurse was still there to help her, Robert assisted her up the stairs, then I helped her get into something more comfortable and suggested she try to take a nap. Like an obedient child, she climbed beneath the covers and closed her eyes. "I'm going to stay with her for a while," I told him. "She's been through a lot."

"Can you believe she's Diamond's mother?" he whispered as he bent to kiss me good-bye.

"No. That news really shocked me. But it all makes sense now. What a life Diamond must have lived. I actually feel sorry for her. I think, once things have settled down, I'm going to take her a Bible. She'll probably throw it at me, but maybe after I'm gone, she'll read it."

"Good idea. If anyone needs to settle their account with God, it's Diamond. God is her only hope. Her future looks pretty bleak."

"I know. She needs our prayers."

"That she does. But we've seen Barbie accept the Lord, why not Diamond? We have to have faith."

"We truly do reap what we sow, don't we?"

"Oh, yes. No one knows human nature like our God. I'm just glad He's more patient with us than we are with ourselves."

"Me, too. We all have our faults and shortcomings."

He kissed me again, then tiptoed out of the room.

Though I tried to spend as much time with Barbie as I could, the next three weeks flew by so rapidly I barely had time to check the pages on my calendar as we worked with Pastor Wyman, the bridal shop, the wedding planner, the caterer, the photographers, and all the other folks necessary to pull off the kind of wedding we wanted. It was fortunate the sale on the house closed right on time, because Robert had decided the walls should all be painted and new carpeting put down in the dining room and our bedroom before we moved in. Plus, he insisted we shop, not only for new bedroom furniture, but for new living room and family room furniture, as well. Though he never mentioned it, I was sure it was because he felt those were the three rooms that would most remind us of our spouses and maybe even cause a barrier between us on our wedding night.

Barbie made giant strides with her health as the effects of the drugs continued to move out of her system. She was soon back to nearly her normal self, although she tired more easily than before, and the old zip had gone out of her life. I knew she was well on her way to recovery when she complained that she didn't have a thing to wear and needed to go on a shopping spree for new clothes. The fact that Jake stopped by to see her each day, usually with a bouquet of fresh flowers from his garden, helped.

I really hoped those two would get together. Now that she was a Christian, they had so much more in common. Barbie confided in me that most of their conversations, when together, were about the Bible, which really pleased me and let me know she had been serious in her profession of Christ.

All in all, life was good. Not just for Robert and me, but for my friends, as well. Though Sally was still hurting from her breakup with George, she was adjusting to it and was actually returning smiles to other men in our church instead of running in the opposite direction. I knew she was lonely, so I continued to pray for her, asking God to send another godly man into her life. He'd done it for me and for Reva, so why not Sally? And even though Reva was still seeing Chuck on the sly and feeling guilty about it, she hadn't done a single thing toward moving Mrs. Billingham into a nursing home. But we all knew it was just a matter of time before the woman would be nearly bedfast and that choice would become a necessity.

"Maybe I've pushed you too hard, insisting we get married as soon as possible when you wanted to spend time with Barbie," Robert said one evening after a particularly trying day as he rubbed my shoulders. "You're really stressed out. Your muscles are in knots."

I pressed my shoulder against his rotating thumbs. "Mmm, that feels good. Ah, right there. That's where it hurts the most."

"You're still concerned about Barbie, aren't you?"

"Yes. She's so ridden with guilt...but it's Diamond I can't get off my mind. I keep thinking of her being locked up in a cell, knowing it's almost certain she'll have many years to come in prison.'"

"You've got to put that whole thing behind you, Valentine."

"Don't you see? I can't. I've always felt God sent Barbie into my life for a purpose. What about Diamond? Perhaps He sent her into my life, too. Maybe there is still something I can do to lead her to the Lord. I've got to get a Bible to her."

Robert seemed to give my comment thought. "Her heart is really hardened, Valentine. She's going to be tough to reach. She may even refuse to see you."

"I've thought of that, but I know if God wants me to reach her, He'll soften her heart. If I can get her to take a Bible, with all the time she'll have on her hands, she just might read it."

"Maybe." He moved directly behind me and began to massage my neck. "Wow, you *are* tense. I don't want you to stress out on me." He paused. "Although I'd hate to delay our wedding, I guess we could put it off until September or even October," he went on. "It's not worth—"

I twisted in my chair to face him. "No! Please, Robert. I'm fine. The worst part is over. Although Barbie is still chafing from her ordeal with Diamond, she's getting stronger physically every day, so I no longer have to worry about her health. When I mentioned I'd like to take a Bible to Diamond, she said eventually she'd like to see her, too, and try to establish some sort of relationship with her, which really surprised me. Everything else in my life is under control. I don't want to change our wedding date. It's what has kept me going. Preparing this week for our wedding is going to be the most fun I've had in a long time. I've caught the kindest, most considerate, romantic man a woman could ask for, and I am counting the minutes until Pastor Wyman performs our marriage ceremony."

JOYCE LIVINGSTON

As Robert rose to go home, his cell phone rang. Though I couldn't get the full gist of the conversation by hearing only one side, I knew it had something to do with Diamond.

"You're not going to like hearing what Detective Lopez just told me." He placed his phone back into his belt holster. "It seems your suspicions were right. Diamond wasn't a widow after all. She'd been married three times, and her last husband, a very wealthy man by anyone's standards, divorced her several years ago. Since they had been married in California and were living there at the time, she got half of everything he had as a settlement. So money hadn't been an object."

I was livid. "She wasn't a widow? And to think we welcomed her into the Widows' Club."

He shrugged. "Guess you're going to have to start doing a background search on everyone who wants to join. She not only invaded our lives under false pretenses, she invaded the Widows' Club."

"And we all welcomed her with open arms."

"He mentioned something else. When they questioned her about the book you'd found in Barbie's nightstand, she laughed and said she thought it would be a nice touch if you found it and thought Barbie was interested in witchcraft."

"I have to admit it did throw me when I found it." I gave my head a sad shake. "It seems Diamond's entire life was built on nothing but lying and cheating."

He pulled me close and gazed lovingly into my eyes. "Let's forget about those women and talk about us."

I stood on tiptoe and pressed my lips to his. "What a wonderful idea."

306

"Since you're using two matrons of honor, what do you think about me having two best men? Jake and Ward?"

I gazed dreamily into his eyes. "I think it'd be great."

It was almost uncanny the way the last-minute wedding details fell into place, probably because the wedding planner we chose was so efficient. She left me with barely anything to do. Good thing, because I tried to spend a little time with Barbie every day. I was glad she hadn't died in that fall. I really wanted her at my wedding. I just hoped she wasn't upset because I hadn't asked her to be a third matron of honor.

Despite the fact we had extended an open invitation to the entire church congregation, our friends outside the church, business associates, neighbors, and the members of the Widows' Club, we had decided on a fairly simple ceremony. After all, this was the second wedding for both of us.

On Friday night, we had a short rehearsal followed by a wonderful buffet dinner, which Reva, Sally, Wendy, and a number of other women in our church insisted on providing. I had to laugh when Sally came to me all teary-eyed. "Valentine," she said, taking hold of my hand, "I just realized, once you and Robert are married, you won't be able to belong to the Widows' Club!"

I gave her hand an affectionate squeeze. "I mentioned that to Robert. You know what he said? He said that even though I would be married to him, I'd still be a widow since I'd lost Carter. So, unless our membership disagrees, I'll still be a part of the Widows' Club."

She breathed a sigh of relief. "Oh, good. It wouldn't be the same without you."

When Robert took me home, held me in his arms, and kissed me good night, I knew it would be the last time we'd be together like that, until I met him at the altar, and I wanted to make the most of it. "You do know I love you, don't you?" I wrapped my arms about his neck and wove my fingers through his hair. I loved being close to him. "And that I want to be everything you could hope for in a wife?"

He nodded, then leaned his forehead against mine. "And you know I love you? And that I would never say or do anything to hurt you like I did to Lydia."

I hurriedly put a finger to his lips. "Please, dearest, we're never to talk about that again. It's over, in the past. We can't do anything to change it. God has forgiven you, I have forgiven you, and if Lydia were here and she knew the facts and how repentant you are, I'm sure she would forgive you, too. I know you're still having a hard time forgiving yourself, but as your wife, I am going to do everything I can to make that happen."

"I know you will, and I love you for it." He reached into his pocket and pulled out something folded up tightly in a single sheet of tissue paper. "For you, my darling. Something new to wear on your wedding day."

I let out an, "Oh, Robert!" as I pulled aside the paper and held up a single twinkling diamond pendant that dangled from a sparkling platinum chain. "The jeweler said the diamond was flawless, just like you."

I laughed as I lifted my hair so he could place it around my neck. "A diamond in the rough, maybe, but certainly not flawless!"

"You'll always be flawless to me. The beauty of that diamond pales in comparison to your beauty, my love."

I had never been happier than I was at that moment. "I pray I'll never disappoint you."

"I'm sure you never will. See you tomorrow," he whispered against my lips. "You are a gift from God, Valentine. Only He could have brought us together. By tomorrow night at this time, we'll be husband and wife, Mr. and Mrs. Robert Chase."

My heart did a cartwheel at the thought. "I know. I can hardly wait."

He freed me, then slowly backed out the door, closing it gently behind him. As I turned to go upstairs, I stopped long enough to glance about the home I had loved so much. The home I almost let stand between me and that amazing man. Though it still looked beautiful to me, it no longer had the attraction that had kept me mentally chained to it. After tomorrow, it would no longer be my home. From tomorrow on, my home would be wherever Robert was—the house on Windmill Road, or wherever God would lead us. I didn't care where. I just wanted to be with my man.

 CHAPTER 22

S top shaking." Sally grabbed hold of my hand to still it as we stood in the bride's room at the church the next evening. I was glad we'd opted to have our ceremony there instead of in my yard. Though my yard would have been the perfect place for it, somehow, I felt I needed to be married in the church that had brought us together.

Reva grabbed hold of my other hand and interceded in my behalf. "Leave her alone. Every bride gets the jitters before her wedding. Let her enjoy it."

The way those two had been mother-henning me all afternoon, I began to wonder if having two matrons of honor had been a good idea. "Do I look all right? Is my headpiece on straight?" I ran my tongue over my teeth, then curled up my lips. "Do I have lipstick on my teeth?"

Dina Bradbury, the wedding planner, stepped between me and my friends to adjust the tiny heart-shaped brooch I'd chosen for my something old. "You look lovely, dear. I'm so glad you decided on that simple pink-lace gown. It's perfect on you."

Barbie stood back to admire my dress. "She's right. You look lovelier than I've ever seen you. I do wish you the best. You know that, don't you?"

I gazed into the full-length mirror. "I feel lovely. I can't tell you how happy I am you're here. Our wedding wouldn't have been the same without you."

She blew me a kiss as she backed out the door. "I'd better get seated. I wouldn't want to miss seeing you walk down the aisle. I love you, Valentine."

"I love you, too." And I did. She was not only my friend, she was now my sister in Christ.

As the organ began to play, Dina gestured toward the door, then gave her hands a clap. "It's time. Everyone, get into your places." She grabbed onto Maria, our pastor's six-year-old daughter, who had agreed to be our flower girl, and maneuvered her to the head of the line. "Sally and Reva, you two ladies are next, but instead of walking down the aisle single-file, don't forget to walk side by side."

I smiled at my friends. They looked absolutely gorgeous in their hint-of-pink lace dresses with a pink rose each tucked into their hair. The wedding planner made a wide sweep of her arm. "You next, lovely lady."

I clutched my bridal bouquet even tighter. I wasn't sure my legs would hold me up, but they did, so I moved up behind Sally and Reva as told.

As I stood there, I ran a quick mental check. Something old? The tiny heart-shaped brooch Wendy had given me for my birthday, the one that had belonged to her mother. I'd tried to refuse, but she'd insisted I have it. Something new? The beautiful necklace Robert had given me after the rehearsal dinner. Something borrowed? The long pale pink slip I'd borrowed from Barbie. Something blue?

I panicked! I'd forgotten to bring the tiny piece of blue ribbon I had planned to pin to my bra strap. I had to have something blue. But what?

"Are you okay?" Apparently Dina had seen the look of terror in my eyes.

"I don't have anything blue!"

She, Sally, Reva, and I looked around the empty foyer. There wasn't a single item of blue in sight!

"I don't have anything blue!" I said in a voice much louder than intended.

"But, dear, there isn't anything blue here, and you certainly don't want to delay your wedding while someone goes to find it."

"Even a piece of paper, a wad of lint, anything blue! It's not that I'm superstitious, but all brides have something blue on their wedding day. It's a tradition."

Sally stepped forward with a giggle. "I have something blue, but I'm not sure you'll want it."

"Don't be silly. I don't care what it is. Hand it over!"

She glanced around toward the hall leading to the foyer and, seeing no one but the five of us women, lifted her skirt and ripped off a piece of the pale blue lace edging her long slip. "Here ya go!"

I laughed aloud as I grabbed the lace and tucked it into my shoe. "Sally, that lace is not only something blue, it's a real keepsake, and will go into our wedding album as something to remember you by."

We all straightened and ceased our giggling as the music began to swell. Dina gave us our final instruction, "Chin held high, walk slowly, and smile." Then she gave the flower girl a slight nudge to get her started. After each of my friends gave me a quick, loving peck on my cheek, Reva and Sally moved into the aisle, side by side.

"When they reach the front, the organist will begin to play 'Here Comes the Bride,'" the planner reminded me. "That will be your cue. Remember, Valentine, this is your day. Yours and your beloved's. Relax and enjoy it."

I sucked in a deep breath and waited. All nervousness suddenly disappeared. There was only one thing on my mind. Robert was waiting for me at the altar.

As the strains of "Here Comes the Bride" sounded, I mouthed a thank-you to the wedding planner, lifted my chin high, smiled, then walked toward the man I loved.

ABOUT THE AUTHOR

Award-winning author Joyce Livingston is a Midwest native who lives in Kansas. She has six adult children, all married; twenty-five grandchildren; and fifteen great-grandchildren. In 2004, she lost the love of her life, the hero of every book she writes, her husband of many years, Don Livingston, who was also her #1 fan.

Before becoming a published inspirational author, Joyce was a television broadcaster for eighteen years doing two variety/talk shows daily. Using much of the information she learned there, she went on to publish numerous magazine articles on a variety of subjects.

Her first published inspirational romance novel, *Ice Castle*, was released in November 1999 by Heartsong. She now has nearly thirty books in print with more to come. Three of her books have been voted Contemporary Book of the Year. A fourth book was named 2004 Short Contemporary Book of the Year by the American Christian Fiction Writers, and she was voted Favorite Author in 2003 and 2004 in the Heartsong Readers' Poll.

Joyce says, "God has been so good to me. With Him, every day is an adventure."